PRAIS
TOO BIG

D0371063

Received an Honorable Mention in the Genre
Fiction category, *Writer's Digest* International
Self-Published Book Awards

"I have read (*Too Big to Miss*) and I loved it! It is a mystery but
it is also very funny."

—Cindy Quinn, President, Massachusetts
Paralegal Association, Inc.

"I think (Jaffarian's) going to be a big-selling author. . . . (She's)
an excellent, funny, beautiful, talented lady."

—Ed Mitchell, author of
Gold Lust and *Gold Raid*

"A tight, well-plotted story, with enough twists and turns to
keep me up past my bedtime. . . . Recommended."

—Linda Linguvic, *Greenwich Village Gazette*

"Love a good mystery? Order a copy of *Too Big to Miss* for
yourself, then settle in for a great read."

—SizeWise.com

An Odelia Grey Mystery

Sue Ann
Jaffarian

TOO BIG
TO MISS

MIDNIGHT INK
WOODBURY, MINNESOTA

FIRST EDITION
Third Printing, 2009

Book design by Donna Burch
Cover design by Ellen L. Dahl
Editing and layout by Rebecca Zins

Midnight Ink, an imprint of Llewellyn Publications

Library of Congress Cataloging-in-Publication Data
Jaffarian, Sue Ann, 1952–
    Too big to miss / Sue Ann Jaffarian.—1st ed.
        p.   cm.—(An Odelia Grey Mystery)
    ISBN-13: 978-0-7387-0863-8
    ISBN-10: 0-7387-0863-1
    1. Overweight women—Fiction. 2. Women detectives—California—Fiction. 3. World Wide Web—Fiction. 4. California—Fiction. I. Title.

PS3610.A359T66 2006
813'.6—dc22

                                                                2005054123

Midnight Ink
2143 Wooddale Drive, Dept. 978-0-7387-0863-8
Woodbury, MN 55125-2989

www.midnightinkbooks.com

Printed in the United States of America

ALSO IN THE ODELIA GREY SERIES

The Curse of the Holy Pail

Thugs and Kisses

Booby Trap

For Rudy

ACKNOWLEDGMENTS

Writing can be a lonely occupation, but it is never done entirely alone.

Thank you with all my heart to "Team Odelia"—my agent, Whitney Lee of The Fielding Agency; Barbara Moore, my acquisitions editor; Rebecca Zins, my production editor; Ellen Dahl, my cover designer; Kelly Hailstone, my publicist; and all the folks at Llewellyn Worldwide/Midnight Ink for believing in this book and in my ability to tell a good story.

And for their patience and continued love and support during this long and very bumpy journey, I want to thank my friends Marlaine Burbank, Kevin Gillogly, Susan Groeneweg, Dennis Pollman, Glen Ratcliff, Susan Schwartz, Laura Thomas, Kate Thornton, Lori Tillman, and my web master and nephew, Tom Jaffarian.

And a special thank-you to the members of the Los Angeles chapter of Sisters In Crime.

ONE

My weekend was D.O.A. . . . dead on arrival.

Two o'clock on a bright Sunday afternoon, and I was already counting the hours until I could go back to work. Now that's sad.

Stopped at the corner of Newport Boulevard and Seventeenth Street in Costa Mesa, I waited to complete a right turn. It was a busy intersection, even on a Sunday. I tapped my fingers impatiently on the steering wheel and looked around.

Size Does Matter!

The giant advertisement caught my eye like a hook in a trout's lip.

Behind me, someone honked. I dragged my attention away from the billboard and saw that the traffic light was green. I hit the gas and turned the wheel of the car sharply, causing the vehicle to swerve as it rounded the corner.

"Careful, Odelia," I cautioned in a low tone, "no need to season your foul mood with a crunched fender."

There it was again: this time on a billboard overlooking the grocery store that was my destination.

Size Does Matter!

It was all the sign said. Just three words emblazoned across a gargantuan advertisement for a new model of sport utility vehicle; as if the damn gas guzzlers couldn't get any bigger.

Without much trouble, I found a parking spot near the front door of the market. Turning off the engine, I smoothed the fabric of my sundress across my ample lap and sat quietly in the car to think. Not about the groceries waiting to be bought, but about the three words now burned forever into my brain.

Size Does Matter!

You bet your sweet ass size matters. It matters a lot, though how and to what it is applied is ambiguous. Size seemed to matter in random chaos. No hard and fast rules, just whatever fits your needs at the moment. Jumbo burgers, super-sized fries, and biggie drinks were a good thing. Small paychecks were bad. Big houses, good. Small diamonds, bad.

From the first time Adam noticed shrinkage and explained it to Eve, men have been trying to tell women that size *didn't* matter when it came to their manhood. Small penis. Big penis. Made no difference. Both were good. The same men have been telling women that size *does* matter when it comes to breasts, butts, and hips. To add to the confusion, big and small could also be good and bad at the same time. Big smile, good. Big ass, bad. Small waist, good. Small tits, bad.

It was a puzzle. A girl needed a scorecard or, at the very least, a seminar with a syllabus to make any sense of it.

I was feeling sorry for myself. On top of licking wounds from a particularly confusing date the night before, I had just come from visiting my father. Poor, sweet Dad, I thought, shaking my head. That recent memory alone was enough to entice me into restarting my engine and driving my old but dependable car right through the plate glass window of the grocery store.

Giving a deep sigh, I took a minute to think about it. I wasn't the type to look at life through rose-colored glasses, but neither was I a doom and gloom sort. Yet I'd been on edge all weekend. And it wasn't PMS—I'd ridden that roller coaster last week. No, it was something else. Disenchantment maybe, possibly disgruntlement. *Rut* was written all over my life: R-U-T in big, bold letters, outlined in neon tube lighting. It competed for attention with the now-important *Size Does Matter*. For better or for worse, I definitely needed a change. Standing still wasn't an option any longer.

Stuffed in my wallet were two dollar-off coupons for my favorite comfort food, Stouffer's Macaroni and Cheese. Later, I was going to throw myself a pity party . . . a big one . . . catered by Sara Lee and all her friends from the frozen food section.

"Odeliaaaaa," I scolded audibly, drawing out the last syllable in a menacing tone. "Eating this stuff is not going to help matters."

No, it wouldn't, but change could start tomorrow. It seemed natural, new beginnings on a Monday. Diets always began on Monday; why couldn't other improvements? You never hear of anyone starting anything of importance on a Tuesday or a Wednesday.

By the way, Odelia is not my imaginary friend. I am Odelia, Odelia Patience Grey, and I tend to talk to myself when alone, though why I do this is beyond me since I never listen. I am hardly a scintillating conversationalist in the best of times, and I can be a real nag when my mood is less than sunny. Like now.

Turning the usual deaf ear to my own lecture, I hoisted myself out of the car and wandered into the store. The brightly lit aisles of the market beckoned me with specials and new and improved items. I strolled down each one, gripping a red plastic basket in one hand. It was my misguided opinion and denial of choice that if I used a smaller, hand-carried basket rather than a full-size cart, I would be less apt to load up on junk food. Sometimes the theory worked. Most of the time I just experienced shoulder pain from lugging a too full and too heavy basket.

Meandering the well-stocked aisles, I plucked items from my list off the shelves. Tea bags, two bars of bath soap, and several cans of cat food for starters. I also picked up an assortment of things not on the list—E. L. Fudge Cookies (the vanilla ones with the chocolate centers) and the much sought-after large-size macaroni and cheese in the red, rectangular box. Out of guilt, and with a bow to nutrition, along the way I tossed in a bag of prewashed salad mix, a few tomatoes, and a small bunch of bananas. The next stop was the frozen dessert section, where I debated between a carton of Cherry Garcia ice cream and cheesecake, with the latter already in my hand. Using one leg to support the now-heavy basket, I deliberated my choice.

"Put down the Sara Lee and nobody gets hurt."

I gave a little jump at the unexpected but familiar voice. Turning around, I held the chilly box in front of me like a hostage in a shoot-out.

"You'll never take me alive!" I declared.

A few feet away, wheeling her own full cart, was Zenobia Washington, my dearest friend. She approached me, slowly shaking her head side to side.

"Girl," she said firmly, "you were supposed to call me this morning and let me know how it went last night."

Zenobia, called Zee by everyone but her father, a man fiercely fond of the unusual name he had chosen for his only daughter, fixed her large, liquid brown eyes on me and placed a hand on a generous hip. It was an intimidating stance; a posture that worked on most people, it only made me roll my eyes in childish defiance.

"Is it a safe assumption," Zee continued without waiting for an answer, "from what's in your basket, that the date was a bust?"

I nodded. I have known Zee for almost fifteen years, dating back to the time we both worked for the same law firm. We were more than good friends. At times we were each other's conscience, a mirrored reflection of life's measurement, both good and bad. But I can say truthfully, and without envy, that Zenobia Washington's image portrayed a more noble character than my own.

Zee knew that had my date been a success, my basket would have held lots of fresh fruit, vegetables, and fish. As a rule, my grocery shopping habits rode the roller coaster of my emotions. Like arthritic knees predicting rain, my purchases could foretell a sagging spirit with unfailing accuracy. Zee knew this and suffered a similar affliction.

"I was going to call you later," I said, not lying. "I had lunch with my family today."

"Lunch with your family!" She laughed heartily, her large body jiggling with an almost Santa-like bowl of jelly quality. "Then I'm surprised you only have one package of cheesecake in your hand."

We were almost identical in size. Both of us are about five foot one or so. Both tip the scales in the two-fifteen, two-thirty range and wear size twenty. We are even about the same age, with Zee at forty-two and I the elder at forty-five. The only difference is our color. Zee is the color of a creamy semi-sweet chocolate bar, while my skin tone resembles the cookies in my basket, minus the fudge filling. Zee's husband, Seth, often refers to us as his favorite salt and pepper shakers.

"So what's this one's story?" Zee asked, referring to my date the night before.

"The usual," was all I blandly responded, knowing that I did not have to go into the gory details with Zee right this minute. It was the same old story, different cast.

It had been a fix-up, a blind date set up by a well-meaning skinny coworker who had no clue that most men in Southern California placed overweight women in the same category as serial killers and believed them worthy of the same punishment—the death penalty. I finally had given in to her assurances that this man and I had a lot in common. Which, sadly, we did. But I saw the look of disappointment on his face when he entered the restaurant and realized that I was his date. I had seen that look before. It was unmistakable disgust encased in civility. Like a dead fish wrapped in clean white butcher paper, the covering kept your hands from being soiled but could not stop the stink.

As soon as the check was paid, he had walked me to my car. When he asked for a goodnight kiss, I thought that maybe I was paranoid about his chilly behavior. When his kiss became passionate, I was sure that I had read his signals incorrectly. But after washing and waxing my tonsils with his tongue in the darkness of the parking lot, he shrank from any suggestion that we should get together again. After four decades, I knew the score. If I had offered him my body, he would have slept with me, as long as he did not have to be seen with me.

Zee sighed deeply and reached out a hand to warmly touch my arm. "I'm sorry, sweetie." She took the cheesecake from my hand and put it back into the freezer, receiving no protests. "Seth can't be the only decent man out there."

Screwing up my freckled face in a most unbecoming way, I demonstrated my lack of faith in her statement. I wanted to be a good sport about it, not a childish whiner. But no matter how you slice the cheesecake, size *does* matter. How could one argue with a billboard?

"Why don't you join us for supper tonight?" Zee asked. "Just roast chicken, but it's a lot safer than going home and devouring that crap in the dark. Not to mention, you haven't spent an evening with us in a while."

Just as I was about to accept, Hannah, Zee's daughter, trotted up. Her gorgeous seventeen-year-old face looked serious. In her hand was a cell phone.

"It's Daddy," she said in a rush. She looked at me, surprise registering at my presence. Zee reached for the phone, but Hannah stopped her. "He says he's looking for Aunt Odie."

Zee and I shrugged together, as if on cue. I took the phone from the girl.

"Seth, it's me, Odelia. I was shopping when—" I stopped talking and listened. As his words entered my ear and saturated my brain, I felt my face cloud over and my lower lip tremble.

"I'll be right there," I finally said stiffly into the phone, then handed it back to Hannah.

Without looking at Zee, I leaned in close to her and uttered the news Seth had just relayed. My voice was low and raspy. My hands shook.

"The police just called your house looking for me," I told her. "Sophie London committed suicide."

Zee being Zee, she kicked into action like a general whose troops were under attack. She turned her cart over to Hannah. "Here, take the car keys and my ATM card, you know the code. Finish getting the stuff on this list, then go right home and stay there. I'm going with Odelia."

Hannah hesitated, her young face going from mine to her mother's with unasked questions. "But—," she started to say.

Her mother cut her off, but not unkindly. "Just do as I say, child. And while you're at it, pay for Odelia's things, too."

She took the red plastic basket from my grasp and hoisted it on top of her own cart. When Hannah started off, Zee stopped her. Opening the freezer door, she took out the cheesecake she had just put back and tossed it into the basket before sending the girl away.

"We're going to need that," she told me before taking my arm and leading me out of the store.

Sophie London did not have much, if any, family. I often envied her solitude and filial independence. Sophie's life seemed easier, less complicated and frustrating than my own. But then I have never thought about, much less attempted, blowing my brains out.

When Sophie had asked if she could use me as her emergency contact, I happily agreed. Zee was the secondary emergency contact, which is why the police had called Zee's house when they could not locate me. The detective told me that he got our names and numbers from the front of Sophie's address book, the page where you list emergency information.

Zee and I met Sophie nearly three years ago at a fashion show sponsored by Abundance, a store in Newport Beach specializing in large women's fashions.

Sophie London is—was—gorgeous, funny, and vibrant. But what attracted us most, especially me, was her confidence. She was big. She was beautiful. She was proud. Her battle cry was *I'm too big to miss.* She had even painstakingly cross-stitched the saying on linen, framed it, and hung the completed project in a prominent place in her living room. We were also about the same age, and since both of us were single, we often went out socially.

The news of her suicide rocked my tiny, rut-filled world.

About a year and a half ago, Sophie started a support group for large people called Reality Check. A small core group of mostly women met in Sophie's home every other Wednesday night to talk about the social and emotional problems of being overweight. Reality Check is not a diet club. If people want to lose weight, the group supports them in their efforts. If someone needs dating tips, fashion help, interview guidance, or résumé suggestions, it's provided. We're friends going through the same issues and helping each other with the solutions. Sophie's charisma and positive outlook guided us all. She was our ideal BBW—big, beautiful woman—our mentor and banner carrier in a world idolizing size four and under. Now Sophie London was dead, and by her own hand. It did not make sense.

After Seth's call, Zee and I drove to the Orange County coroner's office. They wanted us to identify the body. They also wanted to ask us questions. Seth, who's an attorney, met us there and guided us through the process.

I had expected it to be like on TV. A sheet-covered body rolled out on a gurney. The sheet slowly and dramatically pulled back to reveal the lifeless body of the loved one. The swooning and falling into each other's arms. I was equally relieved and disappointed.

Instead, Seth, Zee, and I were shown Sophie's waxen face via a television monitor. We were told that she had put a gun into her mouth and pulled the trigger, and I expected to see destruction. But her face was untouched, her features perfect. She looked like she was asleep.

After being questioned by a detective, we went back to Zee's for the promised roast chicken dinner, followed by cheesecake for dessert. We ate quietly, going through the motions. Zee and Seth campaigned hard for me to stay overnight, but I finally convinced them that I'd be fine at home alone. Seth particularly didn't want to see me leave. Somewhere during our years of friendship he had adopted me as a younger sister, with all the rights of advice-giving and protectiveness afforded a real older brother. He could be downright annoying at times, but tonight his concern felt as warm and soothing as a mug of hot cocoa.

Once at home, I wearily fitted my key into the front door lock of my townhouse and turned it. I repeated the action with the dead bolt located higher up. From the other side of the door, I could hear a half meow, half growl.

I'd like to say that I own a cat, but those of you who are familiar with cats would know that I'd be lying. So I'll simply tell you that I *live with* a cat: a one-eyed, raggedy-eared, greenish feline named Seamus.

I have never been a cat person. Actually, I'm not much of an animal person. It's not that I don't like animals, it's just that I have never been around them much. But even my lack of expertise in the animal kingdom wouldn't allow me to turn a deaf ear to a beast in trouble.

This past St. Patrick's Day I had come home from work, arms full of grocery bags, to discover some of the children who lived in my complex tormenting Seamus. He wasn't Seamus then, of course, just a nameless stray who lived by his wits among the brush and vegetation surrounding the nearby bay.

Somehow the kids had managed to capture him, bind him, and dye his shaggy coat green with what I later learned was nothing more than food coloring. By the time I intervened, the animal was out of his mind with terror and anger, and none of the little hoodlums dared to release him.

As soon as I yelled at them to stop, they scattered like roaches. I shook my head and approached the green ball of spit and fury cautiously. Hoping he was more hungry than angry, I pulled some tuna from my grocery bag, one of the small cans with a pull-tab lid. It did the trick. Once the animal was busy eating, I gnawed through the cords with a pair of cuticle scissors I keep in my ever-present tote bag, freeing him as he finished. Picking up my groceries, I went home, my good deed done.

Before I knew it, the cat had taken up lodging on my patio, and I began leaving out little snacks for him. I named him Seamus because he was green and I had met him on St. Patrick's Day. Then one night, during a bad spring rainstorm, I saw him hovering and shaking under the plastic patio table and invited him in. He has never left and seems content with his new life.

Two months later, Seamus is still as green as the Emerald Isle.

As soon as I entered my home, I dropped my tote bag and groceries to the floor and scooped him up. Plopping down on the sofa, I clutched the animal close, burying my tearful face in his soft, colorful fur.

TWO

UP AND DOWN, UP and down. This was how I spent the first night after Sophie's death. I paced the taupe carpet in my townhouse half alive, seeing and feeling little to nothing. The clock moved slowly, each digital minute changing slower than ketchup pouring from a new bottle. Seamus, disgusted with the disturbance, left his usual spot at the end of my bed and went in search of quieter sleeping quarters.

The Home Shopping Network beamed brightly from the small television in my bedroom. A woman, much too chipper for the middle of the night, was peddling pink tourmaline earrings.

It just didn't make sense.

Sophie's death, that is. It didn't make sense to sell earrings at two in the morning either, but the jewelry lady was on her own.

It was difficult to drag myself to work the next day. But drag I did, pushing aside the idea of calling in and taking a personal day. I negotiated with my tired and confused body, telling it that the diversion of work might do me good. The compromise was that I would go to work, but would skip my usual morning walk.

Each morning several of us meet at six o'clock for a loosely scheduled walk around a section of Newport Bay, a protected estuary just a few minutes from my home. There is no set group of participants, just an understanding that at six each morning a walk around the back section of the bay begins, and all are welcome. We have had as many as ten people at a time, sometimes as few as no one. No one waits for anyone to show up. At six each morning walking commences, no matter who is or isn't there. This casual exercise group has been going on, rain or shine, dark or light, for about a year. It was started by Sophie.

It wasn't just fatigue that kept me from my exercise this morning. Most of the walkers were part of the Reality Check bunch, and the idea of seeing the faces and fielding the questions of our friends made me queasy.

Sophie's death had been on the news last night and in the paper this morning. It was turning into a titillating gossip piece, something worthy of a supermarket tabloid.

Online Sex Star Kills Self As Dozens Watch! was how one television station had hawked the lead story for their eleven o'clock news the night before.

An *online sex star?*

I was still in shock over Sophie's death. Now I was reeling from the knowledge that she had owned and operated an adult web site. I was only glad that the police had broken the news to us instead of the media vultures.

According to Detective Devin Frye, the homicide detective who interviewed us at the coroner's office, Sophie's site was called Sassy Sophie. It was an Internet site set up with a camera that allowed viewers into her home via computer. Classified as a pornography site, for nineteen dollars and ninety-five cents a month, members could watch Sophie dress, shower, sleep, and even have sex.

Surfing the Internet, I had seen those sites before. Naked or scantily clad men and women played to their audience in front of a camera. Usually they tapped out messages via the keyboard and took requests. Many used a headset and spoke directly to their viewers. In some instances, the image was delayed, taking a few seconds for it to reach watchers around the world. But now, with streaming video and high-speed Internet connections, almost all sites and activities on them were instantaneous. At the end of his day, a man in Cairo could watch a woman in Los Angeles take her morning shower.

Detective Frye told us that as many as forty-five or fifty people, maybe even more, had seen Sophie put a gun into her mouth and pull the trigger. My blood iced over every time I thought about it, so I tried not to.

Seth said he would call and keep me informed about what was next concerning Sophie. One of his law partners, a man versed in estate matters, had drafted Sophie's will a while back. He promised to contact the attorney this morning and see if there were any instructions on her personal matters. Zee and I knew almost nothing about Sophie's family, just that both of her parents were dead. We were her emergency contacts but knew of no one else who should be advised of what had happened.

I work in a law firm as well, but we do not handle wills or trust work, mostly corporate and business litigation. The work on my desk faded in and out of focus as I struggled to keep a grip on my emotions.

For seventeen years I have been employed by the firm of Wallace, Boer, Brown and Yates, or Woobie as we inmates refer to it. I serve as the legal assistant to Wendell Wallace, one of the firm's founding partners, and as a corporate paralegal. This is the same firm where I met Zee. She worked here for a few years before becoming a full-time mother and part-time sales representative for Golden Rose Cosmetics.

I have worked for Mr. Wallace, who just turned seventy-two a few weeks ago, for almost fifteen years. He recently announced that he will retire at the end of this summer. It makes me wonder what will become of me when that happens, although I have been assured by our office manager that I will be given full-time paralegal work.

My position also puts me in contact with Michael Steele, which is a good name for him considering his lack of natural warmth. Steele is a senior associate who handles most of Mr. Wallace's clients. Saying I'm not overly fond of Mike Steele is an understatement. He has his own secretary, or rather succession of secretaries, but I do his paralegal work and also get saddled with some of the more sensitive clerical work his practice demands. I would leave my job rather than be assigned to him solely.

I was pondering my future at the firm sans Wendell Wallace, anything not to think about Sophie, when a thick file landed with a heavy thud smack in the middle of my desk. It jarred my thoughts back to the present.

"Grey, I need this copied," Steele ordered as he began walking back to his office. "Now."

"I'll have the copy center take care of it," I informed him politely but coolly.

I'll say it again. I do not like this man, having never found anything redeeming about him except his single-minded devotion to law. Steele is cocky and arrogant, a pretty boy in his mid- to late thirties who likes to play hard when not working hard. His clothes are impeccable and his taste in women favors models and centerfolds.

He's known to wine, dine, and dump women at a record-breaking pace, although office gossips claim that the real truth is that the women dump him for lack of substance.

"No," Steele said, coming back to stand in front of my desk. He looked me in the eye. It was the same look a schoolteacher might give a student who just said something fresh. "I want you to do it personally."

I looked at the file. It would take an hour or more of standing in front of a copier to painstakingly copy the documents. I looked at my already piled-high desk. We had a whole department devoted to tasks like copying, binding, and filing. That the file might be of a highly sensitive nature crossed my mind. Although all Woobie employees were required to sign a confidentiality agreement upon coming to work at the firm, some things were even too sensitive for most employees to see. I was often called upon to do work of this nature.

"Unless you'd rather take over your friend's porn site," Steele said with a lewd sneer.

The remark took me aback. I didn't realize Steele knew who my friends were. He paid so little attention to me, except to dump work on me, that sometimes I wondered if he even knew my name. I said nothing, but gave him a look that I hoped would convey "shut up" loud and clear. But either he couldn't read my look or chose not to, because he didn't let up.

"Hey, maybe she'll leave it to you in her will. After all, those paying customers of hers are going to miss all those love handles. Could be a whole new career for you, Grey."

My hands itched with the urge to belt him into next week. But lucky for both of us, I was now holding the documents he had given me. For a brief moment, I considered assault and battery with an expanding file. This one was over three inches thick and would probably leave a good-sized dent in a man's skull. Instead, I clutched the file to my chest and walked away from Steele, leaving him to chuckle at his own stupid comment.

Once in the copy room I told myself, sensitive or not, this was a simple, uncomplicated task. It was busywork that could keep me occupied while I waited for Seth to call. Mr. Wallace was out of the office this morning, and his work occupied less and less of my time these days, while the corporate paralegal work occupied more of it. I was too antsy to focus on anything detailed.

The awaited call from Seth came while I was at lunch. In his deep, oboe-sounding voice, he left a message to stop by his office after work.

At quarter of six, I sat in a conference room across from Seth and one of his law partners, Douglas Hemming. Zee was there too, seated next to me, twisting a tissue in her hands. It was her only outward sign of grief.

I had met Doug Hemming several times, if only briefly, at a few of Seth and Zee's annual Christmas parties. I guessed him to be younger than Seth, with pale, splotchy skin that looked like it would burn easily with minimal sun exposure. He was lean and lanky with an inconsequential chin, which he tried to round out with a goatee of reddish hair. The sparse hair on his head was a little lighter than the color of his beard. He held a document, which he peered at through wire-rimmed glasses; then he peered at me, then at Zee. Suddenly, and for no reason at all, I remembered that his wife's name was Nina and that she was a pediatrician.

"This," Doug began, indicating the few pages in his hand, "contains Sophia London's burial requests and arrangements. I thought it best to start here."

Sophie, or rather her body, was at the morgue. I hadn't thought of how or where she would be buried. What surprised me was that she had made arrangements ahead of time. We were pretty much the same age. Did that mean I should be thinking about the disposal of my remains? Should I have a will? I swept the morbid thoughts out of my head like so many dust bunnies.

"Sophia London wished to be cremated," Doug informed us. "She already made arrangements to take care of that and paid for the services in advance. She requested that you," he said, indicating me, "should take care of her personal matters."

I couldn't believe that Sophie had committed suicide, but here it was right in front of my nose, tons of evidence pointing to the obvious. A self-inflicted gun shot to the head and preplanned, prepaid funeral arrangements. As if reading my mind, Zee spoke up, asking the question that hovered on the tip of my numb tongue.

"When were these arrangements made, Doug?"

Doug looked at the papers again. "This directive was signed last October, the services paid for in full about the same time, according to the receipt attached." He rummaged through a small stack of papers briefly until he found another document. "Her will was drawn up and signed in October also."

Eight months ago.

Last September, just one short month before that, Sophie and I had taken a long weekend trip together. We drove up the California central coast, visiting Cambria, Hearst Castle, and Morro Bay. I racked my brain but couldn't recall her being depressed or preoccupied with death and dying, only a brief comment about needing a will. The trip had been lighthearted and relaxing, with lots of laughter.

"We took a short trip together last fall," I mentioned. "I remember Sophie asking me if Seth knew someone who could draw up a will. I gave her his office number."

Seth nodded.

"Yes," Doug said, "that's when Seth referred her to me." He put down the documents and took off his glasses, wiping them clean with a small tan cloth he retrieved from his inside jacket pocket. His face seemed sad and drawn, his small eyes droopy. "She was such a lovely woman. So tragic." He returned his glasses to his face, transforming himself back into Mr. Professional Lawyer. Picking up the other documents, he went back to Sophie's business.

"Has her family been notified yet?" he asked.

Zee and I looked at each other with surprise.

"We didn't know she had family," Zee said for us both.

"The police asked, but we had nothing to tell them," I added.

Doug sighed. "Sophia London is survived by an ex-husband and one child, a son. She never told you?"

We shook our heads in unison. It was another secret she had not shared.

"She gave me her ex-husband's phone number and address when she signed the will," Doug said, pulling a piece of yellow legal paper from the stack.

Stunned, I sat in the leather conference room chair like a piece of petrified wood. A husband. A son. An adult website. I had always assumed that Sophie, like me, had never been married. Not mentioning the porn site I understood. It could have been embarrassment, shame, or even the assumption that I might not understand. Which I didn't. But I certainly would have expected her to mention an ex-spouse. We had talked about and trashed various men in our pasts with regularity. Even when I shared with her the horrible engagement I had broken off just a few years earlier, she never gave the slightest indication that she had once been married.

"What about her work, her employer?" Doug asked. "Do they know yet what has happened?"

I shook my head. "Sophie was self-employed. Some kind of consulting work, computers I think."

"She also modeled from time to time," Zee added. "Sometimes she did fashion shows for large sizes."

"That's right. That's how Zee and I met her. She was in a show for that store in Fashion Island, Abundance."

The adult website was not mentioned audibly, but its existence loomed in the room like an embarrassing relative.

I didn't realize that I had been crying until Zee handed me a small purse pack of tissues. Taking them, I smiled my thanks. Her face was wet, too.

"If you like," Doug said, putting down the papers and shuffling them into a neat stack, "I'll call her ex-husband." He looked at his watch. "It's almost six-thirty. I'll try right now."

"I think that's a good idea, Doug," Seth said. "As her attorney, it might be best coming from you."

Doug picked up a file from the table and left the room. Seth came to stand behind Zee and placed a hand on her shoulder, giving it a slight squeeze. Then he put his other hand on my shoulder and did the same.

"You girls stay put," Seth told us. "I'm going to join Doug."

Minutes after Seth left the room, Ranita, his secretary, came in with a tray. On it were a couple of stylish mugs, a carafe, and a small basket containing an assortment of teas, sugar, and sweetener.

"I thought you ladies might like some tea," she said in a sweet somber voice with a slight but unfamiliar accent.

"Thank you, Ranita," Zee told her. "But it's time you went home." Zee reached out a hand and softly patted Ranita's arm. "Please don't stay for us. We'll manage."

Ranita bent down and she and Zee exchanged an affectionate hug.

"I'm sorry about your friend," the young woman said, looking at both of us as she unconsciously rubbed her pregnant belly. She wasn't more than twenty-five years old, with an open, dark face, just slightly lighter than Zee's. Here and there it was marked with small acne scars. Her eyes were big and soulful. It was easy to see that the comment came from her heart.

"Thank you, Ranita," I said.

After Ranita left, Zee opened up a mint tea bag for me and an Earl Grey bag for herself and placed them in mugs. I added hot water from the carafe. We were sipping tea in silence when Doug and Seth returned. Doug took his place on the other side of the table. Seth sat next to Zee.

We waited expectantly for Doug to speak.

"Well, we spoke to the ex-husband," he began. "His name is Peter Olsen." He looked at Seth before continuing.

"There are some unusual circumstances," Seth added.

"Unusual," I heard myself say. It wasn't in the form of a question, but more of a parroting remark. This whole matter had been unusual from the start. And there was more to come?

"Yes," Doug continued. "Except for a few personal items she bequeathed to you, Zee, and a few others, Ms. London left her entire estate to Mr. Olsen, as trustee for their son."

"But that's not unusual in the case of children," I commented.

"No, Odelia, you're right. It's not. Ms. London's son is twenty years old now. His name is Robert. She gave me that information when she made the will."

"What's unusual," Seth added, hesitating a single heartbeat, "is that her son thinks she's been dead for years."

"Yes," Doug continued, "and Mr. Olsen wants to keep it that way."

My head was spinning. I took a sip of tea, holding the cup in hands that shook slightly. I felt drained, and last night's lack of sleep was finally catching up to me. Right now, pink tourmaline earrings seemed like a swell idea.

"You okay?" Zee asked me.

"Yeah, I'm fine. A bit thrown off track maybe, but I'm fine." I looked at her and Seth. "Did you two know any of this?"

Both shook their heads.

"Only Doug knew about the son and the ex," Seth explained. "As her attorney, of course, it was confidential."

With our collective and varied legal backgrounds, everyone in the room knew all about attorney-client confidentiality.

"But she didn't even tell me about the . . . well, the other part," Doug said. "Apparently, that was a personal agreement between her and Olsen. He claims she knew that her son believed her dead."

I played with my hair, twisting it around a finger. "Now what?" I asked, feeling totally stumped.

"You, Odelia," Doug explained, "are named as the personal representative of Ms. London's estate. But just because she indicated you, it doesn't mean that you have to accept."

It would mean a lot of work. Personal representatives were in charge of winding up all the affairs of the deceased. The law firm would help with the legalities, of course, but the arrangements to dispose of her personal items and business affairs would fall on me. Until yesterday, I had never seen a body or known anyone close to me who had died. Sophie's funeral, if there was one, would be my first.

I seriously questioned if I was up to the task, but knew in my heart that I couldn't refuse. Sophie had done a lot to bolster my self-esteem in the time I'd known her. To refuse her this last favor would be unthinkable on my part. I nodded my consent.

"I'll do it. It's what she wanted."

Zee reached over and put a tender hand on my arm. "Seth and I will help you."

THREE

It's amazing, this profession of serving the dead. Everyone seemed positioned to help, solicitous and sensitive, causing as little emotional friction as possible. The business of death operated like a well-oiled machine and was as organized as a Fortune 500 company. It seemed more orderly than life, making me wonder why the business of living couldn't run as smoothly as that of death. Maybe if it did, there would be fewer self-inflicted gunshot wounds.

On Tuesday, with a few short phone calls from the office, I was able to set up the memorial service. It would be Friday afternoon at four o'clock. Following the service, everyone would be invited back to the Washingtons' for a light buffet. I also placed an obituary in the *Orange County Register*.

Zee was tasked with calling everyone we knew who would want or need to know about Sophie's death. I would send e-mails to others tonight after I got home.

Seamus was his arrogant self when I came through the door after work. But he did rub my legs and purr to let me know he'd missed me a little. After receiving some well-placed scratching behind the ears, he followed me into the kitchen where I made myself a quick sandwich. Carrying my plate and a diet soda, I headed upstairs to my spare bedroom where I kept my computer and desk.

First I checked for phone messages. There were two, one from my stepmother. In her usual disapproving voice, she reminded me to pick up a cake at the supermarket for Mother's Day, less than a week away. It annoyed me to think that she felt it necessary to remind me. It annoyed me even more to know that I had forgotten, just as she'd expected. I wrote myself a note and stuck it to the front of the computer, then wondered why, knowing full well that she'd call again with another reminder.

The second message was from Glo—Gloria Kendall. She was one of the mainstays of the Reality Check group. Glo is a delightful character with a big heart and cornpone Southern accent. Her voice sounded sweet and kind as she asked if she could help with the upcoming memorial. I made another note, this one reminding me to call tomorrow and accept her offer.

After listening to the messages, I started up the computer. I hadn't been online in over a week and needed to check my e-mail. With a few strokes to the keyboard, I found myself properly connected to my online provider.

My e-mail box held a whole slew of new correspondence. Most were from Reality Check members, dated within the last two days. Our regulars would have received a call today from Zee, so I wasn't too concerned about responding right away.

Some of the other e-mails were from concerned online friends who hadn't heard from me in a while. These were friends from around the nation who only knew me from the Internet. I wasn't much for the chat room scene, finding it boring. But I loved to play backgammon online, as well as hearts and cribbage, finding the games a nice diversion from television. Over the years I had made many acquaintances this way. My online handle, or screen name, is OdieWanKanobie. Go ahead, laugh, most do.

Reality Check also had a web page that promoted equality for all shapes and sizes. It had been set up and operated by Sophie, and my name and e-mail was one of the contacts for more information. This web page was something else that would need attention. I didn't know much about computers and web design, but Sophie was very organized, so I felt sure that Zee and I would find information about the site among her office papers. If not, we knew people who could help sort it out.

Suddenly I found myself wondering about the future of Reality Check. Would the group continue? Sophie London was more than the group's founder and leader, she was its heart.

Instead of answering each and every e-mail inquiry about Sophie individually, I drafted a short note about her upcoming memorial and sent it out to my entire Reality Check address list, as well as a few others who had contacted me through the website. I thought about posting something nice on the web page, but didn't know how. *Later,* I told myself. It didn't all have to be done tonight.

A hot shower and bed beckoned me. I was still exhausted from lack of sleep. Monday night had been better than Sunday, but only marginally. Another restless night and I would be comatose.

Just as I was about to sign off and answer the pleasant call of hot streaming water, a tone sounded. It was the signal informing me that a new e-mail had just arrived. The sender was someone named Rocknrlr. No one I knew, but I remembered the screen name from one of the earlier e-mail inquiries about Sophie. I had just sent this person memorial information. The subject line for the new e-mail read *Suicide????*.

I opened the e-mail with a tentative click.

"Hello Odelia," it started. "My name is Greg Stevens, a friend of Sophie's. I was one of the people who saw her die."

My right hand trembled. The news stories, both in the papers and on television, had been full of the horror. Some programs had even rustled up people anxious to talk about it. Last night on the eleven o'clock news, I had watched a skuzzy, middle-aged man relay how he had tuned in to Sophie's website expecting to see some skin, only to watch her blow her brains out. He had been zealous and graphic in his description, like a bystander describing a drive-by shooting or a beating.

Now, here in front of me was another viewer willing to talk. What was the purpose? Titillation? Attention? I didn't know and I didn't care. I felt violated. My memory of Sophie was being ransacked and pillaged, replaced by carnage up close and personal. I didn't want to know about the mechanics of her death. It was gut wrenching enough to know that she wouldn't be coming back. There'd be no more dinners, or discussions about movies, or leaping tall buildings in a single bound for the right of fat girls to wear spandex. It was over, and I had no patience for people interested in the sideshow that was her death.

Still . . .

I wrapped my fingers tighter on the computer mouse as I read on.

"Sophie spoke a lot about you," the e-mail continued, "so I almost feel like I know you. I don't believe she committed suicide. Do you? If you knew her as well as I think you did, there is no way you could. I'd like to talk to you about it. Please call me at (714) 555-1821. Call anytime."

At this point, most people would have made themselves a drink. Wine perhaps, maybe scotch on the rocks with a twist of lemon. Not me. Instead, I padded downstairs and rummaged through my refrigerator. In answer to my emotional needs and agitation, I located a box of Girl Scout cookies in my freezer. Thin Mints. My favorites. And they're even better frozen.

FOUR

SUICIDES ARE TREATED BY the police as homicides until concluded a suicide. This I discovered from Detective Frye. Hmmm, guess it's true, you do learn something new every day. It only took a few days for the police to determine and declare that Sophia London had died by her own hand. That was about the same length of time it took me to decide to *not* call Rocknrlr. Instead, I deleted his e-mail and his phone number.

One of the most difficult tasks ahead would be the dismantling and disposal of Sophie's personal things. As soon as the police allowed us into her home, I called her housekeeper, Cruz Valenz, and asked her to meet me and Zee there.

I had requested Friday off as a personal day. At the firm we each get an allotment of five a year. So far I had taken none. Since I was off work and Zee was self-employed, we set the time for Friday at eight in the morning to begin the task. It was the same day as the memorial service.

Cruz was also my housekeeper. A small, stocky woman in her mid- to late fifties, every other week she shows up at my two-bedroom, two-bath townhouse and works her magic.

To me, having someone clean my home is an outrageous luxury. I certainly am able-bodied enough to do it myself. But earlier this year I came down with a bad flu and was barely able to drag myself between work and home for what seemed like weeks. During that time, Sophie hired Cruz to come in and give my place a good cleaning, top to bottom. She came twice during my illness. By the time I was one hundred percent well, I was also one hundred percent hooked.

Cruz got to Sophie's first. Zee and I found her sitting on the sofa in a crumpled, sobbing heap. She was babbling in what we in Southern California refer to as Spanglish, a mixture of Spanish and English words. Every so often she crossed herself. Usually Cruz is unflappable. As a mother of eight and grandmother of the same, she has seen most everything. Or so we thought.

Sophie lived in a charming single-story house in the older part of Newport Beach, near the border of Costa Mesa. The house was painted blue gray with a white picket fence and matching shutters. Shrubs and flowers grew along the fence and walkway. It was only a mile or two from my place.

When we arrived, the sliding door to the back patio was wide open, letting fresh spring air into the stuffy house. Past the patio was the small yard. Cruz's husband, Arturo, was Sophie's gardener. He came by every Tuesday to mow and edge the lawn and tend the flowers.

I sat down next to Cruz and put an arm around her. "Are you all right?" I asked.

She wiped her face with a green, striped dishtowel that she held in her hands. "*Sí*," she answered in a shaky voice, then nodded. "Yes," she assured me again, this time in English.

Zee went to look around the house while I calmed Cruz. She walked back toward the living room and signaled to me from the hallway. Her cocoa face looked ashen. It was the first time I'd ever seen her look truly pale.

"I'll be right back," I told Cruz quietly before going to Zee.

"We might want to hire someone else to do the cleaning," she whispered when I reached her.

"I know," I said. "Cruz might not be up to it. She was very attached to Sophie. Been with her for years. We'll hire a service. Or I could even do it."

Zee looked me squarely in the eyes and held my upper arms in a firm but kindly grip. "That's not what I mean."

She turned her head so that her gaze was directed to one of the other rooms. My eyes followed hers and suddenly I knew exactly what she meant. My knees threatened to buckle. Zee tried to guide me back to the living room where Cruz was still sitting.

"No," I said weakly, slipping away from her and heading toward the room Sophie used as an office. "I want to see it."

"Don't do this, Odie," Zee begged. I knew she was especially concerned when she referred to me as Odie. Only her children had been granted special permission to call me that annoying nickname. Not even my family dared.

"No, Odelia, don't," I heard Cruz sob. "It's an evil place."

Ignoring them both, I walked slowly down the hallway heading toward the back of the house. The master bedroom, with its private bath, was at the other end of the hall toward the front of the house. I passed the guest bedroom and the second bathroom. Glancing briefly into both, I could see that they were undisturbed. Each was immaculate and beautifully decorated in designer prints and accessories.

The last room at the end of the hallway was the third bedroom, the one she had used as an office. I opened the door, which Zee had apparently pulled shut, and gasped.

The furnishings were just as I had seen them many times before. The L-shaped desk took up most of the room, with the main arm facing the door. On it were her computer monitor, keyboard, and various papers. On the shorter section, which was against the wall, sat the fax machine and printer. Across from the desk, on the same wall as the door, was the closet, its white, slatted folding doors ajar. The wall to the right of the door held a large window. Under the window was a stylish love seat with a small table at one end. A short bookcase was behind the desk. The same photos and prints decorated the walls and surfaces as when I was last here.

What was different was the blood.

There wasn't as much on the back wall as I had expected, just a light spray tattooing the bookcase and Van Gogh posters directly over it. The real eye popper was the chair. We were told that she had been found slumped backward in it. It was a light blue swivel desk chair with short arms and a high back, a costly lumbar type, adjustable to fit the various curves of the back.

Blood must have leaked from the exit wound at the back of her head. The high back of the chair had been soaked, making an overlay of dark brown on top of the light blue tweed. There was blood on the carpet, too. A pool, though not particularly large because the chair's fabric had acted like a huge sponge, mopping up Sophie's life as it had drained from her. An odor of musty metal hung in the air.

Seeing Sophie's body on the monitor at the coroner's had made her death seem unreal and the corpse staged. This brought it home.

On wobbly legs, I turned around and closed the door behind me. Zee was right, we needed to hire a cleaning crew for this. The chair could be easily tossed and the carpet and walls cleaned. But not by us, not by any of us who knew and loved her. Some things are best left to strangers.

I don't know how long I spent slumped on the toilet in the guest bathroom with a cool cloth pressed against my face, but it was long enough for Zee to knock on the door and check on me.

"You okay?"

"Yeah," I answered weakly.

She opened the door and looked me over with great concern. I was thankful she didn't say "I told you so."

"When you're ready," she said gently, "we have company. But don't rush it. You're going to need your strength for this." She started to close the door, then stopped. "And I've sent Cruz home. Didn't think you'd mind."

I shook my head, then freshened the cloth and reapplied it to my forehead.

After resting for another few minutes, I joined Zee and our mystery guest in the living room. As soon as I saw who it was, I wanted to run out the back door and abandon Zee to her own devices.

"This is Iris," Zee said, introducing us. "Iris . . ."

"Somers," the woman added. "I live next door."

Iris Somers obviously did not recognize me. We had only met once and that was in the driveway one night when I came over to visit Sophie. But I could never forget her. She was extremely memorable. And not just from my own one encounter, but from the countless stories Sophie told over coffee.

Iris Somers sat in one of the side chairs that had been uphol-stered to match the sofa. With her body perched on the edge, she re-minded me of a sparrow, nervous and fragile, waiting for a cat to pounce. Her eyes darted with edginess as she spoke. Surprisingly, her voice was clear and softly demanding in its tone. Age was diffi-cult to guess. Her makeup-free face looked about mid- to late thir-ties, but her posture and clothing suggested elderly. She had dark hair laced with gray, and she wore it long and pulled back into a ponytail. In her hands she held a small umbrella, nothing more, re-ally, than a child's parasol. It was covered in aluminum foil both top and underside and looked like a personal satellite dish.

"I can't stay," she informed us, holding the parasol open and moving it slowly—first up and over her head, then back in front of her. Then she took the same calculated route again, as if sweeping the air with a homemade metal detector.

I sat down on the sofa and looked at Zee. She was standing near a curio cabinet, fussing with some knickknacks. I could see her lips were pressed tight, her eyes crinkled. I knew that she was intention-ally not looking at me or Iris.

"I just came by," Iris said, continuing her sweep of the air, chang-ing the pattern of the parasol's orbit ever so slightly, "to see what you were going to do about the beams."

"The beams?" I asked.

"Yes, of course, the beams."

She pointed to a small gizmo positioned on the wall near the door. I recognized it as a sensor for the alarm system. It was a mo-tion detector that could set off the home security system if acti-vated. There were several positioned in the living and kitchen areas of the house, as well as sensors on the windows and outside doors. I remembered when Sophie had had the alarm installed; it was just a few months ago. Right now the alarm was turned off.

"Now that Miss London is gone, I'll expect you to do something about them. She never did. Just ignored my complaints. Didn't care a bit that I was sick and injured."

"I don't understand," I said to her. "What was she supposed to do? Does the alarm go off and disturb you?"

Iris Somers gave a slight huffing sound that I assumed was to let me know she thought I was stupid. She stopped her parasol's travels just long enough to inaudibly convey the message.

"Security systems," she said, pointing again to the sensor, "give off rays of energy that are damaging."

Sighing, I shut my eyes. My friend was dead. My memory had just been imprinted with the sight of her blood. This was not a good day to be talking to me about beams, rays, or any such crap as that—and it was an even worse day to be speaking to me as if I were a five-year-old.

"So what does that have to do with you, Ms. Somers?" I asked, with a slight edge to my voice. "These sensors are inside the house, nowhere near you." I was trying to be patient, really working hard at it.

Missing the tone in my voice, Iris continued. She gave me another deep huff. Zee, though, didn't mistake the tightness in my words. She stopped moving bric-a-brac and turned to fully listen.

"These beams are very harmful. Don't you know that?" Iris was becoming agitated. "It doesn't matter that they're inside. They still shoot out into my property. They strike my body and my head, causing a great deal of discomfort. I have suffered considerable harm ever since Miss London installed her security system."

"You *do* know that Sophie London is dead, don't you?" Zee asked. Her words were low and calm, but I detected a strong note of sarcasm.

"Yes. Exactly my point," Iris said, pointing her umbrella first at me, then at Zee. "And I don't want to be next. Those electrical rays struck her over and over, like arrows, until she was driven insane. That system caused her to shoot herself."

"Ms. Somers," I began, trying to rein in my anger and disbelief. Getting up, I went to the front door and opened it. "I can assure you that this harmless security system has no bearing on the death of our friend or on your own discomfort. Please seek mental health assistance. You obviously need it."

Iris Somers correctly read the open door and my suggestion of counseling as an invitation to leave. She stood up and, with her parasol sweeping about, made her way out the door.

"Don't say I didn't warn you," she said, turning to stand on the small outside landing to address me. "You'll be hearing from my attorney."

"Great. Call her husband." I jerked a thumb at Zee. "He's an attorney. He'd just *love* to hear what you have to say."

Iris Somers had just started to say something else, her words accompanied by a pointed finger, when the door slipped from my hand and slammed in her face. Since we didn't hear a scream from the other side, I felt it safe to assume that she was standing far enough away to avoid a broken nose.

Honest. The door just slipped.

FIVE

"What if she's right?" I asked Zee.

We were having lunch at a favorite little restaurant located on Lido Island. We had settled ourselves on the patio rather than in the small dining room, taking a table overlooking the boats in the bay.

After Iris Somers left, we had thrown ourselves into the sorting and packing of Sophie's things. Our industry was more to distract us from the morning disturbances than to accomplish anything constructive. Shortly after noon, Zee suggested that we break for lunch. Afterward, we had a memorial service to prepare for and attend.

"What if she's right?" I asked Zee again as I squeezed fresh lemon into my iced tea.

"Who? That nut case?" Zee took a big sip of her Coke and giggled. Then she did a double take. "You're not serious, Odelia?"

"No. Not about the beam-me-up-Scotty crap. But, about . . ." I took a drink of my iced tea before continuing. "But what if something *did* drive Sophie to commit suicide—something far-fetched and unexplainable? It just doesn't make sense that she killed herself. She wasn't the type."

We sat in silence and watched the water and the gulls until our food came. I hadn't told Zee yet about Greg Stevens' e-mail and wondered what she'd make of it.

"Don't tell me you haven't been thinking about it," I said, finally breaking the silence.

Zee still didn't answer. She took her time assembling her grilled chicken sandwich just the way she liked it. First, she removed the gourmet lettuce mix, dismissing it as weeds. Next, she tore the two bacon slices into smaller pieces and rearranged them so that they covered the chicken breast more evenly. Then came the extra mayo and the thinning of the red onion slices. She went through this ritual every time she ordered food out, never taking a bite until it was exactly the way she preferred it. Normally, I found it amusing. Today, even though I knew that Zee was taking this time to think, I found it maddening.

With my patience as limp as the lettuce she had discarded, I waited while she cut the sandwich into two more ladylike halves. When she salted her steak fries and picked up the ketchup, I knew we were nearing mission accomplished. Finally, she took her first bite and chewed slowly and thoughtfully. I toyed with the black olives and feta cheese in my Greek salad and waited for her comments.

"Yes," she answered after dabbing at her mouth with her napkin. "Of course I've thought about it. In fact, I've thought of little else lately. Sophie killing herself doesn't add up at all."

"I knew it!" I slapped the table with my left palm.

"But," Zee interrupted, pointing a thick fried potato strip at me, "neither does that porn site. When you think about that, and the fact that she had a hidden family, a grown son, maybe we didn't know her as well as we'd like to think. Maybe, just maybe, she was a very unhappy and depressed person hiding behind an outgoing, bubbly persona. It happens all the time."

"The jolly fat person who's really miserable inside?"

"It could happen. And it does happen. Now don't get me wrong. I'm just as shocked and puzzled by all of this as you are." Zee hesitated and took another sip of her soda. "And like you, I need and want some answers."

I watched quietly as a gull bobbed up and down on the water, lazily going with the flow. After a few moments, I turned my attention back to Zee.

"Even with all the secrets oozing out of the nooks and crannies of Sophie's life, my gut tells me that there's more to this than meets the eye."

"Even with dozens of eyewitnesses?" Zee asked.

"Even then."

I decided to come clean about Greg Stevens. First, I took another drink of tea.

"I received an e-mail from one of the guys who saw her die," I told Zee. "He got my name and e-mail address off the Reality Check website."

"Lord, no." She put down her sandwich and wiped her mouth and hands with her napkin. "Odelia, don't go getting mixed up with one of those sick crackpots. You've seen the news. They're feeding off this like sharks."

"I know. But I can't put this guy out of my mind. He says that Sophie talked to him about me. He told me he doesn't believe Sophie committed suicide."

"Odelia, if you truly think that there is something else going on here, why not talk to that nice detective. Frye, wasn't it? You are not a private investigator or law enforcement. This is their job."

I knew she was speaking with the voice of reason, but I couldn't let it go. Greg Stevens and his e-mail continued to nag at me in spite of my decision not to respond.

"The police have already determined that it was a suicide," I told her, hoping it would soothe her concerns. "But I'd still like to poke around a bit. You know, ask some questions. Nothing more. I feel I owe it to Sophie to at least find out something about that morning."

"Well, I guess asking a few questions won't hurt." Zee raised her glass in a toast. "To Sophie and to the truth."

I toasted back with my iced tea. "Just one more thing," I told her. "Don't tell Seth. He'll just nag me about being careful. You can do the job for both of you."

We laughed together. With no further discussion, a thoughtful silence settled over us as we returned to our food.

Maybe the Iris Somerses of the world aren't the wing nuts of our society. Maybe people like her are right on the money about such things as beams, little green men, and mental probes. Maybe it's those of us who think we're normal who are really going round the bend. We all laugh at the strangely dressed man in the street who holds up a sign saying the end is near. Could it be that he has the inside track, while the rest of us are running endlessly in a hamster wheel?

Maybe somewhere along the line, Sophie discovered this theory to be true, and the truth had been too harsh to bear.

Afraid that she'd throw the salt shaker at me for being ridiculous, I didn't voice this thought to Zee. But it occupied my mind like thoughtless guests in the next bedroom.

After lunch, Zee went home to get ready for the gathering after the memorial service. I decided to go shopping. I didn't need anything in particular, but a new outfit for the service later today would be a nice pick-me-up. Like food, shopping often served as an outlet for my anxiety.

That morning we had made some good headway on sorting Sophie's things, starting with tagging the items left by Sophie to specific people in an attachment to her will. I was left three items—her Lenox nativity set, her thirty-inch strand of pearls, and the cross-stitched sampler. She had left Zee an antique rocking chair as well as her peridot earrings and pendent, knowing that the green gemstone was Zee's favorite.

The nativity, which consisted of about sixteen or more pieces, including several stable animals, was made of smooth, creamy porcelain decorated with elaborate jewel-toned raised dots. I already have a growing collection of unusual nativity sets and had openly coveted her expensive set each Christmas when it adorned her buffet table.

Something about the willed gifts nagged at me. I had the list in my purse and dug it out after finding a parking space at Fashion Island. I went down the list, name by name, item by item. Most of the bequeathed items went to friends in Reality Check. A few went to people I didn't know. Scanning the list, I found what I was looking for and what I hadn't noticed this morning during our mechanical bustle. Greg Stevens was on the gift list. He was to receive a framed portrait. So he wasn't just an anonymous sex voyeur. He had been telling the truth about being a friend.

According to Sophie's will, all items not specifically given to someone were to be sold, with the proceeds added to her estate. Unsold items were to go to charity if no one wanted them. The house, too, was to be put on the market. In the end, after all expenses were met and the probate court satisfied, the liquidated estate would be given to her ex-husband for the benefit of their son.

Doug Hemming informed me that Peter Olsen didn't want to know anything about Sophie's estate. Nor did he want to be involved. He just told Doug to send him a check if there was anything left.

Sophie had a lot of stuff. It would take us about two to three weekends to properly ready everything for disposal. Before going to lunch, I had called a professional cleaning crew. We were anxious to have the office scrubbed before entering it again.

As I locked my car, leaving it in the Fashion Island parking lot with the driver's window cracked against the heat, I glanced at my watch. I had just over an hour to find something new. If I failed in my mission, I could always wear my navy blue and white two-piece summer suit as a backup.

Today I skipped Abundance. I shopped there so much I knew the stock by heart and had not found anything special the last time I was there. Thinking back, that would have been last Saturday, the day before Sophie died. I was in a funk and she'd dragged me out shopping to lift my spirits.

I thought about that. Sophie had tried to improve *my* mood. I didn't recall her being down. In fact, she'd been annoyingly chipper. It was one more thing that didn't feel right.

Most major department stores had sections for large women. The racks of clothing, sized fourteen through twenty-six, were usually tucked away in some remote corner of the store, far from the other women's clothing departments and well out of view of the general buying public. Zee and I had dubbed these hidden women's clothing areas Invisible Women Departments.

Although none of these stores seemed shy about taking my hard-earned money, they did seem embarrassed about displaying the clothing I wanted to purchase. Kind of like a so-called family-oriented store that sold smut from a back room with a look of apology, but still smiled when they gave you your change and told you to come back again soon.

I entered one of my favorite department stores and made the trek from the ground floor up several levels of escalator to the women's department located on the fourth floor. In this particular establishment, it was lurking in a distant corner, tucked between Fine China and Small Appliances. Across the way was Furniture; to the far left, Linens. It was the only clothing department on the entire floor.

The store's management must think that since women wearing these sizes are as big as houses, they would be more comfortable buying clothes next to household goods. It was the only logical explanation I could think of.

After roaming the familiar racks with no success, I left, riding the escalator down to the land of the normal and acceptable.

Walking around the charming outdoor mall with its courtyards of clever fountains and kiosks, I felt a stab in my chest. It wasn't indigestion from lunch, that I knew. I placed a hand over my chest and pressed. It was a glob of grief, sitting just over my heart; a big, solid wad of pain and emotions that would have to come out sooner or later, like a hairball. Sophie and I had shopped this mall together regularly. Many Sunday afternoons, we had sat beside the koi pond sipping designer coffee, watching children play in the water while their parents kept a watchful eye from behind carefully chosen Ray-Bans.

Those days were gone now, lost in a single trigger pull.

A dress caught my eye in the window of a large, well-known chain featuring only women's clothing and accessories. It was an upscale shop, larger than a boutique, not quite a department store, known for high mark-ups and celebrity clientele. Not a store in which I regularly shopped. Stepping inside, I let the air conditioning bathe me while I wandered around. I fingered silky, rich materials and examined different displays, occasionally holding a garment up to my frame in front of one of the many side mirrors. The activity was calming my nerves. The lump in my chest subsided.

A clerk approached me. She couldn't have been older than early twenties, wearing an expensive ensemble all in black. Her legs were long, her body tall and lithe. She might have been pretty except for the thick makeup and severe hairdo, making her look like something out of a rock music video. Her name tag said Jody.

I looked at her and smiled pleasantly. She stared back at me expressionless, her facial features as tight as the sweater on her back.

"We don't have your size here," she informed me with an air of superiority.

Not sure I heard her right, I said, "Excuse me?"

"I said, we don't carry your size here."

There it was again. I had heard right. Stunned, I put the silk blouse in my hand back on the rack with a sharp snap of my wrist.

Not even a damn *good afternoon, may I help you* first?

"I don't recall asking if you had my size," I replied, correcting my posture while I spoke. "Perhaps I'm shopping for someone else, or for a handbag or a scarf."

The little snit didn't even bat an over-mascaraed eyelash.

"Well, are you?" she asked, raising her nose a tad higher into the air. Her insolence slapped me hard.

"No, *miss*, but that's hardly the point."

With a roll of her black-lined eyes, she turned on her four-inch heels and strode away. My face turned as raspberry as the silk blouse I had just admired.

With my head down to hide my embarrassment, I left the store and scurried back to my car. Once inside, I dropped my face into my cupped hands and broke into sobs of humiliation and personal grief. This was exactly what Sophie fought against. It was what she stood for.

Weight was the last acceptable prejudice. People of girth, especially women, were open targets for jokes and comments. It was still politically correct to assault and ridicule fat people.

I thought about Sophie and felt ashamed. She wouldn't have let that little snot intimidate her. No, Sophie would have demanded to see the store manager or the vice president—hell, the owner! She would have demanded an apology. And she wouldn't have let up until she had gotten one.

I, on the other hand, had made a feeble attempt at indignation, then ran with my tail between my legs.

Where was our champion now?

SIX

WEARING MY NAVY BLUE and white suit, I quietly greeted people as they filed into the small nondenominational chapel to say goodbye to Sophie London.

The late afternoon sun was still high and blazing when the service began. I felt my underarms progress from damp to wet in spite of the building's air conditioning. There were more people at the memorial service than we had expected. Many Zee and I didn't know.

The pastor from Zee's church, Pastor Hill, said a few words of comfort. Zee read Scripture and I recited one of Sophie's favorite poems, "Phenomenal Woman" by Maya Angelou. Glo Kendall sang a stunning arrangement of "The Lord's Prayer." It was a very moving service.

At the front of the chapel stood three different photographs of Sophie. They had been blown up and arranged on easels, surrounded by the many flowers that had arrived.

Her ashes were back at my house, sitting in an urn right next to the Lenox nativity set she'd left me. We hadn't decided on how to disperse her remains, and Sophie had provided no direction on that. It seemed to be the only loose end she hadn't tied. The thought of having the urn on display at the service gave me the creeps. I wanted people's last memory of Sophie to be as she was displayed in the photos.

The center one was a beautiful professional pose, the same as she used on her modeling résumé. The one on the right was a more casual photo taken at the beach. But the photo on the left was my favorite. It had been taken on her last birthday, almost exactly a year ago. A few of us had surprised her with a male stripper. The photo in the chapel didn't show the nearby naked man, of course, but was a close-up of Sophie's expression. She had her glasses on, but pushed down on the bridge of her nose. She was looking up over the top of the rims, her mouth hung open in surprise. It was a comical pose and probably a better representation of her true personality than the others.

The eulogy was given by Anna Garcia, owner of Abundance. Sophie had modeled for Anna many times. Like Sophie, Anna was an activist for the rights of large women. Her words at the memorial were touching, funny, and thoughtful.

The service began at four o'clock and was through shortly after five. The pastor made an announcement that all were welcome to attend the light supper following the service at the home of Mr. and Mrs. Seth Washington. Directions to the Washingtons' could be found on the table in the back by the guest book.

I had ridden to the service with Seth and Zee. Their children did not come, but would be at the house later. Zee and I stood by the car, accepting and giving condolences, shaking hands and passing hugs, while Seth supervised the packing of the flowers and photos for moving to the house.

Among those greeting us were Glo Kendall and her husband, Blaine. As much as we loved Glo, her husband was another matter.

I suspected that he would fit in nicely with my stepfamily, and I generally referred to him as Tennessee trailer trash. Zee chided me for being so mean, but I noticed that she never stood up for him with positive comments.

"Beautiful song, Glo," I said to her. "Thank you so much. Sophie would have loved it." I gave her a big hug. After me, Zee gave her another.

"Y'all know my husband, Blaine," Glo said in her thick accent.

"Honey," she said to her husband, "this is Zenobia and Odelia. I think you've met them before."

"Yeah, I have," he said in his own thick accent.

He pulled a baseball cap out of a back pocket of his trousers and put it on. It was a red cap with the emblem for the Tennessee Smokies on the front. I was mildly surprised that he hadn't worn it in the chapel.

"I always remember you two," he said, once the cap was in place, " 'cause of your peculiar names. Hey, I've been meanin' to ask ya. With those funny names, you two aren't kin, are ya?"

I smiled tightly at him, very tightly.

"Why yes, Blaine," Zee answered, her voice dripping with honey. But I noted that the underlying tone was as plastic as my smile. "We're sisters. Same daddy, different mothers."

"I thought so," he declared with pride. Full of satisfaction for the mystery solved, he nudged Glo and headed toward the parking lot. Glo smiled weakly and trotted after him.

I turned to Zee. Her face was strained, her patience shot. I could tell that Blaine Kendall's stupidity did not set well on top of recent events. My own patience was at ground level as well. Following my failed shopping expedition, I had gone home and sobbed hysterically for almost an hour. It had been cleansing but exhausting. Right now, I just wanted to get through today.

"Well, at least you know he's just ignorant and not a bigot," I said, trying to lighten both our moods.

Before she could answer, a commotion started not too far from us. One man was about to get into his car. He stood with his hand on the handle of a late-model black Mercedes with the door slightly open. He was very tall and elegant, and dressed expensively. I was struck immediately by how handsome he was with his wavy salt and pepper hair and beautiful yet rugged face. He looked like a middle-aged movie star; maybe even the next James Bond.

Another man stood next to the Mercedes and had grabbed the door. He was thin and wiry and about a half-foot shorter than the other man. He was dressed nicely but not costly. His face was plain, his hair thinning. The two looked about the same age. I didn't know either. The shorter man stood facing the other, his face distraught and contorted.

"You happy now?" the shorter man said. He wasn't yelling, but the anguish in his voice carried the sound to the rest of us.

The other man didn't answer. His face wore contempt as well as his body wore the tailored suit. He stood towering over the man accosting him, sneering openly.

"She's dead now. You happy?" the smaller man said again. The pain in his voice was as real and solid as the blacktop covering the parking lot.

Without answering, the taller man pulled his car door open even farther. He started to get in but was stopped by the other man, who lunged forward and gripped his upper arm.

"I know you, Hollowell," the shorter man yelled. "I know you had something to do with this."

The man he called Hollowell shook off the hold easily. With a quick move, he grabbed the lapels of the smaller man's jacket, almost lifting him up.

Like lightning, Seth Washington was between them, loosening the grip and breaking them apart.

"Gentlemen," he said, his voice deep and full of authority. "This is not the time and place for such things."

"He killed her!" the smaller man cried. "He may not have shot her, but he killed her just the same."

He tried to get past Seth to throw a punch at Hollowell, but Seth quickly grabbed him and held him back. Hollowell never said a word during the whole exchange, but instead chuckled. It was an ugly, mocking sound, the type of self-satisfied snicker that made me want to throw a punch at him myself.

Seth continued to hold on to the angry man. He firmly but gently steered him away from the Mercedes as Hollowell got in and drove off. I went over to where they stood. The man was crying softly, his head lowered in grief as Seth loosened his grip and released him.

"Now what was that all about?" Seth asked him.

With grace, Zee broke up the onlookers and directed them to head on over to the house.

I moved in closer, not wanting to miss the man's response. This was about Sophie, about her death. This man had accused Hollowell of killing her, and Hollowell had offered no rebuttal. I felt my hands shake as it dawned on me that this might be Greg Stevens, Rocknrlr from the e-mail.

"She's gone," the man said quietly to Seth, looking directly into his eyes with overwhelming grief. "She's gone forever."

"Mister," Seth said gently, "why don't you come on back to the house and have some coffee and a bite to eat. You'll feel better."

"We will all miss her," I added, my own cried-out eyes threatening to spill over again. I put a hand softly on his right arm. He covered my hand with his left hand and squeezed it warmly. I noticed that he wore a wedding ring.

"Are you Mr. Stevens?" I asked.

He shook his head from side to side. "Who I am doesn't matter."

He turned back to Seth. "Thank you for the invitation, but I need to get going. I'm sorry that I've behaved so badly. Didn't mean to cause a ruckus."

"No problem," Seth answered. "We've all been upset by this tragedy."

The man still had his hand over mine. He picked it up and squeezed it gently. "I'm so glad Sophie had good friends like you folks."

After shaking Seth's hand, the man walked away. He climbed into a late-model pickup truck. Without a look back, he drove off.

SEVEN

"Who's Mr. Stevens?" Seth asked me on the way back to the house.

"A friend of Sophie's who e-mailed me this week. He said he doesn't think Sophie killed herself. By the way that guy behaved, I thought it might be him."

I sighed with relief when Seth dropped the issue.

Most everyone was already at the Washingtons' by the time we got there, but no one had started eating. Pastor Hill was holding the blessing until we arrived.

Usually when I'm stressed, I'll eat everything not nailed down. Only small children and family pets are safe. And okra—I won't eat okra under any circumstances. But there are times when my emotional arc runs so close to the sun that I can't eat a thing. Now was one of those times.

People lined up at the catered buffet to sample honey baked ham, smoked salmon, and turkey breast, along with various salads. An assortment of desserts, all lovingly brought by friends, were set on another smaller table along with coffee and soft drinks. I picked at a few appetizers and raw vegetables before giving up.

Seth and Zee have a large, lovely home with a roomy backyard, perfect for entertaining. Small tables and chairs were placed outside on the patio and along the pool edge. Many folks were also gathered inside in the living room and den. After making the rounds dictated by courtesy, I took a soda and escaped to the table farthest from the house. Hannah and Jacob, Zee's children, were already seated there, eating their dinner. It was now early evening and the air was beginning to cool down nicely.

"Hey, Aunt Odie," Jacob greeted me, his mouth half full.

"Don't talk with your mouth full," his sister scolded. She rolled her eyes at me. "It's so rude."

Jacob made a face. "It's so ruuuuuuuuuude," he mimicked, then went back to shoveling food from his heaping plate into his fourteen-year-old body.

He was a younger version of his father, and it was easy to see that in a few years he would gain the same height and solid build to his body. Both children had their mother's beautiful smile.

Hannah picked at her food. "Aunt Odie, why would your friend kill herself?"

"Mama said it's a sin," Jacob chimed in. "No one but the Lord should take a life."

"I don't know why Sophie killed herself," I answered truthfully. *Maybe she didn't,* I said to myself silently.

Hannah sighed. I could see that recent events were bothering her. "I met her a few times with Mama. She didn't seem sad."

"She didn't seem sad to me either, sweetie. And I knew her very well."

"She didn't look like a porn star either," Jacob said as he took his last bite.

"Jacob!" his sister snapped.

"Well, she didn't."

"So, Jacob," I asked, "you've seen lots of porn stars?"

He didn't answer. Instead, he buried his face in his cup, pretending to drink, avoiding my eyes.

"Maybe, Hannah, we should do a little search and seizure of your brother's room."

She snapped her fingers in the air. "Just give me the word and I'm there."

"I swear, Hannah," Jacob said, getting worked up. "You touch my room and Pastor Hill will be saying a few words over *you.*"

"I'm gonna tell Mama you said that."

"Kids, kids, kids," I said, trying to bring order to the situation. "Calm down. No one's telling. No one's searching. We were just teasing."

We moved on to the topic of school, which I thought would be a safe discussion. In a few minutes the bickering started up again. This time it centered on a boy that Hannah liked. Jacob thought he was a butthead and said so. I was so busy soothing teenage ruffled feathers, I didn't notice someone approaching our table. Jacob saw him first.

"Hi," he said to the man.

"Hi back," the man answered.

I turned around to see a man in a wheelchair. A nice-looking man, a very handsome thirty-something actually. I remembered seeing him briefly at the memorial service. But like many in attendance, he was unknown to me.

"I hope I'm not intruding," he said.

"No, not at all," I answered, giving him a slightly embarrassed grin. "We're just having a little family discussion."

The kids didn't seem to recognize him either, so I made introductions.

"This is Hannah and Jacob Washington. Zee and Seth's children."

He held out his hand and the kids politely took turns shaking it and saying a proper hello.

"And I'm Odelia Grey."

He took my hand, shook it, and held on, looking straight into my eyes. "I know. I'm Greg Stevens."

I withdrew my hand quickly, as if burned. Well, butter my buns and call me a biscuit. Here was the man himself, and it wasn't the little guy at the service.

I fought the urge to laugh out loud, to cackle insanely until someone subdued me with chemicals for my own safety. From start to finish, today had been too much. I wanted to put some of it aside, on account so to speak, to deal with later when my emotional reserves weren't so spent. But I had no idea when that time would be, so I gathered myself together for the next round.

"We need to talk, Odelia," the man named Greg Stevens said to me.

As if on cue, the kids rose to leave. A part of me wanted to tell them to stay, but I knew that eventually this man and I would have to speak. I also knew that the children were upset enough, and there was no need for them to hear this discussion.

"I have some homework to do," Hannah said. She leaned over on her way by me and gave me a kiss on my cheek before departing. "Hang in there."

"Thanks, sweetie."

"Later, Aunt Odie," Jacob said, walking away with his empty plate.

"You too big now to give me a kiss?"

Jacob walked back, rolling his eyes for Greg's benefit. Greg chuckled. Dutifully, the boy bent down and pecked me on the cheek. I pecked him back. He lingered, his mouth close to my ear. I smelled after-shave and wondered to myself when had he gotten old enough to wear it.

"We're not gonna find out you're some sorta closet porn star, too, are we?" the boy whispered in my ear.

"What?" I sputtered, then realized that I had given him exactly the response he wanted.

Grinning, Jacob walked away, leaving me flushed and speechless. And alone with Greg Stevens.

"That must've been some remark," Greg commented with a smile.

"Some days, I just want to beat that boy. Out of love, of course."

"Easy to see they love you back. Have you known them long?"

"Jacob was a gleam in his daddy's eye when I met Zee; Hannah was just a toddler. They're almost like my own. Sorry you walked into that family bickering. They go out of their way to torment each other." I fidgeted, not sure what to say.

Greg laughed. "Siblings. It's natural. I have a brother and a sister. I'm in the middle, literally and figuratively. You from a big family?"

I thought about that. The anticipation of another agonizing Mother's Day sat in my stomach like mayonnaise in the sun.

"No," I admitted. "I'm an only child. My parents divorced when I was about thirteen. My father remarried a woman with two kids who are much older than me."

"My parents have been together forty-two years," he said. "And amazingly, they still seem nuts for each other. I've been lucky. You get along well with your stepfamily?"

I thought about it before answering. "If you asked them, they'd say we get along fine. As for me, I keep my mouth shut for the purpose of getting along. I keep the peace for the sake of my father."

"At great expense to yourself, no doubt."

I was tempted to ask Greg Stevens if he was a shrink, but held back. He certainly knew how to get to the meat of a matter and how to make someone comfortable enough to spill their guts. Under the stress of recent events, I was ready to lay back on a couch and talk over my problems for hours. I wondered how much this man would charge and if I had enough in my savings to cover it.

"I'm sure you didn't come here to discuss my childhood," I said instead.

He shook his head. "No, I didn't. I came to say goodbye to a good friend." There was a pause. "And I came to meet you."

Again, a quiet lingered between us. It wasn't an awkward silence, but, strangely, a comforting one. There was definitely something soothing about this man. He seemed so self-assured, so genuine. I looked him over, wondering what his relationship was with Sophie. Was he yet another secret?

He was definitely attractive. Not beautiful like Hollowell, but good-looking in an athletic, wholesome way. Except for his lifeless legs, his body was toned and strong, especially his upper body. His hair was medium brown, worn on the long side, but well cut and styled. His eyes were hazel and sparkled with life, in spite of his obvious grief. Dressed in a nice shirt and lightweight sports jacket, he looked successful but not wealthy. Independent rather than mainstream.

"You really saw her die?" There it was, the bonus round question.

"Yes, I did. I was the one who called 911."

Detective Frye had told us that one of the watchers of the website had made the emergency call. I found myself giving quick thought to who this man was and why he was watching Sophie that morning.

"You didn't really know her, did you, Mr. Stevens? Not in person anyway."

Bottom line, this was a paying customer of an adult website. He wasn't a friend of Sophie's, he was a guy who watched her sexually. Suddenly, I wasn't feeling all that warm and fuzzy about Greg Stevens.

"No, unfortunately, I never met her in person. But I knew her well."

I leaned in toward him, not wanting my voice to carry. "I seriously doubt if jacking off to an image constitutes knowing someone."

I got up to leave, but he reached out a hand to stop me. "You're right about that, Odelia. It doesn't." His voice was firm but kind. "But I spoke with Sophie at least once a week by phone. And not phone sex either, so don't even go down that road. I worked with her on her website. This is the cyber age. You don't need to meet someone in person to know them and work with them. We were friends, just like you and she were. We just never went shopping together."

I winced at the mention of shopping.

Shaking his hand off my arm, I started once more to walk away. My face burned with frustration sprinkled with anger. I wondered how many more of Sophie's cyber fans were here, eating, talking, and discussing her like they truly knew her.

"I knew she had a kid," he called after me. "And I know who Hollowell is."

I stopped dead in my tracks. My head swam with confusion, pushing aside the anger for the moment. He knew she had a son, but I didn't. Why would she tell him that and not me? Or even Zee? For some reason, Sophie didn't trust us. That hurt. I wanted to keep walking but the second half of his remark prevented me. He knew Hollowell, too. My personal feelings were fighting with my curiosity. I was never going to get to the bottom of this if I behaved this way. Then I remembered that Sophie had left this man something in her will. Reluctantly, I walked back to the table and sat down.

His remark had been used as bait, and I was biting. I only hoped that I didn't wind up dipped in cornmeal and pan fried.

"Mr. Stevens, I don't know what your game is, but like you, I have doubts about the suicide."

"There's no game, Odelia. We both loved Sophie. Neither of us believe her capable of suicide. Give me a chance to help."

He reached into the inside pocket of his jacket, pulled out a business card, and passed it to me. It was for a business in Huntington Beach called Ocean Breeze Graphics. The card said "Gregory W. Stevens, Owner."

"That's my company. Check it out, then call me. And please tell the Washingtons thanks for their hospitality."

He turned his chair around and started off. I didn't make any attempt to stop him, but, instead, watched as he wheeled out the back way and started down the driveway.

EIGHT

THE SOUND OF BREAKING waves filled my ears as I walked along the street from the public parking lot. On the other side, across Pacific Coast Highway, was the beach. I was searching the store fronts for a restaurant. Finally, I spotted it—The Gull. It was a small café with most of their seating outside. Greg Stevens saw me and waved.

It was eight in the morning—way too early for me to be up and out of the house on a normal Saturday, but my life was anything but normal these days. I was meeting Zee and Cruz later to continue sorting and packing Sophie's things. Glo was coming by to help as well.

On my way home from the memorial the night before, I had stopped by Sophie's house. The cleaning company had promised to send a crew by on Saturday morning to clean the back room and the kitchen. I had to pay extra for the Saturday service, but considered it necessary. I made the arrangements with the owner of the company. After describing the delicate nature of the job, he tacked on another premium, saying that he would have to send special people.

Tomorrow would mark a week since Sophie's death. By the time a month passes, I thought of how it might seem as if she'd never existed, except in our memories.

I hadn't realized how truly simple and small our lives are until now. Sophie was forty-seven years old when she died. Her forty-eighth birthday would have been in a few weeks. The fact that even after nearly forty-eight years, an entire life could be sorted, labeled, and packed in the span of a few weekend days astounded me. A whole lifetime processed and wrapped like sliced turkey sandwich meat. When the package is empty, we just move on to the maple-flavored ham until that, too, is used up. I found it depressing to think about disposable humanity. It felt too much like disposable diapers.

I had walked around Sophie's house the night before, touching and caressing her things. They were all that was left of her. In a moment of courage I went to the back office and opened the door slowly. I reached in first, felt the switch on the wall near the door, and snapped on the light.

The chair, stained with the dark pattern of Sophie's blood, stood as a silent memorial.

Later last night, after I was home, I had called Greg Stevens and set up a meeting. It had been almost midnight, but he picked up the phone on the first ring. I didn't care how late it was, I had to make the appointment before I chickened out. He didn't seem to mind. In fact, he didn't seem surprised at all by my call.

He held out his right hand to me as I approached the table. I took it and shook politely, but not before noticing a very large golden retriever by his side. As I've said before, I'm not much of an animal person. The dog came forward and intently smelled my legs, which were encased in cotton leggings. I must have seemed nervous because Greg pulled him back.

"Wainwright, down," he commanded.

The dog immediately sank to the pavement next to his master. I was impressed.

"Sorry, he loves new people," he said, apologizing.

"He must smell my cat."

"Then that explains it," Greg said with a big grin. "Wainwright loves cats. Though most of them have heart attacks when they see him galloping up to play. What's its name?"

"Huh? Oh. You mean my cat. His name is Seamus."

Greg and I smiled at each other. It was plain to see that he was trying to put me at ease.

After I had called him, I invested some time doing research on Greg Stevens. Being a paralegal has its rewards, not to mention access to and knowledge of public records. What I needed to know, I found right online. You just have to know where to look.

I verified that Gregory William Stevens was the owner and operator of Ocean Breeze Graphics, a printing and design shop located in Huntington Beach. It was a sole proprietorship with a fictitious name certificate properly filed with the Orange County clerk. I also discovered that he graduated in 1985 from Palisades High School, and from Cal State–Long Beach in 1990 with a degree in business. Five years ago he purchased a home in Seal Beach. I even drove by the house early this morning to determine the type of neighborhood he lived in. All seemed on the up and up.

"I hope you don't mind eating here," he said. "The food is very good and it's one of the few places that allows me to have Wainwright with me."

"No, not at all. And it's nice being so close to the beach."

We were making small talk, avoiding the real reason for the meeting. We were here to talk about Sophie; to discuss the possibility of a murder.

As soon as the waitress brought coffee and took our orders, I opened the discussion.

"Did you see Hollowell and that man arguing at the chapel?" I asked.

He took a sip of coffee. "You mean the little guy making accusations and Hollowell ignoring him?"

"Exactly."

"Sure I saw it. Who didn't?"

"So who are those guys? You said that you knew Hollowell."

"No, not exactly. Until that guy called him Hollowell, I didn't know that was him."

"But you said—"

"I said, I know who Hollowell is. Meaning, I know who he is, or was, to Sophie."

"And?"

"John Hollowell was Sophie's addiction. Heroin in human form. Though I have no idea who he is, the little guy was probably right. It's very likely that Hollowell did have something to do with her death. Maybe not directly, but at least indirectly."

Our breakfasts came. Greg immediately began cutting up his eggs, then splashed some salsa over them. While I waited for more information, I watched the yellow yolks and red sauce run all over the plate, mixing with the whites and hash browns. My own avocado and jack cheese omelet went ignored.

He took a bite, chewed, and swallowed before going on.

"Sophie was in love with the bastard. Had been for years, even though she knew he was just using her. She was trying to break it off. I think there was a lot of co-dependency in that relationship."

"You knew about her son?" I cut a small piece of omelet with the side of my fork and ate it without tasting, waiting for his answer.

"I knew she had one. That she hadn't seen him in years, not since he was a small boy. That, too, somehow was because of Hollowell, though she never went into details."

I continued with my twenty questions. "Did you know that her son thinks she's been dead all these years? And that he lives just about an hour from here?"

Now it was his turn to be surprised. We both drank some coffee. He flagged the waitress over for a refill.

"Sherrie, while you're at it, could you get Wainwright a bit of water?"

"Sure, Greg," the waitress answered. She flashed a megawatt smile at him that was more than just good service.

Shortly, she returned with a plastic bowl and placed it on the ground by the patient dog, patting him on the head before leaving. I could hear the animal lapping at the water with great gusto. It made me smile. In the middle of all this crazy intrigue, his eager drinking made sense. It was normal and natural.

"I knew about the son's existence," Greg said. "Nothing more. Because she told me she hadn't seen him in years, I assumed he lived out of state or at least far away."

"The boy and his father live in Santa Paula."

Greg was surprised again. "Santa Paula isn't that far away. Do you think maybe the little guy at the service was her husband?"

I thought about it before answering. "Could be. But the attorney said he spoke to Sophie's ex, and he claimed he didn't want anything to do with her or her estate. In fact, he said to just mail him a check for their son if anything was left."

"So everything goes to the boy?"

"Yes. Except for a few personal bequests. Including something to you, I might add." He brightened a bit at my words, but his smile was tainted with sadness. "Everything else is to be liquidated and given to the father as trustee for the son. I'm told the son is about twenty now."

"Is there much of an estate? I never got the feeling Sophie was rolling in dough, just comfortable."

We had finished breakfast and were sipping coffee. I looked at my watch. I still had another hour before meeting Zee and Cruz.

"More than I expected," I explained. "Stocks, savings, jewelry. The house, of course, which is mortgage-free. A rough initial estimate came in at just over a million."

"Nice," Greg said, sounding impressed. "Sounds like she was a good little saver. You think maybe she was killed for the estate? If so, that would point to the ex or the son."

"Yes, but I don't think so. Supposedly, the boy didn't even know she existed and her ex wants to keep it that way. Since the boy is the only heir, no one else would have benefited financially from her death."

"So money wouldn't be the motive for murder."

Although it was on both of our minds, this was the first time either of us had used the *M* word.

I threw out another idea, one I had been chewing on like a piece of Juicy Fruit. "Maybe the ex-husband wanted to make sure Sophie remained dead to their son."

Greg mulled it over a bit. "It's a possibility. Maybe she was trying to contact the boy and his father didn't like it. That could certainly be a motive. Get her out of the way permanently."

There was something else I had been dying to bring up, but didn't know how without seeming ghoulish. Greg hadn't mentioned again that he'd seen Sophie die. Many others couldn't shut up about it. Leaning forward, I posed it to him in a quiet, almost nonexistent whisper.

"Greg, you said you saw Sophie kill herself."

He nervously ran his fingers through his longish hair, and his handsome face quickly turned from thoughtful to distraught. He looked away, toward the beach across the street.

"Yes," he said quietly. "First she held the gun in her mouth. Then I saw the aftermath."

I had only seen the dried blood, and that had been enough.

"The detective said that the gun was registered in Sophie's name, and that there was gunpowder residue on both of her hands."

Greg nodded. "The residue would make sense if she shot herself. She held the gun with both hands. Like this."

He demonstrated, holding a spoon in both hands and sticking the bowl just inside his lips. The sight of it made me want to vomit. I quickly went back to our conversation about money.

"The only beneficiary is the son, and supposedly he didn't even know she existed."

"Sex and money." Greg was looking out at the beach again. I could tell that he was thinking out loud, rather than speaking to me. "Sex and money," he repeated. "The two most popular reasons for murder."

There it was again, the *M* word.

"What about the website?" I asked. "Perhaps one of the viewers got too close."

More than once it had crossed my mind that maybe Greg Stevens had gotten too close. He said he'd never met Sophie, but that didn't mean he was telling the truth. For someone he'd never met, he sure knew a lot about her. He turned his gaze away from the beach and in my direction, catching me red-handed in the act of scrutinizing him. I felt myself blush and quickly brought my coffee mug up to my mouth, hoping to cover part of it.

"Greg," I said, after taking a couple swallows of coffee, "since we are on such friendly and candid terms now, tell me something. Something that Sophie might have confided in you."

"Sure, doesn't matter now, does it?"

I felt my mouth turn downward.

"Tell me, why did Sophie perform on that site?"

Greg reached down and patted his dog. I could tell he was giving it a great deal of thought. Picking up a scrap of bacon from his plate, he fed it to the well-behaved animal.

"Sophie had a lot of reasons for operating that site. Some I know, most I can guess at. Money, for one reason. She was very popular and had a lot of subscribers. Also, I think it gave her a boost emotionally."

"You mean performing like that gave her a rush?"

"Probably. You'd be surprised how many people get their kicks that way on the Internet. But for Sophie it was more than that." He paused, weighing his words carefully.

"Both you and Sophie did a lot of work promoting equality for overweight women. If you haven't looked at the site yet, you should. Her message is loud and clear, even there. All women are beautiful, no matter what their size or shape. Also . . . ," he drifted off.

"Also, what?" I asked, urging him on. He was talking about a friend I knew, yet didn't know. "Did she ever say anything specifically about the site?"

"Yes, one night she and I talked until dawn about a lot of things." He rolled his wheelchair closer to me, and I found myself leaning in closer to him.

"The same bigotry that faces you as an overweight woman often faces the disabled. We are viewed differently, as something apart. People are nervous around others who are not quite the same as they are."

He paused briefly, took a deep breath, and continued. "Just as many people don't view me as a whole man, they don't see you as a whole woman. And you know that's true, Odelia. I'm not telling you something you haven't already experienced."

I nodded. Size does matter. In getting jobs, mates, even seats on buses, it's always a factor. Even shopping.

"It doesn't matter if it's weight, a disability, religion, or the color of someone's skin," Greg said. "It's all based on ignorance. Most of the men who frequented Sophie's website adore larger women, including me. That night she told me that chatting with them, getting e-mails and fan mail, made her feel truly special. After giving so much to everyone else, this was where she received her support. Her refueling, so to speak."

It was my turn to gaze out at the ocean. I stared at the sand and surf across the street and took several deep breaths, each time filling my lungs with the salty fresh air until they could hold no more.

"It bothers you that she confided in me and not you, doesn't it?" Greg asked.

I nodded without looking at him.

"Maybe I can explain it better. You ever go online, like in chat rooms?"

Again, I nodded my confession. "Yes, a few times. But I usually find them pretty stupid."

"Ever meet someone, man or woman, and find yourself talking to them about everything?"

I didn't have to think long before remembering JersyLil. Her real name was Lillian Ramsey. We'd met playing backgammon online and spent hours one evening just playing one game after another and talking. We still meet about an hour a week to play and chat. Though she doesn't live that far away, in all this time we've never met. I had confided things to her even Zee didn't know. It was dawning on me where Greg was going with this.

"Yes. I have an online friend like that."

"That's how Sophie and I were. We were faceless confidants, although I knew what she looked like. I came across her webcam site one night, then started corresponding and chatting with her regularly. Since I have design and computer knowledge, I helped her with the site on occasion. Later, it became regular phone calls." He sighed deeply. "I begged her to meet me, but she wouldn't allow it."

"Maybe you were angry about that, found her, and killed her," I said, my head down, eyes focused on the murky coffee in the mug I still held like a security blanket. Here I sat, suggesting he was a murderer, and I didn't even have the guts to look him in the eye.

"I could have been, but I wasn't. I understood why she didn't want to meet me. Once the anonymity is removed, the appeal to confess disappears. You become more self-conscious about what people know about you when you have to look them in the eye."

I knew he was right. Inside, I didn't believe he killed Sophie. I wanted to trust Greg Stevens. He was a link to Sophie's secret life and I wanted to make sure I didn't lose that link.

"We're also forgetting something else," he started to say just as Sherrie came by with our bill. Greg gave her his credit card over my protests. "No, this one's on me. Next time, you can treat me by cooking."

Next time? Cooking? This guy was about a decade younger than me and we were knee deep into a discussion on murder. Was that an attempt to flirt or just a courtesy remark? I was so out of practice, I wouldn't have been able to tell unless the comment had come wrapped around a dozen roses. I dismissed it as a simple nicety.

"What are we forgetting?" I asked him, getting the conversation back on track.

"We're forgetting another very important reason for not telling your friends something."

"And that would be?"

"For their own good. To protect them."

NINE

Everyone has a favorite and least favorite holiday. My favorite is the Fourth of July. My least favorite is any holiday that requires me to spend time with my family, with Mother's Day topping the list.

When I was about thirteen, my mother insisted on a divorce. She was an alcoholic with ideas of grandeur and was given to fits of depression. I wasn't happy about the split, but it put a stop to the horrendous fighting, and for that I was glad. Following the break-up, I saw my father a few times a month. After he remarried, I hardly saw him at all.

A few years later, I came home from high school to find my mother's things packed and gone. There was no note left behind, just half-open drawers and a sink full of dirty dishes. I kept going to school, trying to pretend everything was normal. She was just away, I told myself. She went to visit someone and forgot to tell me, I said to my reflection in the mirror every morning before school. Three weeks after she left, I finally called my father. That was almost thirty years ago. To this day I still don't know if she's alive or dead. My father is reluctant to speak about it. My stepmother takes every opportunity to remind me of it.

After my mother's disappearance, I lived with my father and stepmother until I was old enough to move out on my own. I remember clearly counting the days.

Mother's Day is a two-pronged fork of fire for me. One, it reminds me that my own mother took a powder. Two, it reminds me that my father married Gigi.

I've tried to politely bow out of these holiday functions, but my father gets his feelings hurt every time I try. He seems to forget that they're his family, not mine. I'm not the one who vowed for better or for worse.

My father hadn't married well when he married my mother. With Gigi, he hit the bottom of the barrel. The woman hates me for the single reason that I am my father's child from a prior marriage. When I lived with them, she treated me like an indentured servant. My father, Horten Grey, is a nice enough guy with the spine of a jellyfish and a few bricks missing from his load. But for all his frailties, he loves me and I love him, and it would hurt him to his very core if I just vanished like my mother.

He's seventy-nine now and Gigi is eighty-one. Gigi has two children from her first marriage. The eldest is Dee, who is sixty-three. Gigi's son JJ is sixty. Gigi's family not only reads the *National Enquirer*, they're the sort who believe it. Get the picture?

With a fake smile worthy of a greasy politician, I showed up at my father's house with a cake freshly purchased from the grocery store. Dee took the cake from me as I entered the kitchen area and all but tossed it on the counter. I knew it would never be opened and eaten. Nothing I ever brought or made was. Dee's husband and family were nowhere to be seen. Neither was Nonnie, Gigi's ninety-nine-year-old mother, and the only one in the family I liked. But I didn't expect to see her since she was in a rest home. JJ, wearing an undershirt and dirty khaki shorts, was slouched in the living room watching TV. A can of Coors occupied one hand, the other hand dangled around his balls. My father was asleep in his recliner.

I fought the urge to run screaming to my car and drive nonstop to Montana.

"Where's your family, Dee?" I asked instead.

"At home, where do you think?" she snapped, a cigarette hanging from her mouth. "I'm a mother, too, you know. Only came over here cause Ma would pitch a fit if I didn't."

"Who'd have a fit?" It was Gigi. With hair dyed the color of cotton candy and worn in a similar shape, she shuffled into the kitchen on spindly legs. Her freshly powdered face and sharply arched eyebrows were straight out of clown college.

"You, Ma. I was just telling Odelia how you'd have a fit if she didn't make it over today."

I glowered at Dee, but said nothing. Her specialty was lying, especially if she could shift the blame to me in the process. She lived less than two miles away and seldom visited or called her mother. I lived forty miles away and was usually the one on the hook when something went wrong around the house. I also suspected that I was the only one who regularly visited Nonnie in the rest home.

"Well, it's the least she could do, considering I took her in after that no-good mother of hers left her flat."

I wanted to remind Gigi that I was right here in the room, but since she was looking straight at me as she made the rude comment, I didn't bother. Instead, I bit my tongue and walked into the living room, hoping to rouse my father.

I kissed his grizzled cheek. He moved slightly, then opened his eyes. A small smile crossed his face when he recognized me, and he reached up to stroke my chin. That alone had been worth the trek on the freeway.

He wasn't happy and I knew it. Gigi and her family dominated him like playground bullies. Her children berated him to his face. Once they made the mistake of doing it in front of me. Only once.

"How are you doing, Dad?"

He looked puzzled, then perked up and gave a little laugh. Reaching up to his left ear he turned on his hearing aid. Most of the time he had it off. It was the only way he could get any peace.

"How are you doing?" I asked again, pulling up a chair near him.

"Good, dear. You look so pretty today. You always look so pretty." He beamed at me, flashing a smile that showed off the fact that he still had most of his own teeth.

"Thanks, Dad, you ol' flatterer."

"Hey Odelia, what's the story on that friend of yours?" The question came from JJ, who was still slumped on the sofa.

JJ was currently living with my father and Gigi. He had been divorced for over twenty years and his children lived back east somewhere. None of them wanted him. He hadn't held a steady job since I'd known him. Instead, he scratched out a meager living by working the angles, always looking for the easy way out. He gambled, cheated, and ran scams, anything to get his hands on a few dollars. Anything to avoid an honest day's work.

If his question referred to Sophie, I wasn't in the mood to discuss it. This was the type of stuff Gigi and her brood thrived on. They would make a meal out of this at my expense. I ignored the question.

"Hey, I said," JJ persisted. "What's with your friend Sophie?"

74

"She died recently, JJ," I said bluntly.

"Died, hell! She blew her friggin' brains out! And right on the Internet. A friend of mine saw it."

I wanted him to shut up. "Have another beer, JJ. You need it."

"Who died?" my father asked.

"Somebody dead?" Gigi hollered, racing as fast as she was able into the room. "Who? Who died? Who?" She sounded like an owl on speed. Dee was right behind her. Gigi turned around and clutched at her daughter. "Oh God, Dee, someone died."

"What?" my father asked, adjusting his hearing aid. "Did someone die or not?"

"A friend of mine did," I said loudly, aiming for his left ear.

"Yeah, some porn slut friend of Odelia's blew her brains out," JJ added, raising his voice above the others.

I shot him a scowl, sorry that he was too old to be shipped off to military school.

Each participant in the debate spoke louder than the last to make sure they were heard. The din was growing, making my head hurt.

"A friend of yours?" asked Gigi. She turned her attention back to Dee. "I bet it was that little colored gal she's so chummy with."

My father tapped my arm to get my attention. "Did I ever tell you about the time I was in the army? Saw a lot of people die in the war."

Much more of this and *I'd* be blowing my brains out. Right here, right now.

On the wall behind me hung a black velvet and neon colored rug depicting John F. Kennedy and the White House. It had been there for as long as I could remember. I suddenly pictured it spattered with thick red liquid and lumpy gray matter. Being the sick puppy I am, the imagery seemed fitting and logical, and it made me feel better.

Hoping to head off any more wild assumptions, I decided to make a statement. I stood up and addressed the inmates of the insane asylum, holding out my arms as if directing traffic.

"Quiet, everyone, please," I began with a shout, as if trying to be heard over a hundred people. "My friend Sophie London, *not* my friend Zee Washington," I announced, directing the last few words at Gigi, "committed suicide last Sunday. I did not know she operated an adult website. I repeat, I DID NOT KNOW about her website." The last statement was made to JJ.

"Website?" Gigi asked. "That one of them sex things on the computer?"

I hung my head in despair. The idea of grabbing my elderly father, slinging him over my shoulder, and racing out of the house suddenly crossed my mind. Like rescuing a child from a burning building, you don't think about it, you just do it. It might even snare me a medal from the AARP.

"Yeah, Ma," JJ told her with a grin. "This friend of Odelia's, some big ol' fat blonde, stripped in front of a camera. And for money."

Gigi looked horrified. She stared at me as if I were the one with the porn site. "Now why in heaven's name would any man pay to see a fat girl naked?"

"Oooh," said Dee, "that's gross and disgusting. I could see a man paying to see a slim, pretty girl."

"Sophie was *very* beautiful," I said loudly to Dee.

Pausing while they bantered ignorantly, I got a grip on myself. I didn't need to defend Sophie, myself, or anyone else to these louts. They were off and running again, and I was helpless to stop it. Might as well be a toddler trying to halt a runaway train.

"Odelia," Gigi said, laughing, "girls like you can't even get a man to look for free. What made your friend think any guy would *pay* to see her?"

"More like paying to see a circus side show, if you ask me," said JJ, scratching his privates.

"No wonder that girl killed herself," Dee said with a clucking sound. "I'd kill myself, too, if I got that fat."

While they were cackling and feeding off of Sophie's corpse like vultures at a banquet, I bent down to kiss my father goodbye.

I had been there long enough.

His eyes were red and wet.

TEN

My skin was crawling and tight after I left my father's house. I felt encased in a rubber wet suit two sizes too small on a hot day. It was how I usually felt after time spent with my stepfamily.

Instead of going home, I decided to head over to Sophie's. At least I could continue sorting and labeling items. The work, depressing as it was, would keep my hands busy. I was afraid, if left on my own, I'd inhale half of the supermarket's inventory of Ben & Jerry's ice cream.

With Sophie's radio playing in the background, I made a considerable dent in the packing. Later, I dashed out and brought back a grilled chicken sandwich and a vanilla shake from the closest drive-thru restaurant. During this break I called Greg. As I had expected, he wasn't home, this being Mother's Day and all, but I left a message asking him to call me on my cell phone if he got home soon. He called about an hour later and eagerly accepted my invitation to come by.

I had invited Greg over to help with some of the office stuff, particularly the computer. It was also an awkward and very amateur test. My trust level in Greg Stevens was about eighty-five percent to the good, but there was still room for error. He had said that he'd never met Sophie. That also meant that he had never been to her home. The murderer, if there was one, would have been here before.

It was my plan to watch him closely, to observe any spark of recognition or familiarity when he entered the house. So far, he was passing. When I intentionally failed to provide the address, Greg asked for it. Then he asked for general directions from the freeway. It either meant he was telling the truth or that he was a criminal on his toes, so to speak.

I was in the kitchen wrapping dishes when the doorbell rang about thirty minutes later. In spite of my trap, I felt my insides leap at the thought of seeing Greg again. I scolded myself. He's much younger than I am, and let's not forget he's a viewer of Sophie's sex site. And a possible murderer. I liked the man, no doubt there, but cautioned myself to keep the fantasies on the back burner—at least until I was one hundred percent sure he wasn't the murderer.

Even with these other obstacles out of the way, he was in a wheelchair. I had never been attracted to a man in a wheelchair before and wasn't sure how I felt about it, deep down inside. His comment about the disabled and the overweight being treated in a similar fashion had played itself over in my mind a few times. Perhaps it was true, to a certain extent. While many people consider the overweight targets for ridicule, the disabled are often treated with pity and misguided condescension. But I also reminded myself that with a lot of hard work I could change my weight to some degree. Greg would never be able to change his situation. But opportunity for improvement aside, in general, neither are treated as true equals with valuable skills, capable of significant contributions. Both are feared as personal possibilities or punishments to be rained down like the plagues of Israel.

There but for the grace of God go I.

A thought suddenly smacked me upside the brain. If Greg was the murderer, I had invited him here to be alone with me at the scene of the crime. I stopped in my tracks in front of the door. Was a murderer on the other side, separated from me by only a few inches of wood and paint? How stupid could I have been? I looked around, feeling very vulnerable.

The doorbell rang again, this time in two staccato blasts.

"Odelia," I told myself in a barely audible whisper, "you've really gotten yourself into a mess."

I did a quick study of my predicament. Dashing out the back and hiding in the shrubbery became a distinct possibility. Then I took stock of the positive aspects of the situation. Greg was in a wheelchair, and even I could outrun and outmaneuver a man who couldn't walk.

"Odelia, you gonna outrun a bullet, too?" I asked myself in a hushed tone.

I heard voices from the other side of the door. Voices, in the plural. I breathed a sigh of relief. Before I could unlock the door, the bell rang again. This time the blast was long and pleading. Whoever it was seemed eager to come inside.

Opening the door a bit, I peered out and found myself face to face with a small and varied crowd of three. Greg was there, sitting in his wheelchair. Fortunately, or unfortunately, depending on the outcome of his visit, Sophie's house didn't have a series of steps up to the front door. Next to him, sitting obediently, was Wainwright, who wagged his tail politely when he saw me. The third party was Iris Somers. She was talking a mile a minute to Greg. I caught the word *beams* here and there.

I groaned inwardly, hoping that none of my annoyance audibly escaped my lips.

"Greg, have you met Sophie's neighbor, Iris Somers?" I asked with false perkiness.

"Just now," he said, his eyes pleading with me for rescue.

I stepped aside. Wainwright trotted in first. There was a small lip from the landing up to the main floor of the house. With his guidance, I gave Greg a bit of assistance to get over it, amazed at how easily the chair responded to contact. It was compact and lightweight, the metal tubing painted in a bright purple, black, and silver design. It was the type of wheelchair I'd seen athletes use.

Once he was inside, I quickly stepped into the frame of the doorway, blocking Iris's entrance. I thought about slamming the door in her face, but didn't. Doors don't *slip* twice. That would be too much of a coincidence. And I certainly didn't want my dark side exhibited to Greg. She wasn't carrying her parasol today. Instead, she was wearing a hat, a bonnet with a brim entirely covered in foil. Her head resembled a turkey about to be shoved into a moderate oven for a few hours of roasting.

"What can I do for you, Iris?" I asked, dispensing with formalities and using her first name. Even I heard the frost in my voice.

She sighed her signature sigh. "The beams," she said simply.

I didn't answer, just looked at her blankly. Maybe if I ignored her, she would dismiss me as a fool and go away. It was worth a shot. I glanced back at Greg, who was seated just behind me. He was listening, but his head was also turning around, looking at the place. To me, he looked like someone seeing it for the first time. It was a good sign and helped me relax.

"The beams," Iris said again. She looked behind me and addressed Greg. "The rays from these home security systems are very dangerous, you know. I've incurred quite a few doctor's bills because of this system, and she," she said, pointing a knobby finger at me, "doesn't do anything about it. Just like her dead friend."

Greg visibly bristled around the edges. It reminded me of the way Seamus reacts when irritated. Just as quickly, I saw Greg ease up. He propelled his chair closer to the door, positioning himself beside me.

"In the future," he said to Iris with calm authority, "if you feel you are being injured by the security system, please report it to the alarm company. It's their system, their issue."

"I have. After dozens of complaints, they finally sent someone out to check on it. But he didn't do anything." Iris repositioned her finger in Greg's direction. "Those beams are what caused your friend to kill herself. They get into your brain, mixing it all up."

"Please call the company," Greg said again, firmly. "And stop bothering Odelia with this nonsense. She has enough on her mind."

He retreated his chair a bit and gave me a sign with his head to shut the door. I followed his direction, being careful not to slam the solid piece of wood, as I wanted. Just as the door started closing, I caught Iris's last words.

"At least *last* weekend the alarm guy wasn't so rude."

My head jerked toward Greg. His eyes, round with surprise, found mine and locked. I yanked the door open.

"Iris," I called out. She was already halfway down the walk, heading for the gate. She turned when she heard her name. "The alarm guy was here last weekend?"

She didn't say anything, just looked at me.

"Well, was he?" I asked again, my voice taking on a tone of urgent demand.

Greg reached out and touched the small of my back lightly. Then he took over.

"Iris, forgive us," he said, smooth as silk. "We didn't realize that someone from the alarm company had stopped by. When exactly was he here?"

She looked at Greg and smiled coyly from under her silver head-dress. Her gaze moved to me and she scowled. She looked back at Greg and addressed him in her usual soft yet firm voice.

"He was here Saturday. As soon as I saw the truck, I came out to speak with him. He said he came by to check the system."

"Did you see him with Sophie London?" I asked.

Iris Somers rolled her eyes at me. Clearly, she thought me the village idiot. Maybe my initial plan was working too well.

"No, she wasn't home. He said he'd have to come back. He came by Sunday morning, too, but he wasn't here long."

I placed a hand on Greg's shoulder and squeezed gently. He continued with the delicate interrogation. "Iris, did the police talk to you after Sophie died?"

"Yes, they came by. I told them I heard the shot. Well, I didn't know it was a gunshot at the time. I was in bed suffering from a migraine, from the beams, of course. They had been very active the night before." She looked at me defiantly. "I told the police about the beams. I told them how Ms. London refused to stop them."

Under my hand, I felt Greg lean forward. "Did you tell them about the alarm guy?" he asked her.

Iris had to think about that. "I don't think so. I told them about hearing a loud noise. Then I showed them where the beams from the system shoot into my property. Right after that, they told me they had enough information."

I wanted to strangle her. The police probably figured she was useless as a witness upon hearing about the damn beams. I imagined yanking on one of the imaginary beams and twisting it around her scrawny neck, tying it into a big bow to go with her foil parasol and foil bonnet. This demented woman definitely did not bring out the best in me.

"Think about it, Iris," Greg gently coaxed. "Do you remember what time the alarm serviceman was here?"

She pursed her lips. I was sure she was whirling the question around in that beam-damaged brain of hers.

"Not exactly."

"Was it before or after you heard the shot?"

"Before, I think. No, maybe right after. Hard to tell since I didn't know what I'd heard was a gunshot." She gave it more thought. "But I think it was before."

Greg thanked her for her help and assured her that he would do whatever he could to stop the beams from injuring her again.

With a final look of triumph tossed my way and a flick of her foil-wrapped turkey head, Iris Somers walked down the walkway and out the gate. Greg and I watched her as she turned left on the sidewalk and proceeded to her own walkway next door.

I was happy to see the back of Iris Somers. And I was even more glad that Greg had been here to deal with her. He had handled her well, much better than I could have.

That over and done with, I turned to see Greg wheeling himself deeper into Sophie's house, looking around as he made his way. Suddenly I wished that we hadn't been so diligent with the dismantling and packing. I was sorry that he hadn't been able to see her home as she had kept it, with her sweet personal touches and warmhearted mementos. The living room and kitchen were both scattered with boxes, filled and well labeled.

He stopped in the dining room, his attention focused on something specific. Coming up behind him, I saw that he was looking at a portrait of Sophie, a small fine oil in a simple but elegant frame. The artist had truly captured her beauty and personality. It was the item she'd left him in her will.

"She was so beautiful," he whispered with reverence.

"She left you that painting," I said, equally as quiet. "You can take it home tonight, if you wish."

He looked at me and beamed. "Really?"

The pleased look on his face made me happy, but something else was nagging at me.

"Greg, why would an alarm company send out a service guy on a Sunday morning?"

He thought about it. "Maybe for an emergency."

"You mean like a repeated false alarm? Or something like that?"

"Probably."

"My townhouse has an alarm, and my service is with the same company as this house. Normally, they would have made an appointment with Sophie before coming out on Saturday, and Sophie wasn't the type to blow off appointments."

I headed for the office. Greg followed.

The cleaning people had done an excellent job of scrubbing the walls and the carpet. There was just a ghost of a stain left on the floor behind the desk. That I could live with, if I kept my head up. The Van Gogh prints and the chair were gone, disposed of by the cleaning company. Everything had been wiped down. Books and papers were set aside, awaiting review.

Sophie had used a combination appointment and address book. The police had gone through it shortly after finding her. Now it was closed and on the desk. I picked it up and turned to last weekend. Saturday and Sunday were on the same side, each allotted a half page. There were no entries for either day.

"What do you make of that?" I asked Greg, showing him. I held the book up, but he wasn't paying attention. His eyes were on the floor, studying the shadowy stain on the carpet.

He smiled weakly and looked at the calendar. After quickly noting the absence of an entry, he shrugged.

"Maybe she didn't remember the service guy was coming. Or maybe it wasn't important enough to write down."

"Perhaps," I said. "Or she didn't know he was coming."

"The company could have dispatched him just to get Iris Somers off their back."

"But on a Saturday *and* Sunday?" I dug into my memory. It had been quite a while since I'd had any reason to call the company for service. In fact, I hardly ever remembered to set my system. "If this was just a routine check on the system, they would have done it during the week. Sophie worked from home usually, so scheduling on a weekend would not have been necessary. And I doubt if they would view a crackpot like Iris as an emergency."

I started pulling open desk drawers. So far, we had only gone through Sophie's things in the other rooms. I wanted to call the alarm company, but I knew that they would never speak to me about her account. I would have to find her abort code for them to release any information. Or I could contact Detective Frye.

I wasn't ready to do the latter. The police had determined the case a simple suicide. Asking them to look into a security company technician who *might* have been here before Sophie pulled the trigger didn't seem like such a good idea. Especially since our only witness was a nut with self-proclaimed electrocuted brains.

"If I can find Sophie's alarm information," I explained to Greg, "I can call and ask about recent service dispatches."

"You think the guy from the alarm company had anything to do with this?" he asked. "Iris said she thinks he left before the shot."

"I don't know, Greg, but what I do know is that he was probably the last person to see her alive. At the very least, he might be able to tell me what her emotional state was that morning."

He nodded. "I'd really like to know that myself."

As I expected, Sophie was as organized in her office as in everything else. If she didn't have her alarm information handy, it would surprise me. I started going through files in the bottom left-hand side drawer of the desk. Each file tab was neatly printed with a one- or two-word description. This drawer mostly contained files on the computer and her website. I pulled them out for us to review later. I went to the bottom drawer on the right-hand side. Again, the files were well labeled. These were her household and personal files. There was even a copy of her will in one of them.

The last file was simply labeled Security. I yanked it from the drawer and went through it. There was a copy of her contract and other documents that she had signed when she purchased the system. Finally, I found the abort code, the secret numbers or words that are plugged into the panel by the door to stop the alarm. The security company also uses this code as identification when a customer calls about their account.

Walking to the kitchen, I put the file in my tote bag, which I'd left on the table. I would call the company tomorrow and try to get some information on the service guy. When I returned, Greg was going through the files containing the computer information.

"These should help us with handling the website," he told me, not looking up. "Since I helped her from time to time, I have some of the access codes at home that I used for editing the site, but nothing about the billing or host company. You're going to need that."

Greg turned out to be a great deal of help with Sophie's computer stuff. How it should be disposed of and who I should call about it were my top questions. By going through her files, we were able to determine our next steps.

Sophie had treated her adult website like a real business, which, Greg kept reminding me, it was. All pertinent information was organized and filed neatly, including profit reports, member lists, contacts, and tax information. I was shocked to learn that the site earned more each month than I did at the law firm.

Greg said he would help out by contacting the host company that provided the Internet access for the site. He said he would also call the subscription billing company. The records revealed that the hosting fees for May had already been paid, so the site could operate until the end of the month without another payment. I glanced quickly over the agreements with these companies and asked him to see how much notice was required prior to shutting down the site and canceling services, especially under such unusual circumstances. After discussion, Greg and I agreed that we would use the next few weeks to post an appropriate memorial and to notify the paid subscribers. We also found the information about the Reality Check website, and he agreed to design a fitting memorial piece to post there as well.

Leaning back on the loveseat, I watched him eagerly examine the files. Greg Stevens was proving to be a major help. His good-guy percentages were rising.

When he asked if I had ever seen Sophie's adult site, I admitted that I had not, nor did I want to. He told me I should before he started editing it for the memorial piece and offered to open it up right then and there. I declined.

When I got home that evening there was an e-mail from him with a link to the site. He certainly felt strongly about my need to see it, and I felt just as firm about my decision not to see it. But sometime in the middle of the night, when my mind whirred like a turbine engine powered with caffeine, I gave in.

Okay, like I've already confessed, I've visited adult or pornography websites from time to time. I've even participated in cyber sex. But when I opened the Sassy Sophie website and came almost instantly face to face with Sophie's smiling image, it was too much to bear. Quickly, I signed off without going any further.

The rest of the night I wandered my townhouse trying to piece together all the information, like a giant jigsaw puzzle. Hollowell. Olsen. Her son. The man who confronted Hollowell. The website. Even Greg. Each had unique edges and curves that fit into Sophie's life in a particular way.

The great unknown was the murderer, if there was one. I still didn't believe that Sophie was suicidal, at least not in the conventional way. I was anxious to speak with the alarm company, hoping it might provide more insight. But how could it be murder when Sophie had pulled the trigger herself? Yet Greg kept insisting that it had to be murder. I just felt something wasn't right.

A murderer with a motive. This was the stray detail, the missing puzzle piece that invariably falls to the carpet beneath the table, making you search on your hands and knees so that you can complete the puzzle, be satisfied, and finally return the one thousand cheaply cut pieces back to their cardboard box.

In my mind I organized what I already knew, arranging the information in my head like Post-It Notes on a blank wall. Mentally moving them around, I looked for common threads and repeated themes. In my work as a paralegal, I often review materials in such a way. I'm trained to look for cracks in contracts and inconsistencies in provided facts. But there was one little difference: the work at the firm didn't involve a close personal friend or challenge my faith in what I believed was a heroic spirit.

ELEVEN

As USUAL ON A Monday morning, traffic on the San Diego Freeway heading north was heavy, especially approaching the vicinity of the airport and heading deeper into Los Angeles. I concentrated on my driving and read all the major billboards along the way—anything to keep my mind off what I was going to say to Peter Olsen once I reached Santa Paula.

The idea for making this trip blew across my sleep-deprived mind sometime between three and three-thirty this morning, after which I finally fell asleep for a few hours. About eight, I left a voice mail for Tina, the firm's office manager, saying that I needed to take another personal day off to tend to some business. Mr. Wallace wouldn't mind, but Steele, I knew, would be furious. Too bad. I didn't work directly for him anyway.

Before leaving for Santa Paula, I called the security company. But after being put on hold and waiting for fifteen minutes, I gave up. I was anxious to find the technician who had stopped by Sophie's on the day she died, but I was more intrigued about meeting Peter Olsen. I made a mental note to call the alarm company later.

Bits and pieces of Sophie's unknown life were surfacing. With each question asked and each drawer opened and gone through, her life's baggage was floating to the top like oyster crackers in clam chowder.

In Sherman Oaks, I made the transition to the Ventura Freeway and headed away from the sprawl of Los Angeles. I was about halfway there and knew I needed to take the remaining time to put together a plan. On the seat next to me was Sophie's address book. Olsen's addresses and telephone numbers for both home and office were listed, written neatly under the O's. Hollowell's numbers were in the book, too, along with mine and Greg's.

A box sat on the seat next to the address book. It contained photos and trinkets. Most of the photos were of the same boy at different stages, typical grade school poses. They were the same type of color shots most parents display proudly year after year, chronicling their child's progress through the educational system. It wasn't hard to conclude that the boy in the photos was Sophie's son. Even as a young boy he was the spitting image of his mother, right down to the honey blond hair and slight dimple in the left cheek. His eyes were clear blue with a bit of an almond shape, his nose straight as an arrow.

Late last night, I had sat at my kitchen table with a cup of hot herbal tea and arranged the photos in chronological order as best I could. The school shots had been easy since most had his name and the grade on the back—*Robbie, Grade 2*, etc. As he aged, he still looked like Sophie, but with a more angular and masculine line to his jaw. The last photo was a high school graduation shot with a young man in his cap and gown. He was smiling but looking slightly downward at the ground. I studied the picture and the others over and over. He seemed shy and reserved, unlike his vivacious mother.

None of these photos had been on display in Sophie's home. Zee found them while cleaning out a closet in the master bedroom on Saturday. I had brought them home to look through, then forgot until last night.

The box was decorated with fabric, lace, and tiny silk flowers. They were treasures kept in a special place for special viewing. Also in the box was a large silver locket containing a few wisps of hair and a tiny photo of an infant, and a pair of worn baby shoes. The shoes had been placed in a plastic resealable bag.

I couldn't help but wonder how often Sophie had taken this box out of its hiding place, lovingly touched the contents, and cried herself to sleep.

What had surprised me most had been the newspaper clippings and copies of school report cards. Robbie Olsen had been a track star in junior high and high school. Local newspaper articles, now yellowed, reported on regional track meets. His name had been carefully underlined wherever it had appeared. His report cards showed him to be an able but not gifted student.

According to the bits of information Doug Hemming had, Sophie had not seen her son since he was about three or four. Yet someone had helped her keep in touch. The boy may have thought his mother was dead, but his mother had kept tabs on him through the aid of someone close enough to provide her with this information.

Sophie once told me that her father had died when she was very young and that her mother had passed away when she was nineteen. She said she didn't know of any other family members. Her mother had told her that just before she had been born they had moved to California. Who was left if the ex-husband wanted nothing to do with her?

As I approached Camarillo, I reached over and lightly touched the top of the fancy box. Did my own mother have such a keepsake? Did someone send her my high school and college graduation photos? Quickly, I shoved the thought aside.

I passed through Oxnard and entered Ventura. Every town along this part of the freeway seemed to host factory outlet malls. I quickly glanced at the map and saw that the turnoff for Santa Paula was coming up soon. Highway 126 was what I needed. I flew by a road sign informing me that Highway 126 was two miles ahead.

Santa Paula is a town of about twenty-six thousand located in the Santa Clara River Valley. It's primarily an agricultural area, also known as the Citrus Capital of the World. I drove by acres and acres of citrus groves, separated now and then by fields of some type of vegetable growing low to the ground. Workers, heads covered with an assortment of straw hats and baseball caps, toiled under the hot, baking sun.

I exited the highway and drove into town. Following the map I had downloaded from MapQuest, I headed for Olsen's house. It was about eleven in the morning. I didn't think he would be at home, but I wanted to get an idea about how he lived. You can tell a lot about a person by his choice of residence—maybe not if he's a killer or not, but at least his taste and station in life.

The Olsen home was a large ranch-style house tucked away in a wooded clearing on a very small street that could be taken for nothing more than an alley. The whole neighborhood was like that, a honeycomb of small streets that bobbed and weaved in all directions, canopied by large, old trees. Many of the houses were half hidden. Most seemed roomy and well maintained. It was a very good neighborhood and probably housed most of Santa Paula's professionals.

I cruised by Olsen's house slowly, trying not to look like a crook casing the joint. There was a car in the circular driveway, a new Oldsmobile. Satisfied with my findings, I worked my way back to the main street and headed in the direction of Olsen's business.

In my digging, I had discovered that Peter Olsen owned a retail store specializing in farm equipment. When I drove up, it reminded me of a car dealership, but instead of the latest models in two and four-door sedans, the showroom and parking lot contained the most up-to-date farm implements and machinery.

I parked my car on the street, but before getting out I powered up my cell phone. Rummaging in my bag, I found Greg's business card and dialed his number at Ocean Breeze Graphics. I had told no one about my last-minute trek to Santa Paula. Zee would worry all day if she knew. Seth would pick up on that and worm the truth out of her, leading to me sitting through a long and heated future lecture.

Still, I felt that someone should know . . . just in case.

As usual, Zee was right. I wasn't the police or a detective. I was just me, a middle-aged, overweight, nosy woman. I was no more equipped to interview and cope with a conniving murderer than I was to play basketball with the Los Angeles Lakers. But I was hell-bent on finding out the truth about Sophie's final hours, and that single-mindedness alone made me a formidable opponent. At least in my fantasy world.

The phone was ringing on the other end. A man answered. He sounded young. When I asked for Greg and told him my name, he said to hang on.

"Odelia?"

I was only a hundred miles away, yet his voice felt like home. The desire to turn the car around and head back was engulfing me like a fast-moving storm. I steeled myself against it. I had made a commitment to get to the bottom of this and would see it though.

"Um, hi Greg," was all I could muster.

"What's up? You on a cell phone?"

"Yes, I'm in my car. In Santa Paula."

Silence on the other end.

"I'm going to talk to Peter Olsen," I said quickly. "Sophie's ex-husband." There was a pause. I filled it with a little white lie. "I was wondering if there's anything you'd like me to ask him, something I might not have thought of."

"Why didn't you tell me you were going?" he asked. "I could have gone with you." He sounded worried.

Half of me wished I hadn't called him. The other half wanted to wait by the curb in front of Olsen's business until he got here.

"Odelia, you have no idea whom you're dealing with. He might be the killer."

"You could have been the killer, too. But I gave you a chance." I heard him sigh. "This is important to me, Greg. I need to speak with him." Then empty air, making me wonder if I'd lost the connection. "I'll be all right," I added and heard the sigh again.

"Guess it's too late now to talk you out of it," he finally said. "But I still wish you'd waited for me."

"I'll be careful."

"It's almost noon now. I want you to call me by two no matter where you are. And give me your cell phone number. And the description of your car and license number."

It all sounded a bit dramatic and paranoid to me, but comforting all the same. I gave him the information he wanted and hung up after swearing I'd call by two.

As soon as I walked into the showroom area of Olsen's, I was approached by a paunchy middle-aged man wearing a knit shirt with *Olsen's Machinery* stitched over his heart.

"Mr. Olsen?" I asked.

"Back office," the man said, indicating the direction with a jerk of his head. My eyes followed the route of his chin. I could see a glass door leading into an office and headed that way.

Inside the office sat a pleasant-looking elderly woman with a dumpling body and matching face. She wore a cotton dress in a tiny floral print. A strand of pearls cuddled themselves against her thick neck. She looked like she'd be more at home baking cookies and knitting instead of sitting behind a desk answering phones and pushing paper.

"May I help you?" she asked me in a courteous tone. She had a thick European accent, German maybe.

"I'd like to speak with Mr. Olsen, please."

"Peter or Robert?"

The question threw me. I didn't expect to run into Robbie Olsen. In fact, the idea never crossed my mind. I preferred to speak with Olsen senior, but if I could snare a few minutes with Robbie, all the better.

"Whoever is available," I answered.

"And who should I say is here?"

"Odelia Grey. I'm a friend of the family."

Her oatmeal-raisin warmth disappeared as soon as I said the words, and something in the way the old girl looked me over told me not to underestimate her cozy appearance. She disappeared into a back office and returned in an instant, holding the door open for me to enter.

"Peter is out right now, but Robert can see you," she said with more than a smidgen of disapproval in her voice.

Inside the office there were two large wooden desks. One was occupied by a fine-looking young man wearing a company knit shirt. There was no doubt in my mind that this was the live version of the boy in the photos. Here, at last, was Sophie's son. He was beautiful, like having a piece of her in my presence. I fought the urge to fling myself at him and crush him to my hefty bosom.

"Hi, Robbie Olsen," he said shyly as he stood and extended his right hand. "Gram said you're a friend of the family. I'm sorry, but I must confess, I don't remember you." His demeanor may have been modest, but his voice was confident and his words well mannered. Sophie would've been proud.

That he called the old lady Gram wasn't lost on me. No wonder she'd looked me over suspiciously when I said friend of the family. I made an on-the-spot decision. My poker face is nonexistent, so lying was not the best option. I decided to stick as close to the truth as possible without giving away Sophie's secret.

"No, we've never met. I'm an old friend of your mother's."

"Really? Didn't you go by the house? She should be home."

He looked up at a large clock hung on the wall. It was round with a thick wooden frame and plain, no-nonsense face. The whole office looked like it had been decorated in the fifties and never updated.

"Her program is on right now, so I know she'll be there. Would you like me to call her for you?"

Of course, I said to myself. Peter Olsen probably remarried somewhere along the line. And with my luck, Gram was probably the wife's mother and not Peter's. I kept to my commitment of sticking just slightly off-track of the truth.

"No, that won't be necessary," I assured him. "What I mean is that I knew your biological mother, Sophie."

He plopped himself down into a large wooden rolling chair behind the desk, looking not quite as surprised as I thought he might.

"Are you the lady who called a few days ago?" he asked.

In person, he looked even more like Sophie than in the photos. His large blue eyes fixed on me with expectation. I was the one surprised.

"Someone called you a few days ago about Sophie?"

"Yes," he answered, settling into the chair in a youthful slouch. "But I'm guessing now it wasn't you."

I shook my head. "But may I ask what the call was about?"

He gave my request some thought before continuing. "About my biological mother. At least that's what the woman said. She didn't say much else. Only that she had been a good friend of my mother's and wanted to know how I was doing."

My antennae were vibrating at full warp speed. "Do you remember what this woman sounded like?"

He shrugged. "She sounded nice. Normal voice, nothing weird or strange about her that I could tell." He leaned forward in his chair. "But my mother, Sophie I mean, died when I was little. Isn't it kind of odd that two of her friends would contact me about the same time?" The question was asked calmly, with no hint of suspicion, just naive curiosity.

Boy, I'll say. I could feel my nose twitch involuntarily as my brain spun this new information around. "Did this woman give you her name or say she'd call you again?" I asked, trying not to appear overeager for information.

He shook his head. "Nope. We just chatted a bit about stuff. It was a very short call."

"Well," I said, "I'm sure Sophie had lots of friends. It's probably just a coincidence."

I tried to appear nonchalant and wondered if Robbie would buy the idea that it was just a fluke. I sure as hell didn't, but then I'm rather skeptical about a lot of things, including long-lost friends with good intentions.

"All I know," I continued, "is that I'm a friend of hers from a long time ago. I was in the area and thought it might be nice to see how you've grown, and to say hello to your father, of course." I lied like a rug to this nice kid and told myself I'd worry about shame tomorrow.

"Cool," he said, obviously delighted by this unexpected visit. Suddenly aware of his manners, he pointed to a chair. "Please sit down, Mrs. Grey. Dad should be back anytime now."

"Ms. Grey, not Mrs.," I corrected him. "But please call me Odelia."

I sat in a vinyl and metal office chair across from him and placed my tote bag on the floor beside me. Inside the bag was the box of Robbie memorabilia.

"You look like your mother," I told him with a genuine smile.

"Yeah, that's what my dad says." He blushed as he said it. "I have a few old photos of her, but it's hard to see it from them."

"Trust me, Robbie, you're the spitting image."

Once more he slightly reddened. It was easy to like this boy, just as it had been easy to like his mother. It was plain to see that he was well brought up. Whomever had taken over for Sophie had done a very good job.

"How old were you when Sophie died?"

"I was three. But honestly, I don't even remember her. I wish I did though." He swung slightly from side to side in the chair. "Don't get me wrong. Mom, or Marcia, my stepmom, is great . . . the very best. But I wish I knew more about my real mother. Dad never talks about her." He leaned forward eagerly, reminding me of a hungry wolf cub. "What was she like, Odelia?"

I was about to introduce a boy to his mother and wondered if I could do her the justice she deserved.

"She was wonderful. Outgoing and lively. Very beautiful. Very intelligent. She lived to help others."

Before I could tell him more, the door opened and in walked the man from the memorial service. The man who had confronted Hollowell.

"Hi, Dad," Robbie greeted him. "This is Odelia, an old friend of —"

"I know who she is, Robbie," Olsen said, cutting him off. His face was stern and anger flashed in his eyes, but his voice was even.

Not sure where this scene was heading, I decided to take control. Standing up, I held out my hand. "Yes, remember me, Odelia Grey? It's nice to see you again *after all these years.*"

Picking up on my cue, Olsen took my offered hand and shook it briefly. I felt him relax and saw the fire in his eyes cool a few notches.

"Yes, it's nice to see you again, too. What brings you to Santa Paula?"

"A little business, a little pleasure. Thought it'd be fun to stop in and see you and Robbie. See how he's turned out. You've done a wonderful job. Sophie would be so proud of both of you. He looks just like her."

I was babbling like a mountain brook, hoping someone would rescue me before I did major damage. Fortunately, Olsen did.

"It's too bad Robbie's about to take off for school," he said, looking directly into my eyes. His were green, like my own. "He has afternoon classes at the university. But if you'd permit me, Odelia, I'd love to take you to lunch. It'll be fun catching up on *old times*."

The two words *old* and *times* were bolded, italicized, and under-lined by his tone.

TWELVE

THE RESTAURANT WAS ONE of those standard chain restaurants that dot Southern California, providing good but not great food at good but not entirely cheap prices. The waitress directed us to a table near the middle of the dining room, but Olsen quietly suggested the large semicircular booth that stood empty in the back. And that's where we sat.

He looked pretty much the same as the first time I saw him, except that today he looked stronger, both physically and emotionally. Maybe it was the way the *Olsen Machinery* knit shirt clung to his slim but well-developed frame or the fact that here he was in control, while at the chapel he had lost it. I was on his turf, invading his space uninvited, and he was quietly letting me know just that.

Peter Olsen had the kind of face one earns. Deep creases marked the outside of his eyes like parentheses, and lines formed furrows like plowed rows across his forehead. His nose looked like it had once been broken, though not badly. While not particularly handsome, his overall appearance spoke of character and stability.

On the way to the restaurant in his truck, he did not say a word to me. I had offered to take my own car, but he had insisted on driving us both. More than once I wondered if I had made a wise decision. At the restaurant, he didn't speak beyond courteous chitchat until after our iced teas were served. Then he didn't fool around.

"What do you think you're doing?" he asked, getting straight to the point without fanfare.

I quickly took a drink, swallowing it hard. It felt like lumpy oatmeal going down my tight throat. His voice was stern, but not angry. That gave me a glimmer of hope that I would see Newport Beach again.

"I wanted to bring some things of Sophie's to you. I, I . . . ," I stammered. Inwardly, I told myself to get my shit together. "I didn't know you were the man from the memorial service." It was only a partial lie. True, I didn't know that Olsen was the grief-stricken man from the service. And I *was* bringing a few of Sophie's things to him, even though they were merely a ruse to get close to her ex-husband and learn something about her past.

"We don't want anything of hers. She's dead to us. Has been for years."

I didn't like the cold way he spoke about Sophie. It didn't match the sorrow I had seen displayed less than a week ago. Deciding that I had nothing to lose by prodding him, I kept on, hoping to strike an honest nerve.

"Then why did you drive all the way to Orange County?" My tone was a tad sarcastic, letting him know I wasn't buying the tough words. "Making sure she was really dead?"

Across the table, I saw his body clench like a fist.

"That remark was uncalled for," he said in an angry but controlled voice. "Downright mean, in fact."

"Perhaps, Mr. Olsen, but I have a dead friend and a lot of unanswered questions. You see, I don't believe Sophie killed herself. And some of her other friends don't believe it either."

Our food arrived. I crunched crackers into the bowl of vegetable soup that came with my turkey sandwich. The activity was more to hide my nervousness than out of a love for Saltines. I raised my soup spoon to my mouth, watching him carefully while I took my first sip.

His eyes were closed, his head bowed slightly in front of his barbecued chicken salad. I thought he was saying grace, but when he lifted up his face, I could see his eyes were solemn, his mouth turned downward.

"Odelia," he said quietly, "you were obviously a very close friend of Sophie's."

"I loved her very much, like a sister."

"Then let it be, I beg of you." He locked eyes with me. "What's done is done, and nothing will bring her back."

I put down my spoon and fiddled with the sandwich, picking at the crust. "Let me ask you this, then. Why did you accuse Hollowell of having a hand in her death? It didn't look like *you* were letting it be."

He sighed and started poking at lettuce with his fork. "I meant that he probably drove her to suicide, that's all. It never crossed my mind that it might be murder. How can it be, when she pulled the trigger?"

"Did you see it?"

"Heavens no!" His pale face mottled as he spat out the words.

"Did you know about the website?"

This time I denoted a hair's breadth of hesitation before he answered.

"No, not until I heard about it on the news. But it didn't surprise me. Hollowell could talk her into anything. It was probably his idea."

He finally started eating, chewing his salad with determined chomps. I had obviously hit a few sore spots. I wanted to learn more, but wasn't sure how long Olsen would allow me to emotionally poke and prod at him. But what would be the worse-case scenario if I continued? I gave it a quick calculation.

He could storm out and leave me with the check. No big deal, I could afford a turkey sandwich and a chicken salad. He could abandon me here in the Citrus Capital of the World. The restaurant wasn't that far from his office. I was sure I could find my way back to Olsen's Machinery and retrieve my car if I had to. Those thoughts aside, I forged ahead with fresh determination.

"Was Hollowell the reason you and Sophie broke up all those years ago?"

Olsen slightly leaned his head back. "John Hollowell," he began, still looking up at the ceiling, "was the reason Sophie and I got married, the reason we split, and the reason I raised Robbie alone." He lowered his head back down. "Do you believe in time travel, Odelia?" he asked, locking his eyes onto mine again.

I shrugged noncommittally, not betraying that the idea of traveling back and forth between the past, present, and future was a favorite fantasy of mine.

"If you could go back in time," he asked, "what one event would you change if you could?"

It was a good question; one I would have loved to speculate about under different circumstances. One event in all of history; there were so many possibilities. I shrugged again, knowing he didn't really need or want my answer. The question was merely a bridge to something important he wanted to tell me.

"If I could go back in time," he began in a relaxed, storytelling tone, "I would go back to the summer of nineteen seventy-one. Sophie had just turned fifteen. I was sixteen and already in love with her. We were at a pool party given by a kid at school. One of the boys was clowning around. He slipped on the diving board and hit his head on the end as he fell into the water. People were screaming. Everyone panicked. You know how it can be. I jumped in and pulled him out. He was unconscious. I saved his life."

He took a long, slow drink of his iced tea.

"If I could turn back time, knowing what I do now, I would let the kid drown."

"Hollowell?" I guessed.

"Hollowell," Olsen answered, nodding solemnly. "It was at that party Sophie first caught his eye. Soon after, he began shamelessly pursuing her." He paused, then looked me square in the eye. "I have no doubt that had John Hollowell drowned that day years ago, the world would be a better place."

We ate in silence for a short while. I was dying to ask him for more details, especially about Hollowell, but something told me that now was a good time to keep still and be patient. I finished my sandwich, then waited while he polished off his salad. The waitress came by to clear our plates and refill our drinks. It was the height of the lunch hour and the place was almost filled.

The check came and he automatically picked it up. With a wave of work-worn hands, he silenced my protests.

"I can see that you mean no intentional harm to Robbie. And I could tell from the service that you cared about Sophie very much.

But I worry that you might cause my son considerable harm, purely by accident."

I started to say something, but he cut me off with another slight wave of his hand.

"I'd like to show you something." He got up, put some money on the table. "Do you have a little time to take a ride with me?"

"Sure," I answered.

After a short drive through a modest residential section of town, he turned up a small road bordered on the right side by a eucalyptus grove. It led to the local cemetery. It was an older cemetery, small but well maintained, old monuments mixed with new stones. The grounds were scattered with palm trees and a few thick shade trees.

Olsen proceeded up one of the narrow streets and pulled up halfway, parking next to the curb. He got out and headed in the direction of one of the large trees. I followed, stopping when he did. In front of us was a grouping of headstones with OLSEN carved prominently on the largest.

"Those are my parents," he told me, pointing to two flat stones placed slightly to the right front of the family stone. One said Martha, the other Leonard. The dates on the stones told me that Leonard lived long after his wife died. "All of these," he said, sweeping the general area with an open hand, "are Olsens—aunts, uncles, cousins, grandparents. We've been in these parts a long time. But now only Robbie and I remain to carry on the family."

I couldn't see what this had to do with Sophie until he pointed to another flat stone. I swallowed hard. It was positioned just off to the side of his parents and read SOPHIA L. OLSEN . . . BELOVED WIFE AND MOTHER . . . Born 6-7-56 . . . Died 8-14-86.

Olsen sat down under the nearby tree and leaned up against it. I joined him, tucking my denim dress around my legs.

"From the time he first noticed her that day at the party," Olsen began, "Hollowell played with Sophie's emotions. She was a big girl, even then, and because of it not very popular with the boys." He smiled. "Except me. We'd known each other since grade school and were pals even then. She was very insecure about her weight and, of course, the kids always teased her."

Been there, done that, have the scars, I thought to myself.

Suddenly, his voice took on a bite. "Hollowell was one of the most popular boys in school. He was good looking, lettered in all the major sports, drove a sports car, and had girls draped over him most of the time. He was as smooth as ice and just as treacherous. Nothing he did wrong ever caught up with him. He used her, of course. Sleeping with her, debasing her, dangling promises of eventual marriage. He would be seen everywhere with the most beautiful and popular girls, but he kept Sophie on the side, behind the scenes."

Olsen looked at me, his face serious and determined. "Forgive me for saying this, Odelia, but Sophie became Hollowell's private whore. And as far as I know, she was until the day she died." He looked down at the ground and picked at some of the scraggly grass. "I tried to tell her he was no good, but she just said I was jealous.

"When he graduated, Hollowell left for college and promised he'd be back for her. Every summer he would return, crook his little finger, and she'd fly to his bed. Everyone but Sophie knew that nothing would come of the relationship. He was from a well-to-do family. She had nothing. He played around on her, made fun of her, dumped her each fall. The summer between his junior and senior year he didn't come back to Santa Paula at all.

"Sophie graduated the year after Hollowell and I did. A year later her mother died. She had no one else. Sophie moved in with my father and me. I was still in love with her, but the arrangement was strictly on the up and up. She took classes at the local junior college. Spent the rest of her time cooking and cleaning for us, and caring for my father, who was ill. He adored her." Olsen smiled faintly. "I wanted to marry her, but she was in love with that bastard and determined to wait for him."

It was hot, even under the tree. I shifted a bit and fanned myself gently with my hand. Olsen got up and went to his truck, coming back with a small compact cooler. He opened it, revealing a few small bottles of water and a couple of sodas.

"You have to be prepared out here with this heat," he said kindly, offering me a choice.

I took a can of Coke, said thanks, and eagerly popped the top. It felt good going down. Olsen took the other soda and followed suit. I studied him while he drank. He seemed a nice man, a very good man, one used to hard work and self-reliance. As with Greg Stevens, I wanted to believe that he had nothing to do with Sophie's death.

The more I heard about Hollowell, the easier it was becoming to pin the tail on that donkey.

"The following year Hollowell graduated from college," Olsen said, continuing. "He came back that summer but didn't contact her. We'd see him around town squiring a young woman he'd met in college. I think she was visiting him and his family for a few weeks. Sophie tried to call him, but he just ignored her. She was heartbroken. A month later, I convinced her to marry me."

Olsen's narrative disturbed me personally. It was difficult for me to reconcile the confident and bold Sophie I knew with this door-mat caricature he was painting. Yet I also knew, as a fellow fatty, how intoxicating acceptance could be—especially amorous attention from a handsome and charming man.

Most teenage girls are insecure, overweight ones more so. We are all eager and hungry to believe that somewhere out there is a Prince Charming blind to extra pounds, a good-looking, successful chubby chaser toting a glass slipper in a wide size.

In school, I was always asked out by the outsiders and nerds. Had a popular and handsome Hollowell type tapped me on the shoulder, I'm not so sure I wouldn't have followed him like a panting puppy myself.

"But why the empty grave?" I asked.

"I'm getting to that," he answered. "I want you to know the whole story, unless you'd rather not."

"Please, go on." Wild horses couldn't drag me away at this point. I adjusted my legs, smoothed the folds in my dress, and took another gulp of my Coke.

"The first few years we were happy enough. I knew she didn't feel the same type of love I felt for her, but we managed. I was building my business. She finished her schooling. Then Hollowell came back. We'd heard that he'd been living down in Orange County and working for some development company. One weekend we ran into him at a local fair. Next thing I knew, Sophie was gone. She packed a few of her things, told me she was sorry, and left. I remember it clearly."

His voice was beginning to choke. I kept my eyes downward, focused on the grass. He got up from the ground and paced as he spoke.

"She was wearing a pretty green dress with tiny white polka dots. She cried as she told me she loved me, but that he needed her more. There was no telling her different. He was poison to her, like alcohol to a drunk. She couldn't seem to help herself. She moved down south and went to work for him. A year later, the owner of the company died and Hollowell married his widow. Sophie returned to me."

"And you took her back?" I knew my voice sounded incredulous, in spite of my determination to remain neutral on the outside.

"What can I say?" he said sadly. "She was *my* poison. Just like she was convinced that Hollowell would eventually be hers, I was just as sure that in the end she'd be mine. But I was wrong. Couple of years later, she became pregnant. I was so relieved. I wanted children badly, but I also felt it would anchor her, keep her in Santa Paula. I was wrong about that, too.

"When Robbie was two, Sophie took off and joined Hollowell, became his mistress again. She told me that Hollowell was leaving his wife and was going to marry her. I knew that during these years they had been in contact. He just wouldn't leave her alone. I begged her to stop seeing him. Argued with her. Threatened her. But nothing worked. She left Robbie with me and moved for good. This time she asked for a divorce. Hollowell never left his wife or got divorced that I know of, not in all these years.

"Now," he said, looking at me and pointing to the headstone, "we get to this grave here." He walked over and stood next to the grave, as if talking to it instead of to me.

"About a year after our divorce, Sophie was up to see Robbie. She visited him regularly and was a very good mother in most respects. Loved the boy to bits. Spoiled him rotten every time she saw him. After he was in bed, she told me that she wanted me to tell Robbie that she had died. Said I was to make something up. He was just a bit more than three at the time. She was crying and almost hysterical, but said she didn't want him growing up wondering why she'd abandoned him. Said it would be easier for all of us this way."

"And you agreed?"

"Not at first, no. A child needs his mother, even a part-time one. But she kept calling me, insisting that it was the only way. I tried to convince her that this wasn't best for Robbie, but truthfully, I didn't want to face the fact that it destroyed my own hopes. I always thought that one day Hollowell would die, get murdered more than likely, and then she'd come back to both of us. In the end she wore me down. Reluctantly, I finally said yes."

He sighed deeply, his shoulders sagging. He bent down and stroked the glossy stone, picking at a few stray weeds around the edge.

"Together, we concocted a story about her being in a car accident in Los Angeles."

"And people bought that?"

"Sure, why not?" He shrugged. "I told everyone that as she'd wished, her body had been cremated and her ashes scattered along the beach. I had this stone set as a memorial. Not a single person up here questioned it."

Unbelievable.

I knew that people disappeared all the time. They just walked away and started new lives. My own mother, for instance. But that Olsen had actually gone to the trouble to declare Sophie dead and buried totally threw me. Was it really that easy to disappear without a trace?

"But didn't anyone here see the recent news and make a connection? I mean, because of the website, her suicide was all over TV."

He shook his head. "No. You see, London wasn't Sophie's real last name. She changed it after she left us for good. Her real name was Langerdorf. And so many years had passed, no one even noticed."

Without realizing it, I had pulled a thick clump of my hair into my mouth and was chewing the ends. It was a habit I had as a child. My hair was currently just long enough to reach.

"One more thing, Odelia."

I looked at him, waiting for the next installment of weird but true facts of life. He stood up from the grave, walked toward me, and stood leaning against the tree. Every now and then he took a drink of soda.

"The police, of course, questioned me about Sophie. A detective drove all the way up here to talk to me. Guess he got my name from her attorney, considering the will and all. Robbie is her only surviving blood. I told the detective everything about the divorce and the staged death for Robbie's benefit. He said he saw no reason to involve the boy. I'd like you to do likewise."

"What about your wife? Does she know about this?"

He nodded. "Yes, I told her just before we married. At first she was afraid that Sophie would come back. Then over the years she relaxed. She's devoted to Robbie."

I took a deep breath, steeling myself to ask the really big question.

"Did you kill Sophie, Peter?"

He snapped his head in my direction, his mouth hung open in shock.

"God, no!"

His face reddened with indignation and his body clenched as it had in the restaurant. Then he calmed down. I watched his wiry muscles relax, even sag.

"I know it'd be easy to think I had something to do with this, but I didn't. I haven't seen Sophie since her last visit to Robbie when he was a child. Once this stone was set, we cut off all contact with each other. Not once, in all those years, did she ever try to take Robbie. In spite of what you just heard, you must believe that she was an honorable woman."

I nodded my belief. The Sophie I knew had been honorable.

"Robbie told me a woman called him recently saying she was an old friend of Sophie's. Did you know about that call? Or who it might have been?"

Peter Olsen was taking a drink of his soda when the question reached his ears. He stopped mid-gulp to cough. Obviously, he didn't know about the call.

"Robbie told you someone called him about his mother?" he asked as he wiped soda from his chin with the back of his hand.

"He said a woman called saying she was an old friend of Sophie's. He told me they just chatted a bit. Today, when I showed up, he thought it might have been me who called."

"But it wasn't you?" he asked. I felt from his tone he was hoping it had been.

I shook my head. "Wasn't me. Until after Sophie died, I didn't even know either of you existed." I wondered why Robbie didn't tell his father about the call, then remembered the boy saying Peter didn't like to talk about Sophie. "I guess it's safe to assume that Robbie didn't tell you?"

"No, he didn't."

I reached into my bag and pulled out the box. "And I'll bet you didn't send this stuff to Sophie either."

He crouched down in front of me as I opened the fancy lid. He sorted through the photos and clippings with a look of amazement, turning a few of the pictures over.

"No," he told me with a slow shake of his head. He showed me the back of one of the photos. "This is Marcia's handwriting. Marcia's my wife."

The ride home seemed a lot shorter than the trip to Santa Paula. Along the way, I chewed on the information Olsen had given me, masticating it to pulp like a cheap, tough steak. Slowly, I digested each bite of information with my mind, weaving it in and through my brain cells, filing it away after consideration, hoping that nothing crucial got missed in the process.

If what Olsen told me was true, that Sophie had slavishly followed Hollowell for years, even giving up her son for him, I needed to meet this guy face to face, *mano a womano*. If this Hollowell guy was that charming and persuasive, maybe I should get vaccinated before I do. What would I ask for? Bastard serum followed by a bullshit booster? If there were such a thing, women of all ages would camp out overnight on city streets for the shots, with me first in line.

And Olsen's wife had sent the photos and stuff to Sophie. Now there was a kick in the head. Could she also have been the mystery caller? If so, what motive could she have to stir up Sophie's memory so many years later?

Olsen had been as shocked about that as I had been. I could see it in his expression as he held the photos and read the backs. How I wished to be a fly on the wall in their house tonight. But in all honesty, he didn't seem upset by it, just surprised. I found it touching. Marcia Olsen must be one hell of a kind and sensitive woman to have done such an unselfish thing. Or at least I wanted to believe that. In this unfolding tragic story of Sophie's other life, I wanted to believe that she had someone on her side. But the present wife of an ex-husband seemed an unlikely ally. Not impossible, just improbable.

I was lost in my thoughts and flying down the Ventura Freeway at seventy miles per hour when my cell phone rang. I rummaged in my purse, only swerving slightly, mind you, to answer it. It was Greg. Glancing at the dashboard clock I saw that it was two-twenty. I had completely forgotten to call him.

"Now before you get mad," I told him after a quick exchange of hellos and an apology, "you won't believe what I found out." I gave him the *Reader's Digest* condensed version of what Olsen told me.

"I didn't know all the details," Greg said, after I'd finished, "but what little Sophie told me fits Olsen's story."

The connection got patchy as I drove through some fair to middlin' hills. " . . . did say . . . Hollowell hadn't been . . . item for . . . years, but I still felt . . . hold on her."

"Greg," I said, hoping he could hear me. "I have to go, I'm breaking up. I'll call you when I get home." I powered down the phone and went back to driving. And thinking.

Once I transferred to the San Diego Freeway heading south through Los Angeles, I tried calling Greg. This time the connection was clear.

"Greg, would you do me a favor?"

"Sure."

"Would you call the alarm company and ask whether or not a technician was sent to Sophie's last weekend? I tried this morning, but couldn't get through."

He happily agreed to do it. It was the beginning of rush hour and traffic was starting to back up with the usual stop and go. As soon as I found myself in a stopped moment, I read him the account number and abort code from my notes.

"I should be home in about an hour," I told him.

"I'll call you tonight," he said, and hung up.

Then I called Zee and gave her a rundown on my day's activities.

THIRTEEN

Going to work was the last thing I wanted to do on Tuesday morning.

There was so much to be done to get to the bottom of the Sophie matter. Layers in the form of people and events needed to be peeled away like old, faded wallpaper. This mystery had me in its grip and I wouldn't rest until it was resolved to my satisfaction. There were calls to make, people to meet. Not the least of which was Hollowell. But I also reminded myself that I had to get back into my normal routine. It would keep me grounded. So Tuesday morning I got up and went on the six o'clock walk.

Just as I parked my car along the curb at the beginning of the paved walkway that went around the bay, I saw two women waiting. One was Glo Kendall. I didn't know the other.

"Hi," I said, trotting up.

"Hi back," Glo said, beaming. "We haven't seen you here in a long time." We exchanged hugs. She indicated the other woman, who was dressed in biking shorts and a loose windbreaker. "This is Ruth Wise. She started coming to the walk just yesterday."

"Welcome, Ruth," I said, shaking her offered hand.

Ruth Wise was the largest woman I'd ever seen not playing basketball or volleyball in the Olympics. She wasn't fat, just large. With a quick estimate, I judged her to be just over six feet tall and close to two hundred pounds. Her body was solid and fit. She had a young, wholesome face with a straight nose and bright, wide-set brown eyes. Her hair was sandy brown and long, pulled back into a black velvet scrunchie. She couldn't have been much over thirty, if that.

"Thanks," she said with a shy smile, but shaking my hand with a firm grip.

It looked like it was just going to be the three of us this morning. We walked along at a brisk pace, though it seemed for Ruth to be nothing more than a casual stroll.

"How'd you hear about this group, Ruth," I asked. "Through Glo, here?"

With some hesitation, she said, "I found out about the group through the website and always meant to come by." She hesitated again before continuing. "I'm sorry about Sophie London," she said in a respectful voice. "And I'm sorry I didn't get a chance to meet her."

"She was a wonderful woman," I told Ruth. "Everyone loved her."

"That's for sure," Glo chimed in. "I don't know where I'd be if it hadn't been for Sophie."

I looked over at Glo Kendall and smiled. Glo had come a long way since the first time we met. Just over six months ago, she had simply shown up one evening at a Reality Check meeting like a puppy abandoned on a doorstep. She was slovenly, disheveled, and beaten in spirit. She could have been the poster child for the fat slob stereotype that the group fought hard to debunk. She told us she'd learned about Reality Check through a friend.

She and Blaine had moved to Santa Ana from Tennessee just a year before. Back home they'd fallen on hard times when the company Blaine worked for closed down, throwing half of their small town out of work. When a cousin promised him a job if they'd relocate to Southern California, they sold their trailer, packed up the pickup truck, and headed west.

Glo's overall appearance, combined with a slowness of mind and minimum education, had stood in her way of finding decent employment once they settled in the area. But she seemed a sweet and kind person with a good heart, and Sophie had mentored her personally. Now she had a good job as an accounts payroll clerk in a local corporation and held her head high. The change had been remarkable.

"I hope you like us enough to come again," I told Ruth. "We're going to resume the Wednesday night meetings very shortly. They're usually held every two weeks."

Glo perked up considerably at the news.

Zee had informed me on the phone as I whizzed back from Santa Paula that the Reality Check members were asking her if the group would continue. They wanted it to, she told me, and they wanted me to lead it.

I had been shocked. I had always acted as Sophie's backup, but never felt I had the leadership qualities necessary to head a group like this—or any group, for that matter. I had enough trouble managing my own household, which consisted of nothing more than one klutzy human and one crabby cat. Zee had suggested that we set up a meeting in a few weeks and notify the usual attendees. At the meeting we could discuss the future of the group, including who would be best to step into Sophie's size-nine shoes.

There was no doubt in my mind that I wanted Reality Check to continue. It was doing good work and making a difference, one woman at a time. I just wasn't sure I was the heir apparent.

How could I be, after the department store debacle?

The group deserved better.

After taking two days off, I had plenty of mail and work piled up. Mr. Wallace had begun a two-week vacation the day before and had left e-mails and notes with instructions on the few things he had pending. We had already spoken by phone this morning. He and his wife were concerned about me, he had said, knowing what a shock Sophie's death must have been. He encouraged me to take more time off if I needed it. I would miss this man when he retired.

After opening and sorting my mail, neatly stacking it into various piles—to be filed, to be distributed, needs attention, UR-GENT—I looked up the phone number for the local branch of the security company. Since it was the same company that operated my alarm system, I knew there was an office just a few miles away. I found it easily in the phone book. It was on Baker, not far from my office, which was located in a high-rise across from South Coast Plaza, one of the largest shopping malls in the United States.

Greg had been successful in reaching the alarm company's customer service department. He had called the night before to tell me that the alarm company did, in fact, have a record of a service call at Sophie's on Sunday. They would not give him the name of the service technician, just his supervisor's name and the branch telephone number. The number matched the one in the phone book for the office located on Baker.

I called the security company and spoke with the supervisor, a Bill Walker. I asked if I could stop by at lunchtime for just a few minutes. Like all assistants and most paralegals at Woobie, my desk was housed in a cubicle, open and unshielded from prying eyes and ears. It made it impossible to discuss this matter from here. I told Mr. Walker that the matter was confidential, about a friend of mine, Sophia London. He immediately recognized the name and consented, asking if I could come by about eleven-thirty.

The morning sped by as I caught up on accumulated voice mails and e-mails, returning and noting each one. Mike Steele walked by, making a big point of ignoring me. It was his way of expressing his displeasure at my time off. At eleven-fifteen I told the receptionist that I was leaving for an appointment and headed off to meet Mr. Walker.

The corporate offices of the alarm company were located in Pasadena. They also had several branch offices located throughout Southern California, each one housing sales, installation, service, and patrol functions. The Baker Street office served most of Orange County and was located in a large end section of a nondescript strip mall. There was a small customer parking area in the front of the light gray stucco single-story building. I pulled my car into a space and got out. There was a larger parking area at the end of the building reserved for company vehicles and employees. A couple of patrol cars and small trucks bearing the company logo were parked there, as well as about a dozen private vehicles.

Inside the small reception area, the office was plain and sparse. The walls were adorned with publicity posters showing either burglars in action or smiling patrolmen and guards. Brochures on services and equipment were neatly arranged in holders. It was easy to see that this office didn't receive a lot of walk-in customers. Security companies do most of their marketing through ads and telemarketing, with salesmen making in-home appointments to present and close deals.

The receptionist was separated from the waiting area by a wall with a window, like in a doctor's office. The young woman behind the closed glass opening was seated slightly lower than the window and engrossed in her work. I tapped lightly on the window to get her attention.

I asked the receptionist for Mr. Walker and was immediately escorted through the inside door and down a short hallway to a small, private office. The plaque on the door read *W. Walker, Operations Manager* in straight, plain letters of white embossed on a brown background. There were a few other offices along the hallway with similar plaques bearing different names.

Mr. Walker was on the phone when I came in. He waved hello and indicated for me to sit down in a chair opposite his cluttered desk. There was a huge bulletin board on one of his walls, the cork surface all but obliterated with pushpins holding memos, graphs, and messages. On the wall nearest me was an equally large white board with lines drawn in a grid. Names and times were entered into boxes on each line, clearly indicating a schedule of some kind. Among the debris on the desk were a dirty coffee cup, a crumpled McDonald's bag, and several framed photos of children of various ages. As soon as Mr. Walker got off the call, the phone rang again. He answered, said a few words, and hung up. Then he called the receptionist and told her to hold his calls. Finally, with words of apology, he was all mine. He stood up, offered me a callused hand, and told me to call him Bill.

Bill Walker was a black man on the far side of forty with a wide smile and crooked teeth. Both his head and his face were clean shaven, and each earlobe bore a tiny gold hoop. He was average in size, but the soft round tire around his middle told me that he was prone to gaining weight easily. The white knit shirt he wore was similar in style to the ones worn at Olsen's Machinery, but the logo over his left breast was different.

"You're here about that London woman?" he asked after pleasantries. His voice was medium in tone with a bit of a smoker's rasp to it. The faint smell of smoke coming from his clothing confirmed my guess.

"Yes," I said. "She was a friend of mine."

"I'm very sorry."

"Thank you." I took a piece of paper from my tote bag. It was a document Doug Hemming, Sophie's lawyer, had given me. I showed it to Bill Walker. "I'm also her personal representative. You know, the person in charge of closing down her affairs."

He gave me a warm but ragged smile. "You didn't need to come down in person to close her account. You can just call Customer Service. They have procedures for such cases."

"I know. I'm one of your customers as well. But I'm not here for that. In fact, we're going to keep the alarm system operating until the house is sold and the new owners come in."

"Good idea. Don't need vandals trashing the place." He leaned back comfortably in his chair. "So then, Odelia, if this isn't about Ms. London's account, what can we help you with?"

"Well, this is going to sound strange, but Sophie's neighbor has been complaining . . ."

He immediately leaned forward and held up a hand, halting me. "Iris Somers," he said in a deadpan voice, followed by a deep sigh. "Do you have any idea how annoying that woman can be?"

"Yes, as a matter of fact, I do." I gave him a sympathetic smile. "She said that one of your service people stopped by the house the weekend Sophie died."

"Yeah, that was Danny Ortiz." Bill leaned back in his chair again. "Ever since that system was put in, that crazy neighbor of your friend's has been calling us about some damn beams. We've explained to her till we're blue in the face that our system does not utilize harmful beams that travel around and hurt people. I have told her that myself."

"I understand. But why the service call? Did Sophie request it?"

"No, she didn't. Seems this Somers woman sent letters to the big mucky-mucks of the company complaining about these stupid beams. It was the legal department's idea to send a technician out there. You know, just to document that we did look into the problem in case anything comes up later."

It seemed logical to me. The company was covering its ass in the event Iris filed a formal, albeit bogus, complaint.

"Did this Danny see Sophie either of those days?"

"Like I told the police," Bill said slowly and with deliberation, "he first went out on Saturday between calls. Since it wasn't a standard service request, we decided to try and fit it into the schedule when we had time. Your friend wasn't home, so he went back on Sunday morning before his first call, which was nearby. Danny alternates working weekends with other techs. That was his weekend on call."

"The police knew that Danny had been there?" I asked, surprised. I distinctly remembered Iris Somers saying she hadn't had the chance to tell the cops that.

"Sure. Whenever there's a security system present, they contact the company about possible triggering of the alarm or calls to us.

It's standard procedure. They found out Danny had been there and stopped by to talk to him."

"This suicide took us all by surprise, Bill." I shifted in my chair and leaned closer, not wanting to miss a crumb of information. "So what I'd really like to know is what Sophie was like that weekend—how she was acting. Your technician might have been the last person to see her alive, if he saw her."

"He did see her." Bill's face turned somber as he spoke.

He pulled a cigarette package from the middle desk drawer and tapped out a single slim white cylinder. He played with it, rolling it between his fingers. I could tell he was dying to light up.

"I read about your friend in the news," Bill told me. "We like to keep up on things involving our customers. If the witnesses were correct about the time of death, then Danny saw her less than an hour before she pulled the trigger. Danny's a young guy, about the same age as my eldest, maybe twenty-two, twenty-three. He's a sensitive kid and took it pretty hard. He kept wondering if there was something he should have noticed, could've prevented. Kept saying to me that he should've spent more time there, instead of a quick courtesy in and out."

"But he did see her?" I was excited about the news, yet sorry about the boy's trauma.

"Yes, and spoke to her. Then he checked the system. It was working fine, so he left and filed his report. He told me that she seemed okay when he saw her. Cheerful, in fact." He checked his watch. "Would you like to talk to Danny? He's doing a job not far from here, a condo off of MacArthur. He may be at lunch right now."

"Sure, I'd appreciate that, if it's no trouble."

Bill picked up a small handheld radio. "No problem," he said to me. "Glad to help. I think it will help Danny, too, to talk to someone who knew the woman."

While he tried to reach Danny Ortiz, I checked my time. It was noon. MacArthur was just on the other side of the mall, near my office. I could swing by, have a few words with Ortiz, and buzz back to work. Perfect.

"Funny, he's not answering," Bill said and tried again.

The receptionist came dashing in. "Bill, I'm sorry, but the police are on the phone. They say it's an emergency."

He immediately put down the radio. When the receptionist sent the call through to his telephone, he punched the line. I made a motion that I would wait outside and he nodded.

I sat in the waiting area for about fifteen minutes. There seemed to be a lot of commotion going on in the back office behind the separating door. Obviously, something big had happened. I decided to go. Ortiz could wait until tomorrow.

I walked up to the receptionist and tapped on the window, thinking I'd leave Bill a message that I'd call him later. The young woman behind the glass was crying.

"I'm sorry to disturb you," I said to her.

"Oh my God," she said, looking at me as if I were a ghost. "I think Bill forgot you were here!" She dashed back down the hallway.

A few minutes later Bill Walker came through the door. He clutched the cigarette pack tightly in one hand. His face was ashen, his eyes red rimmed. He opened the front door and motioned for me to follow him out. As soon as we were outside, he lit a cigarette and inhaled deeply, right down to his toes. He offered me one, but I declined. He took several long drags before he said anything.

"Danny Ortiz is dead," he announced bluntly and quietly.

"What?" I couldn't believe it. Nonsmoker be damned—suddenly I wanted a smoke, too.

Bill took several more deep pulls off his cigarette, finishing it in short order. He dropped the butt to the ground and mashed it under his heavy work shoe. Promptly, he pulled out another and lit up again.

"About an hour ago, according to the police," he said after exhaling. "Seems Danny was hit by a drunk driver as he was getting into his truck. He was killed instantly. They've arrested the asshole who did it. Some executive named Thomas—Glenn Thomas, I think. Drunk, probably. Most of them are." He coughed a deep, ugly cough and took another big drag off his cigarette.

I squeezed out an inadequate condolence, then started silently crying. Bill Walker touched my shoulder gently.

"Who knows why this shit happens. Danny, your friend. No matter how many people close to us we lose, we never get used to it. Do we?"

He dropped his second butt to the ground and snuffed it out like the first.

"I have to get going," he told me. "The police want me at the scene as soon as possible. I'm sorry you'll never get what you came for." Fighting back tears, he put a hand over his eyes and squeezed gently. "Damn! He was such a good kid."

I held out my hand to Bill Walker. We shook.

"Thank you, Bill. You've been a big help. And, again, I am truly sorry about Danny Ortiz."

I didn't drive back to the office. And I didn't feel like going home. Pulling out my cell phone, I called Woobie, leaving a voice mail for the office manager saying that my appointment was taking much longer than I had planned and I would need to take a half-day off.

Ortiz' death was too much of a coincidence for me to swallow. But they did have the drunk who killed him, so it wasn't like it was premeditated murder. And who knew about Danny Ortiz anyway? As far as I knew, only Iris Somers, Greg, and I knew about the service technician's visit. And, of course, the police. But only I had his name. Greg had said that the security company wouldn't release it to him over the phone.

If Danny Ortiz was murdered, if the accident was really a hit to get him out of the way, then there were only two possibilities that I could see. Either Greg did find out the name and lied to me, which meant that he was back on the suspects list, or that Sophie's murderer was at her house when Ortiz arrived. I prayed for the latter.

I finally decided to drive to Zee's house, hoping to find her at home. She was. I told her about Ortiz.

"You're getting in way over your head," she said when I finished talking. "You know that, don't you?" Her tone was scolding, her look concerned.

I said nothing, just fiddled with the glass of lemonade she'd given me. Lifting up the heavy tumbler, I rolled it across my forehead. The cool, wet drops on the outside of the glass felt wonderful against my warm skin and aching head.

She picked up her phone and handed it to me. "I think it's time to call Detective Frye."

FOURTEEN

DETECTIVE DEVIN FRYE IS a *big* man. It was the first thing I'd noticed about him when I met him at the Orange County coroner's office after Sophie died. Had he been younger or Ruth Wise older, they would have made a physically compatible couple.

He wasn't in when I called from Zee's, so I left a message and asked him to call me at home. Zee wanted to call Seth, but I said no. I didn't want to make a big deal out of this just in case the police determined that Danny Ortiz' death was just a coincidence. The last thing I needed was for the authorities to think I was a hysterical woman with an overactive imagination and an overprotective lawyer. I didn't want to be tagged as another Iris Somers, seeing things that weren't there.

Detective Frye returned my call a few hours later. When I told him about Danny Ortiz, he asked if he could come over later and take a statement. I said sure and gave him my address.

I called Greg and gave him the lowdown. The more I thought about it, the less I believed he had anything to do with the two deaths. More and more I was coming to the conclusion that Sophie's murderer had been in the house when Ortiz arrived to check the security system. I had ruled out any involvement by Iris altogether, deciding she was more annoying than murderous.

Greg, too, thought the accident fishy. When he learned that Frye was coming over, he insisted on being here. He had been interviewed by Frye following Sophie's death and wanted to add more to his take on the whole thing. Two would be more convincing than one, he told me. I agreed completely. As with Frye, I gave Greg my address.

Greg, along with Wainwright, arrived first. Seamus about had a heart attack and scampered upstairs when he saw the big golden dog. On the surface, my cat seems like a bad-tempered bully. But like most bullies, he's a coward. His favorite hiding place is under my bed.

"I'm sorry," Greg said as we maneuvered the step into the house together. "I should have asked first before bringing Wainwright over. It's just that he goes pretty much everywhere with me."

"It's okay," I told him. "Seamus fought off coyotes in the bay before coming to live here. A large, friendly dog should be nothing." I laughed. "I think I've spoiled him. He's gotten too used to the soft life."

"By the way, your cat is green."

"Uh huh," I commented. "I'll tell you about that later."

Something smelled good.

Greg asked me to point him toward the kitchen and off he went. I followed and laughed again when he started pulling cartons of Chinese takeout from the large knapsack that hung on the back of his chair.

"Frye's not due for another hour," he explained with a grin, "so I thought we'd have some dinner first. I'm starved. Hope you like Mongolian beef."

"It's one of my favorites."

"Good. I got that, orange chicken, and shrimp with vegetables, just in case. I figured I'd hit something you like."

"Looks like you're planning to feed an army."

My mouth was getting juicy as the delicious odor filled the kitchen, and my stomach did a jig of joy. With all the commotion over Danny Ortiz, I never ate lunch. Now I was famished. Quickly I set out dishes and flatware. I offered him water, a beer, or soda. He chose the beer, so I got out two.

Just as we were dishing it out, the doorbell rang. Opening it, I found Detective Frye standing there, filling every inch of the opening.

"I know I'm early; hope it won't be a problem," he said politely.

"Ah . . . no, Detective. Please come in. We were just sitting down for dinner."

He followed me into the kitchen. If he was surprised to see Greg, he hid it well.

"You probably remember Greg Stevens," I said, offering Frye a chair at the table.

"Yes, you're the one who called in the nine-one-one on London." The two men shook hands. "I didn't know you and Ms. Grey knew each other."

"We don't," I said quickly. "Or rather, we didn't, until Sophie died. It kind of brought us together."

"A common cause, so to speak," Greg added more calmly.

Police make me nervous. There was no particular reason why. I hadn't done anything wrong. But even the sight of a cruiser waiting next to my car at a red light could make my legs rubbery. It occurred to me that Greg and I together might look suspicious. Oh, hell! *This is stupid,* Odelia, I told myself.

"I see," Frye said, sitting down, his face impassive.

Everything about Frye was large and abundant. His hands, his features, his blue eyes, even his blond hair, which was thick and curly and laced with gray. His voice was distinct, like a cement mixer on low. I placed him in his early fifties. He was chewing gum; another thing I'd noticed the first time I'd met him.

He looked Greg over openly and with no apology. Then he did the same to me. I could tell he was appraising the situation, trying to determine our true relationship in his cop way.

"Would you like to join us?" I offered. There was a slight shake in my voice. I groaned silently.

"No, that's okay. I'm sorry I interrupted you folks. But it's not often I get to leave the office this early."

"How about a beer, Detective?" I asked. His eyes found mine and he gave me a small closed-mouthed smile. I automatically smiled back and felt myself blush. I looked away quickly. "Or a soda?"

"Sure, why not. A Coke, if you've got one, would be great."

"Diet Coke okay?"

He nodded. I handed him a glass of ice and an open can of Diet Coke. He thanked me and took a big swallow right from the cold can.

"God, that's good," he said with pure enjoyment. "It was a scorcher today." He took another drink. With two more swallows he drained the can. I went to the fridge to get another. This time he set the can on the table in front of him. Greg and I looked at each other, waiting.

"You know, Ms. Grey," Frye began, then belched, politely holding it back behind his closed fist. "Excuse me. You know that Ms. London's death was determined a suicide?"

"Yes. But I . . . ," I answered, hesitating. I pointed a finger back and forth between Greg and myself. "We . . . we don't believe it was suicide. And I think that the accident with Danny Ortiz today, the one I told you about on the phone, is somehow connected."

"Yes, I checked that out with the Santa Ana PD. Poor kid never had a chance. Car ran a red light, then swerved into the driver's side of his truck while he was getting in. They're holding some guy on manslaughter. His blood alcohol level was over three times the legal limit. Not his first offense either."

I looked down at my plate, not all that hungry any more.

"I interviewed Ortiz following Ms. London's death. Nice kid, polite. Too bad these things happen."

"Please, Detective, take off your coat and join us," Greg insisted. "We have plenty of food and a whole slew of theories to run by you."

The big man hesitated, sizing up the food with a hungry eye. Before he could refuse again, I got another plate and set of utensils and placed them in front of him.

"Dig in, Detective," I encouraged. "We have lots to tell you."

"Well, I didn't have much lunch and this sure does smell good."

In no time, I relaxed around Frye. He was a very pleasant man, and it was obvious that he knew his business.

Between bites, Greg and I took turns telling him about Hollowell and Olsen, Iris, and Danny Ortiz. Though it was clear that the detective had already met the cast of characters, he took it all in, patiently listening to our side, stopping us here and there to ask a question. Occasionally, he would jot notes in a small spiral pad he'd pulled from his inside pocket before taking off his jacket.

After dinner, I made some coffee, half decaf, and served it in the living room, along with some fresh fruit and cookies. It had been years since I'd had two men over for dinner at the same time. Except for the topic of murder, the evening appeared to be nothing more than a casual dinner among friends. I was only sorry that it had taken Sophie's death to bring such good male company into my life.

About two hours later, Frye got up to leave. He thanked me for my hospitality and shook both of our hands.

"I'll look into everything you've mentioned," he said, standing at the front door. "But honestly, everything still points to suicide. The gun was hers; the wound, self-inflicted. There's absolutely no doubt about that at all. Considering her history with this Hollowell character and her estrangement from her son, maybe she just reached her limit. Unfortunately, it happens all the time."

After Frye left, Greg and I went into the kitchen to clean up. While I scraped plates and rinsed them for the dishwasher, he packed the leftovers and shuttled things from the dining table to the kitchen counter. There was an uneasy silence between us as we worked. Wainwright had followed us from room to room earlier and was currently flopped in a corner of the dining area watching us over crossed paws. Seamus was still missing in action.

"Odelia," Greg finally said. "Did you ever look at Sophie's site?"

Before answering, I put the last dish into the dishwasher, closed the door, and wiped my hands on a nearby dishtowel. I was stalling.

"Yes," I said. "But I only got as far as seeing her face on the opening page. I couldn't go any further."

He wheeled over to me and took one of my hands in his. "I think it's important that you see it. It might help you understand some of the things she did."

"Well, maybe." I sighed. I felt depression edging in on me. Frye still obviously thought it was an open and shut case of suicide. Maybe it was.

"Come on," Greg said, pulling me away from the kitchen. "Let's look at it together. I think you might feel better."

"Okay," I said, giving in.

Whatever was in the site contents, Greg definitely thought I should see it. Why not? It might help me to have someone there when I did. I headed for the stairs, took a few upward, then stopped. I looked down at Greg in his wheelchair.

"I'm sorry, Greg, but the computer's upstairs in the spare bedroom."

He looked perplexed for a moment, then smiled. "We'll just use Sophie's. Her place isn't far from here and the computer's still hooked up, isn't it?"

I nodded and smiled back at him, and off we went.

FIFTEEN

Sophie's house was quickly losing its personality as a home. Without her day-to-day warmth and hospitality, it had been reduced to merely a handsome structure with charming landscaping and a picket fence. Like a shy child reluctant to join in on the fun, it seemed to stand aloof from the other houses on the quiet, tree-lined street.

As soon as we entered the front door, I disarmed the security system and snapped on some lights, hoping that Iris Somers wouldn't notice the activity and decide to come over with more complaints. Greg went straight to the back room and the computer. I followed slowly behind.

While Greg wheeled in behind the computer, I went to the kitchen to retrieve a chair for myself. Together, we waited nervously for the machine to kick into action. He navigated the Internet browser deftly, bringing up the opening page of Sassy Sophie in short time.

I was emotionally torn. On one hand, I did want to see the site. On the other, I wasn't sure I was ready to see it. I decided to trust Greg's judgment that I shouldn't put it off any longer.

Greg had already posted the memorial. Instead of altering the existing pages, he had merely created and inserted a new opening page.

At the top, in a large stylized font on a lavender background, were the words *We Will Miss You!* Below that to the left was the short memorial paragraph that we had drafted together. To the right of the writing was a playful and sexy photo of Sophie I had never seen. She was reclining in a black sheer lace negligee, shown only from the waist up, with her large, round breasts and fully erect nipples bulging for the camera. Her head was tilted back, showing off the graceful curve to her neck and jawline. Like a golden curtain, her hair hung loose away from her head. Her mouth was partially open, and over her full ruby lips she dangled a rosy, plump strawberry.

It was a wonderful photo. Very erotic yet sweet, capturing her impishness. I had to admit, I could see the Sophie I knew posing for such a picture.

Under that section of the page was a small block in which viewers could submit their feelings and sentiments. Greg explained that every evening he would go through the offerings and post the appropriate ones to the site. He scrolled down the page a bit more and there they were, the heartfelt words of her viewers, both men and women, recorded for all visitors to the site to see. I started skimming a few until my eyes blurred from tears.

"These people loved her," Greg whispered to me.

"I'll read them later," I told him with a lump in my throat as big as a grapefruit.

He moved to the next page. This was the beginning of the site as it had been when Sophie was alive, the page I had seen and closed quickly. It was well laid out, with a very feminine and stylish design.

Under the site's large scripted heading was a montage of about a half dozen photos of Sophie in various poses, each one overlapping the other in a very esthetically pleasing format. All of the pictures were cheerful, ranging from playful to boldly erotic. Some were nudes. Others showed her in lingerie. Directly under the photos were buttons for hyperlinks, or shortcuts, to other pages of the website—Members Only, Guest Gallery, Guest Cam, and Mail Bag. Under those had been placed a smartly written paragraph about the beauty of women of all sizes, shapes, colors, and backgrounds. There was even a dedication paragraph in which Sophie committed the entire site to ending prejudice against large and overweight women in particular.

This was what Greg wanted me to see. This had been Sophie's purpose.

I asked Greg to go to the Guest Gallery page. There we found another half dozen erotic and beautiful photos of Sophie. This page also contained words of adoration about women, particularly large women.

I was beginning to understand, though it wasn't the route I would have chosen to make my statement.

"What went on when the camera was running?" I asked Greg.

He shifted slightly in his wheelchair, and I could see that he was getting a bit uncomfortable.

"Well, most of the time she would be nude or near nude in front of the camera and would chat live with visitors to the site in a special chat room. Most of the time she used a headset and spoke directly to them, instead of typing messages. They could see her and communicate with her through typed dialog or voice chat at the same time." Greg looked around the desk until he located an odd round ball that looked like it had three legs. A cable was attached to the back of the ball. "See," he said, showing it to me. "The camera is attached to this tripod and has an extra long cable. That way Sophie could move the camera around the house so viewers could watch her sleep, read, watch TV, and eat. Sometimes they would even get to see her shower."

"They?" I looked at him, my lips tight, trying to keep from laughing.

Normally, I would have been too embarrassed to view such photos with another person, let alone a man I hardly knew. But tonight was way over the top for normal. Looking back, I realized that I hadn't drawn a routine breath since that Sunday in the supermarket when Seth had called with the tragic news.

"Uh . . . ," Greg began, running his fingers through his hair. I had already picked up that this was his particular physical sign of nervousness; a dead giveaway of internal squirming. Fingers through the hair; he did it every time. Right now it was accompanied by an undeniable blush.

"Yeah, okay, you nailed me," he said chuckling. "Yes, we'd watch her in the shower; though I don't want you thinking I'm some sort of perv who habitually visits adult sites. Sophie and her site were different."

"Uh huh," I said, smiling. Actually, I had gotten past the idea of Greg being a sicko with a problem. He was normal and healthy, as far as I could see. "What about sex? Did she perform sexually for the camera?"

He clicked back and hit the Members Only link, then typed in a password at the prompt. I assumed it was his own personal membership code.

Up popped a welcome page with more photos, a short biography of Sophie, and more hyperlinks: Webcam, Archives, and Gallery. Greg clicked on Gallery.

This time the photos were graphic, many even hardcore. There were links to several pages of photos, all erotic and sizzling. Still each page contained words of praise for women of soft, round flesh. Most of these photos were obviously taken with the computer camera, while others looked professional. They chronicled Sophie's domestic life, showing her doing everyday things, mostly unclad or nearly so.

One of the last Gallery pages displayed photos of Sophie in bed with a man. I felt my face go crimson from the neck up until my hair felt like it would burst into flames like dry brush. Yet I couldn't look away.

Totally disregarding Greg, I stared at the photos, wondering who the guy was. In each picture, his face was always well hidden. I motioned to Greg and he clicked on the last Gallery page. Here too, were several photos of Sophie and her partner, again with his face out of view.

Greg broke my concentration. "He likes you, you know."

"Huh? Who?"

"Frye."

Puzzled, I looked at Greg, but he kept staring at the computer screen. *Where in the hell did this come from,* I wondered.

"What are you talking about?" I asked.

"Detective Frye. He likes you, and not in the 'usual suspects' kind of way. I noticed how he was looking at you." His eyes finally met mine. They were crinkled around the edges from teasing, yet sad at the same time.

"You're nuts," I said, returning my focus to the photos. "Besides, he's married. Didn't you see the ring?"

"He had a wedding ring?"

"Yep. Girls always notice little things like that. Gender hazard, or occupational, depending how you look at it."

"Are you saying that you always check to see if a guy is wearing a wedding ring?"

"Do you notice boobs?" I asked, turning to look him in the eye.

He grinned slyly and reddened, giving me my answer.

"Well, there you go!" I declared. "I also noticed that he was doing a great deal of listening and not much talking. Did you catch that? Frye has interviewed all of the people we were discussing, yet he never disclosed one single tidbit about anything he learned to us."

"So, he's a cop. His information is probably confidential."

"Probably," I said. Yet something about Frye's concentration was nagging me. If it was a simple suicide, why was he still so interested in what Greg and I had to say? "But maybe he's trying to tie up some loose ends of his own."

"You mean an 'on his own time' kind of thing?" Greg asked. I could see I had captured his interest in the subject.

"Sure, it's possible. It happens on TV, why not in real life?"

We looked at each other and laughed. Greg and I laughed a lot together. It was one of the things I enjoyed most about our budding friendship.

Greg continued to move throughout the website, coming to rest on a page called Archives.

"The archives," he explained, "hold captured photos from live sessions. You can set the camera to take still shots in timed increments, then post the pictures or use them anyway you like."

"Really?"

This was new territory for me and I was finding it fascinating. The only drawback was that it concerned a dear friend. I pushed the who out of my curious mind and focused on the what.

"Show me," I told him.

He pointed and clicked with the computer mouse. The next page contained dates with a small thumbnail-sized photo showing a sample of the content for each date.

My mind was in overdrive. What if . . .

"Greg," I began, speaking slowly, as my next thought was quickly conceived, incubated, and born via my mouth, "do you think Sophie captured photos the day she died?"

He stared at me, his mouth partially open. His fingers swept slowly through his long, brown hair.

"Shit," he said, "I never thought of that. If she did, they would be in a stored file on the computer. The police would have shut down the computer and the camera. But the photos would have been filed as they were taken."

I watched as his fingers moved the arrow-shaped cursor around the computer screen. He went to the file manager, opening the listing of files on the hard drive, scanning names for clues. My eyes browsed the file names along with Greg's. At one folder he stopped and turned quickly to me.

"Odelia, are you sure you want to see this? I mean, if the photos are here, they will be of the day she died, even of her death itself. I've seen it. It's memorable, but not in a good way."

I hadn't considered that.

"I'd be glad to view the files and photos for you, so you won't have to," he said gently.

I shook my head slowly. "No, Greg. But thanks for the offer. I don't want to see this, but I feel I should. Not to mention, two sets of eyes have a better chance at spotting some offhand clue than one."

"All right." He reached out his left hand and took my right one, squeezing it. "I think this might be it."

He clicked on the file icon and up popped a listing of photos with dates and chronological numbers. The date matched the date she died—May 3.

SIXTEEN

John Hollowell lived in a very expensive, very upscale part of Corona del Mar, a small, unincorporated beach community that bordered the south of Newport Beach. The homes in his neighborhood were gorgeous, painted and landscaped in money.

With Sophie's address book next to me, I identified Hollowell's home and pulled over. It was a two-story modern structure in light coral with large picture windows on both floors. The upstairs level had a deck, which I imagined afforded the residents a spectacular view, especially since the home was situated on a slight rise across the street from a park that perched on a bluff overlooking the ocean. Two large bougainvillaea, exploding in fuchsia, grew along the front of the house.

Glancing at my watch, I noted the time: 6:10. I had an appointment with Hollowell at 6:30. We were meeting in the bar of a restaurant located at Fashion Island. I just wanted to see his home first.

My day at the office had stretched as endlessly as a desert highway. I couldn't wait for it to be over so I could begin moonlighting as a detective. As usual, my heavy workload was a godsend, keeping my mind focused away from the speculations that now clogged my brain like a head cold.

I had arrived at the office early this morning, then worked straight through lunch. Munching on a fluffer-nutter, I continued plowing through the files and projects that were my responsibility. I planned on doing the same tomorrow and the next day until the backlog was caught up. Steele, still giving me the silent treatment, which for me was actually more of a treat, wasn't helping matters by continuing to pile new work on my desk.

For those of you not familiar with fluffer-nutters, it's a peanut butter and marshmallow crème sandwich; a comfort food from childhood that had survived the trip into middle age. Or maybe I had survived to middle age because of comfort foods like these. It was a chicken/egg conundrum. Either way, I still eat them from time to time.

I had missed enough work recently for people to wonder what was going on. Except for the usual vacation days and an occasional sick day, in the past fifteen years I had hardly ever been absent, giving me one of the best attendance records in the firm. Now, in less than two weeks, I had taken two and a half personal days off and had given the office manager a heads-up that I might need a bit more time while Mr. Wallace was away. Shortly before I left for the day, Tina had called me into her office and, after closing her door, asked directly if I was looking for another job. She seemed on the edge of panic.

Woobie's office manager is Christina Swanson. She's close to my age and is as high strung as a Chihuahua on crack. But she's a good manager, treating everyone as fairly as possible. I don't know how she does it. A few years ago, when our last manager left, I was offered the position but turned it down. Attorneys are not easy to deal with, not even when they're on your side. I had my hands full with Michael Steele on a part-time basis; no way was I going to juggle a whole firm of the creatures. Kind of makes me wonder . . . was Tina nervous before she got to Woobie, or did Woobie make her nervous? Guess that's in the same category as the chicken/egg issue.

I planned to be partially upfront with Tina, saying that I was just having a tough time coping emotionally with the death of my close friend and was attending to many of her personal matters as well. The part about playing amateur gumshoe and sticking my nose into a possible murder would be edited out. But before I could say anything, Tina had pounced on me.

"Someone told you, didn't they?" she asked.

I had no idea what she was talking about, so being lost for words, I had simply shrugged my reply.

"It was that darn Michael Steele, wasn't it?" She all but spat out his name. "I warned him something like this would happen. I told him to wait until Mr. Wallace returned and could speak to you personally."

Whatever it was someone supposedly told me and wasn't supposed to, I could tell it was big. And I *hate* being left out of big, juicy news, especially when it concerned me.

"Well, Tina, you know how Steele can be," I had said, ignoring the truth that Steele had childishly not spoken to me for a couple of days. As I said, I have no poker face, so I kept my words brief.

"Odelia," she said, "you're a valuable employee. We don't want to lose you over this, but we need you to be flexible right now. We need you to be a team player."

"When have I ever *not* been a team player?" I asked.

"Always," she quickly confirmed. "That's why it's even more important now that Mr. Wallace is leaving."

I was still stumped, but tried hard not to show it. I already knew that Mr. Wallace was retiring in a few months, but everyone knew that. Again, I shrugged. "What can I say, Tina?"

"Mr. Wallace was going to tell you before he left on vacation, but you were out. But now that you know, I'm asking you to give it a chance."

Tina really thought I was quitting the firm. She was sure Steele had told me something that would make me leave. I combed my brain for what that could be. What would make me leave Woobie after all these years?

Suddenly, my mental fog lifted and I did not like the view. There was only one reason I could think of that would make me want to quit my job. One reason and one reason only: Michael Steele.

I was in shock. Without confirmation from Tina, I knew that they were assigning me permanently to Steele when Mr. Wallace left. Without a word, I got up to leave. Just as I put a hand on the doorknob, Tina spoke again.

"The position comes with a raise, Odelia, a nice one."

I paused and considered it without turning around. Raise? Did someone say raise? Hmmm, but would the extra money really be worth the extra aggravation?

"It's a full-time paralegal position," Tina continued, trying to woo me.

Without taking my hand off the doorknob, I turned slightly around. "But Steele would be my supervising attorney?"

"Yes, that's true," she said quickly. "But for all his faults, he is a brilliant attorney. Think of how much you can learn from him. And, Odelia, Mr. Steele *asked* for you to be assigned to him. He wants to work with you and no one else."

"Lucky me," I said with false gaiety.

Tina smiled tightly at my remark. "Please, Odelia, give it a chance."

I thought about it, quickly turning over the possibilities without losing my lunch.

"I want a private office," I told her. "There's that small one on the floor below." Although most paralegals had to make do with cubicles, some had tiny offices. Anything with a door would suit me. A door could be closed, preferably in the face of an obnoxious attorney. I was getting good at closing doors on annoying people.

But Tina shook her head. "Sorry, but Mr. Steele wants you right outside his office, next to his secretary's desk."

I turned the door handle. "It's been great working here, Tina, but the answer is no."

The door was open and I was halfway through it when she spoke again. "How about the one at the end of the hall? It's a few doors down from Mr. Steele."

I knew the office. It was currently being used for storing case files for a large litigation matter. It was close enough to Steele to be convenient, but far enough away that he couldn't bellow for me from behind his desk. To talk to me, he'd either have to walk down to my office or pick up the phone.

"It's the best I can do, Odelia," Tina said in a strained voice.

I paused, gave it quick thought, and turned to face Tina.

"It's a deal, Tina. I'll give it a chance, but the office is non-negotiable. So is the raise. There will be no horse trading one for the other."

Mike Steele as my supervising attorney; now *that* was something that could make a gal go postal.

After checking out chez Hollowell, it didn't take me long to coast up Pacific Coast Highway to Fashion Island. The restaurant was situated on the outskirts of the mall, on Newport Center Drive, across from a large parking structure and office buildings.

I was nervous. My curiosity was piqued. The Sophie I knew was a warrior of causes, a loving leader who stood tall in the crowd, a doormat for no one. So who was this man and what kind of spells did he weave? I could understand a teenage Sophie being smitten. Even a young woman with a head full of romantic fantasies could be enticed to run off with a dubious suitor. But Sophie had been tied to him for over twenty years and had even given up her son for him. But according to Greg, she'd been trying to break away from Hollowell.

Olsen had said that Hollowell had used Sophie, physically and emotionally, since they were in high school. Greg referred to him as Sophie's addiction. I had lots of questions for John Hollowell. So many, I had entertained the idea of jotting them down on the palm of my hand like crib notes. From what I'd seen and heard of him so far, a bad taste had already formed. But I knew that I'd learn nothing if I came across like a Rottweiler having a bad day. And, after all, it might not have been as Olsen and Greg had said. Jealousy is a powerful motive for spreading blame and dislike. Maybe Hollowell and Sophie had been star-crossed lovers trying to build a life together in spite of unfortunate circumstances.

Yeah, right. My logical side kicked my romantic side in the ass and told it to get real.

Hollowell had agreed to meet me almost immediately after I telephoned this morning. I had baited him, saying that Sophie had left him something that I wanted to deliver in person.

She hadn't left him anything.

Considering that the two of them had been so close, if not bonded in some sick and unholy alliance for over two decades, I had been surprised at the lack of mention of Hollowell in Sophie's final requests. But rummaging through her things, I found something that might be a believable token. It was a thick, gold bracelet with both of their initials engraved on a small, round disk that dangled from one of the large links. I had discovered it at the bottom of one of her dresser drawers, tucked inside a black velvet jewelry case.

The bar was moderately busy. A quick scan showed Hollowell's movie star face nowhere in sight. Over the phone, I had given him a sketchy idea of what I looked like. Sitting at a small table near the bar, I ordered a strawberry margarita and watched the entrance for him.

I didn't have to wait long. He showed up just as my drink was being served. Catching his attention, I gave him a small wave.

Dressed in impeccable casual business attire, he was even more good-looking than I remembered. He strolled over to my table. He was tall and lean, but not skinny. His handsome face was brown from the sun with slight creases feathering the outside of his eyes. If asked, I would have guessed that he either golfed or sailed, or both.

I extended my hand, trying to keep my shakes from being too noticeable. Just as Zee had said, I was out of my league. Sophie had seemed invincible—like Superman, but with red pumps and a handbag to match the cape. I was a mere mortal standing on the precipice of menopause, trying to cruise in an ill-fitting bra.

"John Hollowell, I presume," I said, trying to be jaunty. It came out corny.

"Yes," he chuckled slightly, giving my hand a firm but not tight shake.

His voice was cultured, not too deep, rolling off his tongue with confidence and perfect diction. Had he spoken with a British accent, I would have melted on the spot into an adoring puddle.

Get a grip, Odelia, I warned myself silently. *This man is most likely an emotional predator, possibly a killer.*

"It's nice to meet you, Odelia." He flashed a perfect smile.

I indicated the chair across from me. "Please, have a seat."

Ignoring my offer, he took the chair immediately to my right and pulled up conspiratorially close. Power and control emanated from him like a heady after-shave. It made my nose crinkle and my brain go on alert.

On his left ring finger was a medium-width gold band with a square-cut diamond set flush in the middle. I thought of Greg and our discussion about Detective Frye and smiled.

The waiter came over. Hollowell ordered a Chivas on the rocks, water on the side.

I looked at him and blushed. It was a direct reaction to his uncommonly good looks and proximity. I'll admit it, I'm a sucker for a pretty male face. After spending under three minutes with the man, I was beginning to understand how Sophie had gotten roped in.

Unable to find my voice to start the conversation, he helped me out.

"I remember you from the service," he said, looking at my face, studying it with a slow, lazy smile. Moving only his large brown eyes with their long lashes, his gaze trailed down my neck and rested momentarily on my chest, then traveled back to my face.

I felt naked.

Before I sat down I had taken off my suit jacket. Today I had worn a lightweight sage green suit with a cream silk tank top underneath. I thought about reaching for the jacket, but dismissed the action as too obvious, a sign of discomfort and running scared. I only prayed that the cool air moving through the bar didn't bring up my nipples through the thin material.

"You knew Sophie a long time?" he asked, keeping up his end of the conversation in spite of my silence.

"Almost three years," I croaked out, then repeated it much clearer. "Three years."

Some detective, I scolded myself. *Amateur or not, if you're going to do this, Odelia, do it right.*

"I understand that you knew Sophie since high school," I said, managing to summon some confidence in my tone.

He smiled another slow smile. "Yes, we've been very close all these years." He reached out a hand and lightly patted my forearm. "I'm sorry Sophie never introduced us." My skin sizzled as his cool, dry fingers lingered.

This man was good and obviously knew just what buttons to push. Olsen had called him smooth, but until now I didn't know what *smooth* truly meant. Between his good looks, powerful yet casual demeanor, and silken voice, he was a lethal weapon. I felt my resolve and purpose being sapped.

The waiter came with Hollowell's drink. It gave me a chance to shake the spell off.

I took a long drag on my margarita. After sucking up a fair amount of strawberry-flavored determination, I steeled my shoulders and scooted my chair discreetly away from him just a tad. Then I reached into my bag and brought out the long velvet box.

"I believe Sophie wanted you to have this," I said, placing the bracelet directly in front of Hollowell.

He took the box and opened it, letting loose with a deep chuckle when he did.

"Figures she'd leave me this," he said, his voice edged with sarcasm. He took the bracelet out of the box and dangled it, playing with the fluid links. It cascaded over his fingertips like golden water.

"It's very beautiful," I commented. "I assumed you had given it to her."

"Yes, I did." He chuckled again and looked at me. Again, the lazy, sly smile. "She hated it. Said it reminded her of manacles."

I was silent. Manacles? Chains for a slave?

"So, Odelia, what do you think? An expensive bracelet? Or a single shackle?"

I shrugged. "It's very beautiful, Mr. Hollowell. Maybe it just wasn't Sophie's taste."

"Now, I told you on the phone to call me John."

"Okay, John." I gave him a small forced smile.

With a quick jerk, he pulled off the engraved disk. Then, in a single gliding underhanded motion, he tossed it across the room, away from the other tables. He did it casually, as if skipping rocks on a pond. It struck the far wall of the structure and disappeared behind some potted plants.

Did he dispose of Sophie as calmly? There was no doubt in my mind that he was capable.

"Here, it's yours," he said, offering the jewelry to me.

"Mine?" I was shocked.

"Sure. I certainly don't need it. And it would be a nice keepsake for you to have. Beautiful jewelry should be worn only by beautiful women." Again with the disarming smile. He dangled the gold in front of me as if offering a treat.

Okay, so where was the trick?

"I don't think so . . . John. But thank you just the same." My natural stubborn streak and my built-in bullshit detector were powering up, getting ready to be put into service. "Besides," I lied, "Sophie wanted you to have it. As a remembrance."

He chuckled to himself. So much chuckling. It wasn't a nervous little laugh, but rather a short expression of self-satisfied amusement garnished with a hint of scorn.

"I have many memories of Sophie, but this isn't one of them. Not exactly what I wanted, you might say."

"Well," I said, hoping to sound helpful and innocent, "I am sort of in charge of her things at the moment. If there is something in particular you would like, a photo, item of clothing, or piece of furniture that hasn't already been given to someone else, perhaps I can help you out. Most of her things are being liquidated anyway."

"The money going to the boy?"

"Ah . . . yes, to her son."

At that very instant, I could have sworn that something happened to Hollowell's face. There was a change in his look, an almost imperceptible alteration of his expression. Then it was lost. It happened so fast I couldn't identify the emotion, but I knew I had seen something peeking out from behind the ever-present smile.

"Didn't Sophie leave anything else for me?" he asked in a softly pressing tone, reaching out again to touch my arm. "A letter perhaps? Maybe some words in a note?"

I shook my head slowly in the negative.

"Did you check her safe deposit box?"

"Yes. There was nothing left for you," I said, then quickly added, "except the bracelet."

"You're absolutely sure? Nothing left with her lawyer?"

"No, sorry."

With his right elbow planted on the small table, he lifted his glass to take a drink. His eyes were unfocused, thinking inwardly. He took another drink fast on the heels of the first.

Had I not been on the alert, I might have told him that I didn't believe Sophie had committed suicide. But cautiously, I held my tongue.

It was obvious to me that he wasn't asking about usual items of inheritance or final parting words of regret, but something more specific. And, oddly, he didn't seem particularly disappointed or surprised that there was nothing more. Just curious in a peculiar way. I could almost see his brain working in that handsome head like a fine Swiss watch; the gears grinding, meshing, tick-tocking away.

After a third quick sip, he turned his attention back to me, all smiles once more. The drinking and thinking had taken less than twenty seconds.

What in the hell was he fishing for?

We had gone through most of Sophie's drawers, both in her office and bedroom, and had discovered nothing unusual except for the Robbie box. A bunch of kid's photos and report cards hardly seemed like something Hollowell would expect to receive from a dead girlfriend.

Still holding his scotch, he leaned back casually in his seat and crossed his legs, right ankle over left knee.

"You know, Odelia," he said in a seductive tone, "you are quite attractive."

Huh? How did we get from *whaddaya got for me* to *ain't you cute* so quickly, and without so much as a hint of coming attractions?

"Thank you, John," I said cautiously.

"Yes, very attractive." He was dishing out cool and smooth again, this time in double scoops with chocolate sauce. "And I adore large women. More to love."

I shifted nervously.

"Why did Peter Olsen confront you at the service?" I asked, anxious to get off the subject of more to love.

Hollowell looked at me, his expressionless eyes locked onto mine, not answering.

I decided to shovel some bullshit of my own. "It was so rude of him, and you handled it so well. I was impressed."

His eyes crinkled with amusement.

"Why do you think? Jealousy, of course." He gave a short laugh. "You were a close friend of Sophie's. I'm sure you knew the whole story."

I just smiled at him as I ran my answer silently in my head. *Until recently, buddy, I knew nothing about no one. Not about you, Olsen, Robbie. Nada!*

"Olsen's never gotten over the fact that Sophie left him for me. Pathetic little worm." He leaned in closer, his eyes narrowing, scrutinizing my face. "I'm sure Sophie told you all the gory details."

His last statement was more than a comment, it was a search party. He was pressing me for information, wondering what I knew. God, what did I know? Maybe I knew more than I thought I did. Olsen had told me his side. And Greg had given me a scanty sketch of what Sophie had confided in their talks. But if this was merely a tale about an old love triangle, I didn't think Hollowell would be so curious.

I had seen his type before—had even almost married one, once upon a time. People like this didn't put much effort into wondering what other people thought or felt. To people like Hollowell, emotions, particularly other people's, were nothing more than dead bodies to be dumped on the side of the road after the deed was done.

What was it Greg had said that morning at the beach? Oh yes, that sometimes people keep secrets from friends to protect them. *To protect them.*

Hollowell didn't look like he needed protection. I, on the other hand, felt as vulnerable as a jelly donut at a police station.

"Actually, Sophie never talked about you," I told him truthfully. "I'm sorry."

"She didn't?" He cocked an eyebrow in surprise.

I shook my head and looked at him with false sadness. I needed to get Hollowell off my trail. Sophie had kept silent about this man for a good reason.

"No, in fact, she didn't talk much at all about her past. Not even about her ex-husband or son." I gave him my best tragic sigh. "I think it hurt too much to discuss it. As her friend, I respected that."

There it was again! That same instantaneous alteration of his face I had witnessed before. Like a subliminal message planted in a nature film, his appearance remained relaxed and smiling while other, more intense feelings darted across his face nearly undetected. My gut told me that it was the personality appearing in strobe light intervals that I should be worried about.

"Did you know about Sophie's website?" I asked. "I had no idea that she had one of those . . . um . . . adult sites." I threw in some feigned shock. "Just when you think you know a person."

"Yes, of course I knew." He chuckled.

Ol' Chuckles was beginning to get on my nerves.

"In fact, I helped her set it up. Even gave her the idea." The sexy smile was back. "Why, would you like to take it over?" The question was serious, not a bad joke like Mike Steele's comment. "You'd be a smash on it, Odelia."

His eyes slowly looked me over. Not an open leer, but an appraisal, an almost professional one.

Now it was my turn to chuckle.

"Nooooooo, not me," I told him with an exaggerated roll of my eyes. "My larger-than-life, middle-aged body is not for public consumption. They'd shut me down for being a blight on the side of the information highway."

Hollowell tilted back his head and laughed heartily. It was the first uncalculated and genuine thing he'd done since sitting down. "Attractive *and* funny. That's a good combination, Odelia. No wonder you and Sophie were friends." He uncrossed his legs and shifted forward, leaning in close, giving me an unmistakable bedroom look. "I like spunky women with full curves. Maybe we should get together again? Hopefully soon."

What's a girl to do? Especially a girl who wants to know more about this dangerous man and his relationship with one of her best friends.

I fidgeted with my margarita and took another deep draw on the straw. My eyes were down, my focus buried in the red, slushy liquid.

I felt his touch on my arm again. His fingers stroked and squeezed my flesh discretely, sensuously.

I sucked my drink faster, deeper, until the glass was empty.

SEVENTEEN

THE EARLY MORNING DAMPNESS clung to the shrubs like pavé diamonds set in malachite. I took big, deep breaths while I walked, filling my lungs with gulps of cool wetness mixed with a fresh scent that smelled faintly of licorice. The bay was shrouded in a heavy haze. By noon we'd be enjoying a warm, clear day accompanied by gentle breezes off the nearby ocean.

The walk was invigorating. I could feel my muscles stretching, working to propel my logy ass down the trail. I felt my pulse. My heart was pumping steadily. The whole activity was life affirming, giving me a boost both mentally and physically. *Odelia, you should exercise more often,* I lectured myself silently. Funny how I always forgot how good activity made me feel when sitting on the sofa in front of the TV.

Next to me was Glo Kendall. We were moving at a nice pace, not dawdling, not race walking. A few yards behind us were three other ladies. Two of them were Reality Check regulars. The third walker in the bunch was Ruth Wise. After just a few days, Ruth already fit in nicely with the other women who met casually for the daily walks.

She was quiet yet sociable, exuding a calm confidence that would be an asset to the group. I sincerely hoped that she would attend the meetings once we started them up again.

"You look tired, Odelia," Glo commented.

I looked at her and smiled.

In spite of the cool morning, perspiration was beginning to form on Glo's forehead. Her long, dark blond hair was parted and caught in two pigtails. She had a cute turned-up nose that gave her a slightly pug look, small brown eyes, and thin lips. She was taller than me by three or four inches and lighter by about twenty pounds. And although I was old enough to be her mother, she huffed and puffed considerably more as we kept to our brisk pace. I attributed the latter to her smoking. Glo wasn't what you'd call beautiful, not even particularly pretty. She might be described as a handsome woman, a term I always considered a polite way of saying plain but not unattractive. With Sophie's help she had learned to enhance her best features and create a very appealing and perky look.

Me, people referred to as interesting. Attractive, pretty, maybe even beautiful on a good day, but in a non-classical way. On their own, my features were odd. My nose was long with a slight bump near the bridge and blanketed with a line of freckles. My green eyes were too close and my mouth full on the bottom, thin on top. But somehow it all worked together to give me my own look that over the years many had found pleasing and even a bit exotic.

"Yes, Glo, I am." I rotated my neck, producing a few cracks and pops. "Haven't had much sleep since Sophie died." I turned my head back toward her and displayed a small, tired smile from under the red cap I was wearing. "But it will be over soon. The lawyer has several people coming around next week to appraise the furniture and household goods for purchase. We'll get rid of the whole lot at once hopefully. Then the house will go on the market."

She reached out and gave my arm an affectionate squeeze.

"You've done a might, Odelia," she said in her hick twang. "You've been a good friend to Sophie. If there's somethin' more I can do to help, you just call."

"Thank you, Glo." I smiled at her again. "I appreciate the offer. Most of Sophie's personal things are about packed up. Just a few odds and ends left."

"What are you gonna do with all of it? You know, her clothes, papers, stuff like that?"

"Not sure, maybe donate the clothes to a women's shelter." I looked over at Glo. She was close to Sophie's size, and I knew she could use the extra boost to her wardrobe. "Would you like to have some of her clothing? I'm sure she would've liked that."

She smiled, then said, "Sure. 'Bout the only time I'll ever get to wear such nice things."

We walked along a bit farther in silence. With Sophie gone, I was now the oldest member of the group. Zee and a couple of others were right behind me in age, but many of the women in Reality Check were in their twenties and thirties. They looked to us for guidance as they picked their way through the minefields of a prejudiced society. Giggles could be heard from the small group behind us. I felt maternal watchfulness growing by the minute.

"I met with an old flame of Sophie's last night," I told Glo. She looked at me, her eyes full of interest. "John Hollowell." I caught the quick way her eyes widened, then relaxed. "You know him?" I asked with new curiosity.

She didn't respond for several feet, then she wheezed, followed by coughing to clear her throat.

"Met him once at Sophie's. By accident." She looked up and grinned at me. "Quite a looker."

I nodded. "That he is."

"It was around the holidays, back when I was lookin' for work. Sophie was helpin' me with my résumé one mornin' and he sort of popped in."

Glo had a habit of dropping the *g* in the *ing*.

"Popped in?"

"Yeah, at least it seemed that way. Caught Sophie by surprise anyway. Made her mad, too. I think he was already an ex-boyfriend by that time. Know what I mean?"

That would have been about six months ago, shortly after Glo joined our group. I jotted this new information down in my brain and posted it on my internal bulletin board.

"Did he stay long?" I asked, trying to seem casual rather than interrogating.

"We were workin' at her kitchen table. She took him into her back room. You know, the one she used as her office."

I nodded again. I knew it well. Looking ahead as we walked, I listened to each word intently.

"Anyway, they were back there arguin'. No yellin', just pickin' at each other."

"What about?"

"Couldn't tell ya. But Sophie was real upset. I could tell by her voice. They weren't in there long. When they finished, he headed straight out the front door."

"That's all?"

"Pretty much."

Glo glanced at me. I saw her cheeks redden and pushed my cap back for a better view. Quickly she stared down at the path we were traveling.

"Well, there's more, but nothin' important. Just that Sophie got a call and went back into her office to talk. There was a knock on the front door while she was gone, then it opened. It was John Hollowell again. He came in sayin' he'd left his keys on Sophie's desk. I told him she was on the phone." She hesitated slightly. "He waited with me until she was through, then got his keys and left."

"Did he say anything to you?"

"Chitchat mostly. Kinda made me nervous. Wanted to know what we were workin' on. Told him I was looking for a job and Sophie was helpin'."

The fight could have been about anything. I knew from Greg that Sophie had been trying to break off the relationship. Maybe Hollowell had a hard time letting her go. He didn't seem the clingy type to me, but he definitely seemed the type not to take rejection very well. Hollowell was a man used to winning, someone who didn't take no for an answer. I knew that from recent personal experience.

I had finally agreed to meet him again this Friday night about eight. We were going back to the same restaurant, this time for dinner. He had originally suggested that he pick me up and drive us to a romantic restaurant farther down the coast, but I had nixed the idea. I wanted someplace close, someplace where I could meet him. What I wanted was an emergency exit.

While it is my firm practice not to date married men, I did want to pry into Hollowell and Sophie's relationship more. I had been nervous last night. Oh hell, who was I kidding? I'd been scared nearly deaf and dumb by his manipulative looks and comments.

Also, asking too many questions might have made him suspicious. I came away from that evening a bit tipsy and starved for more data.

I didn't want Hollowell to know, or even to suspect for a minute, that I was investigating Sophie's supposed suicide, at least not yet. Whether or not he was involved with her death, one thing was for sure, he knew something about it. I can't say how I knew this. I just knew it. I could sense it, feel it, even taste it. And trust me, my sense of taste is as fit as a fiddle.

John Hollowell is a very dangerous human being, or I'm a Snickers without the nuts.

Friday will be different, I told myself. It would be my mission to ferret out important clues and information somewhere between drinks and dessert.

"You're thinking about her, huh? About Sophie?"

Startled, I looked in the direction of the question, at Glo. I had forgotten where I was. My feet were on autopilot, putting one in front of the other along the path.

"Yes, I was. I think about her a lot."

"Me, too," she said, almost in a whisper.

We took a few more steps in silence before Glo spoke again.

"Odelia, did you ever find out anything about that box of old photos Zee found in Sophie's closet when we were cleaning?"

"Actually, Glo, I did." I looked over at her. "Turns out Sophie had a son."

"A son?" Glo stopped walking and stood in the middle of the trail. I kept going and she skipped a step or two to catch up.

"Yes, but he lives with his father. Sophie hadn't seen him in a long time."

"Wow," she said, "imagine that. So what's his name? Where's he live?"

Looking forward, I could see that we were about to cross the timber bridge that led up a small incline to where the cars were parked. Another ten minutes and I'd be heading home to shower and get ready for the office.

"How's work going, Glo?" I asked, not wanting to talk anymore about Robbie. Peter Olsen had asked me to leave Robbie out of things as much as possible, and I intended to honor his wishes. "You still enjoy your job?"

She thought about it before answering. "Yeah, sure. It's not what I want to be doin' the rest of my life, but the boss said I have potential." She grinned.

"Great." I beamed at her. She was indeed one of our—one of Sophie's—successes.

"It's just been hard and all with everythin' that's happened lately."

"You mean Sophie?"

"Well, that and that accident a few days ago. You know that kid who was killed by the drunk driver?"

I stopped dead in my tracks and stared at her, barely able to speak. "You mean the young man that worked for that security company?"

She stopped next to me, her face serious and sad. The women behind us caught up and started past.

"Everything all right, ladies?" Ruth asked.

"Yes, fine, thanks," I told her with a small smile. "Just girl talk."

Ruth smiled back and moved on, but I caught her casting a look back over her shoulder as she walked up the slight hill. I turned back to Glo.

"Yeah," she told me, "the one on the news a few nights ago. Well, that was the head of our company. The drunk, I mean. Shook us all up pretty bad. Not that I'm excusin' what he did, mind you."

EIGHTEEN

WHAT IN THE WORLD would southern California do without single-story stucco strip malls? They dotted light commercial areas, painted in various shades of gray, white, and brown, like cheap plastic buildings made for a board game.

Ocean Breeze Graphics was housed in such a structure in Huntington Beach, this one painted tan with Spanish hacienda affectations. The little convenience mall held five small businesses, with Greg's shop taking up the most space. On one side of him was a moderately busy pizza and sandwich joint, on the other side a dry cleaner, beauty supply store, and a nail salon. There was a nice-size parking area in the front.

Inside the shop was a long counter divided into two sections. The left half was normal height, the counter to the right lower by several inches. I immediately realized that the lower counter was to accommodate Greg's wheelchair needs.

At the higher counter, on the work side, stood a college-age kid. He was dressed in full California beach attire—baggy shorts and a loud purple tie-dyed T-shirt. His short, spiked hair was dyed lime green, making me think of Seamus. Completing his fashion statement was a tiny gold hoop piercing his left brow. He was deep in conversation with a conservatively dressed man, discussing layouts for a brochure. The kid glanced my way.

"Be with you in a minute, ma'am."

I nodded at him and sat in one of the several plastic molded chairs lined up against the front window.

Beyond the counter was a very large open area. It was a hive of activity with lots of machines of different sizes and types whirring away. Worker bees were attending to business, chatting and bantering pleasantly among themselves. It seemed like a nice place to work, clean and industrious, and Greg's employees looked happy and relaxed. I imagined him being a good and fair boss.

I only had to wait a few minutes before the man at the counter left and the kid turned his attention to me.

"What can we do for you?" he asked politely, without a hint of the youthful slang usually associated with his colorful attire.

"I'm here to see Greg Stevens, but I don't have an appointment." I stood up and walked to the counter. "I was just hoping to catch him in."

At that moment, Wainwright trotted out from behind the counter and nuzzled my leg like an old friend. I took his boulder of a head in both my hands and playfully rubbed it. His fringed tail wagged like a metronome.

"Hey, Wainwright, how you doing, boy?" I looked up at the kid. "Greg must be in," I said with a laugh.

The kid grinned. "Let me tell Greg you're here. What's your name?"

I told him my name as Wainwright leaned one side of his heavy head into my hand. I scratched behind one ear, then the other, knowing full well that I was going to catch hell from Seamus tonight when I came home smelling like doggie. He hadn't quite forgiven me for letting Wainwright into the house in the first place.

"Looks like you found another sucker, ol' boy."

I looked up to see Greg watching me from behind the counter. He seemed very happy to see me. Upon hearing his master's voice, Wainwright abandoned me to beg attention from Greg.

"You must have ESP or something," he said. "I was going to call you tonight."

"I was in the area attending a meeting," I explained. "Hope you don't mind my dropping in like this?"

It was true. Mike Steele had an afternoon appointment at a client's office in Huntington Beach, not far from Greg's printing company. The client was growing at a fast pace and was looking to expand his business outside the state. Since one of my paralegal duties was to set up corporations inside and outside of California, Steele had asked me to come along. Thankfully, we had taken separate cars. After the news of my upcoming assignment, it was now my turn to present a cold shoulder.

"No, not at all," Greg said. "I have something interesting to show you. But first a quick tour."

He proudly showed me around Ocean Breeze Graphics and introduced me to several people, including the kid from the front counter. His name was Boomer. Like a puffed-up papa, Greg announced, much to the boy's embarrassment, that Boomer was a straight-A college student who had been with him since he was sixteen, beginning with deliveries.

Greg had a right to be pleased with the business and his people. Hard work and success hovered over the place like the hum of the machinery they used. And it was easy to see that genuine affection existed between the workers and their boss. There was an overall camaraderie about the place that didn't exist at Woobie and never had. I wondered with amusement if Ocean Breeze Graphics had an opening for a corporate paralegal.

Greg took me back to his office. It was a large, square room in a corner of the building. One wall consisted mainly of a huge picture window through which he could survey most of the work area. The door to the office was unusually wide, as were the aisles running through the main part of the shop, all tailored to help Greg in the maneuvering of the wheelchair. It was an impressive setup.

"I've been working on the saved camera photos from Sophie's computer," he told me excitedly as he closed the door to give us privacy. "What I've found is very odd."

He wheeled behind his desk and motioned for me to pull up one of the side chairs standing nearby. His computer was already on. I envied his monitor. It was one of the large flat screen models, making mine at home seem no bigger than a Game Boy.

The other night we had located the saved photos taken by the computer camera on the day of Sophie's death. The camera had been programmed to save them on the hard drive at intervals of fifteen seconds. Dates and times were stamped across the bottom of each still shot. The first photos had started close to eight in the morning. The camera had been shut off by the police just after 9:30. In between were numerous photos, including those showing the shooting, according to the time stamp, at about 9:12.

We had gone though many of the pictures that night at Sophie's and had caught some oddities in a few just before the shooting. But the images weren't sharp enough to be sure. Greg burned the photos to a CD and volunteered to enlarge them on his computer at work.

He had done a good job and had created a chronological slide show from the photos taken from Sophie's computer.

"These were taken about 8:20," Greg explained, showing me one enlarged photo on his computer screen, followed by another.

Each photo showed Sophie in front of the camera, her head turned to her left. She looked serious, very tense. I imagined her office, picturing myself sitting behind her desk, moving my head in the same direction.

"She's looking toward the loveseat under the window," I said. My heart started to beat faster as I studied the photo. "Possibly at someone."

"Exactly."

Greg pulled a large pad of yellow lined paper from a stack on his desk. It was the same type of notepad used by lawyers. On it were two times and dates, both circled. One was May 2, 10:50; the other May 3, 8:20. The May 3 entry was also underscored several times.

Greg stabbed the end of a ballpoint pen at each of the dates. "And these are the dates and times Ortiz made service calls to that address, according to the security company. These are my notes from my conversation with them."

I wanted to shout *ah ha!* but felt a need to be cautious.

"Yes, but maybe Ortiz wasn't exact in his report," I said. "Or maybe the clock on the computer was off in one direction or another."

"Wait, Odelia, we haven't come to the interesting part yet."

He moved through the photos quickly until they seemed like a slow-moving video. Most were of Sophie in front of the camera, facing toward the love seat. Throughout the sequence her facial expression changed little, showing her face taut, her eyes narrowed. Sometimes her mouth was open, as if speaking. The times on the photos ranged from 8:15 until 8:32, over fifty photos in all. Following 8:32, the photos showed Sophie looking slightly more to the right, in the direction of the closet. Still her face was stone cold.

"Go back several," I told him. "Then go forward more slowly."

He did as I asked. With each slide, I double checked the date and time posting at the bottom.

"Greg," I said quietly and calmly, "if these photos are correct, then Ortiz . . ." I looked at him wide-eyed.

"Never saw Sophie at all," he said, finishing my sentence.

"But he told his supervisor and the police that he saw Sophie and that she seemed okay. He—"

"Must've seen someone else."

"Yes, someone else. Another woman passing herself off as Sophie when Ortiz stopped by."

My mind did a leap and, surprisingly, landed on its feet.

"If someone else, a woman, was at the door chatting with Ortiz about the alarm system . . . ," I said, the words coming out slow and deliberate as I got the progression straight in my mind, "then some- one else, another person, was in the room with Sophie while these pictures were being snapped."

I threw myself back into the chair and stared at the ceiling.

"We're not looking for a murderer, Greg. We're looking for at least *two* murderers! And poor Ortiz could have been killed because he could identify the person he saw as *not* being the real Sophie London."

"BINGO!" Greg said, slapping his hands together quick and loud like a clap of thunder.

I moved my eyes from the ceiling to Greg. "Holy shit, Greg, what have we stumbled onto?"

"There's more, Odelia. You sure you're ready?"

"Two weeks ago, I was hardly ready to get up in the morning and shower. Today, I'm ready for anything."

Greg clicked on the computer screen and the photos started moving forward again, this time slowly.

"These were taken about the time of the shooting," he said. "About the time I came online."

I had seen the suicide photos the other night, but then they had been small pictures. Now they were more than triple in size. Today, they marched across the screen like surreal images from a pepperoni pizza induced nightmare.

Sophie's face appeared in all of them. Some showed her with the gun, first with it in her hand, then in her mouth. There were three of the gun barrel poised between her lips, the time stamps telling us that it had been about thirty to forty-five seconds between the aiming and the shooting.

The next sequence of photos showed Sophie slumped backward in her chair, her vacant eyes looking upward. There were a number of those pictures, the later ones showing a trickle of blood trailing from one corner of her mouth down her chin. Then another person, a man clad in dark blue or black, a police officer probably, came into the shot. There were a couple of photos of him checking the body for life. Soon after, something covered the camera, blocking the view from the Internet watchers. The next photos were just black empty shots until the end.

"Where's the restroom?" I asked Greg weakly.

"To the right of my office, down a short hall," he told me. "You okay?"

"I will be."

The shop was still full of people as I stepped quickly to the bathroom. Thankfully, it wasn't occupied. After locking the door, I dropped to my knees and hugged the cool porcelain bowl as the remnants of my lunch burst free.

Ready for anything, my big behind.

When the sickness subsided, I stood up and flushed. Moving to the sink, I dabbed my face with a wet paper towel and checked the damage. My mascara was running, my eyeliner smudged. Against my pale, freckled skin my blackened eyes looked ghoulish. With a paper towel and some water, I patted around my eyes, trying to clean up the mess. I only succeeded in pressing it deeper into the crevices of my crow's feet. A fuzz coated my teeth and tongue. It tasted of chocolate and peanut butter. Today I'd had another fluffernutter, followed by carrot sticks and a brownie. None of it tasted good the second time around.

There was a small Dixie cup dispenser attached to the wall. Pulling one of the small cups from the plastic hanger, I used it to swish my mouth out. It only helped a little.

The bathroom was large, without stall walls around the single commode, and the sink was low and open underneath. A metal handrail ran alongside the toilet area. Everything was handicapped accessible and clean. I noticed a large cabinet attached to the wall to the right of the sink and opened it.

Hallelujah!

Inside were several tubes of toothpaste, varied toothbrushes encased in plastic holders, mouthwash, razors, Tylenol, Maalox, bandages, and other hygiene and first-aid items, including a box of Tampax. Obviously, I had discovered the healthcare emergency cache of the employees of Ocean Breeze Graphics.

Using some toothpaste and my finger, I did a quick scrub of my teeth, then poured some mouthwash into the paper cup. I tossed it back like a tequila shooter and swished it around vigorously. It was the kind of mouthwash meant to be diluted with water before using, but feeling the need for industrial-strength action I ignored the directions.

Yowza!

It did the trick. I left the bathroom semi-composed and fully awake, my mouth feeling like it had been rinsed with mint-flavored bleach.

When I emerged from the bathroom I noticed that many of Greg's employees had left. The huge, plain clock hung high on a side wall said five fifteen. I walked back to Greg's office to find Boomer looking at the computer screen over his shoulder. They were discussing something about the photos on the screen.

"You sure you're okay?" Greg asked.

"Yes, I'll be fine. Used some of your mouthwash. Hope you don't mind."

He smiled, but it was a concerned smile. "If you don't want to go on, I'll understand."

"No, really, I'm fine." I turned my attention to the photos. "What was it you found in this batch?" I asked.

"Well, see these photos, the ones with Sophie holding the gun, and then these next ones with the gun in her mouth?" He no longer had a single photo on the screen, but four at a time.

"Yes."

"Boomer was the one who saw something odd right away." Greg looked at the beach scholar standing close by. "Show Odelia what you noticed, Boom."

Boomer leaned over Greg's shoulder for a closer look and commandeered the mouse. Calmly and professionally he surveyed the photos. He pointed to several of Sophie holding the gun.

"See this? In these pictures your friend is holding the gun and looking down at it. Looks to me like she's maybe contemplating what's next. Look closely and you can see what might be wetness on the side of her face." With a double click the photo was instantaneously enlarged. Boomer clicked several more times, each time enlarging the photo until only Sophie's face covered the screen.

Sure enough, it did look like she was crying. I swallowed hard, the mouthwash still burning my mucous membranes.

Boomer clicked some more and the photos returned to smaller, four-to-a-page size.

"In these pictures," Boomer explained, pointing to a photo in the next sequence grouping, "she's got the gun barrel in her mouth." He clicked to enlarge the shot. "But look at her eyes. She's definitely looking at something. This next picture, too." He clicked the mouse to bring up the next photo and clicked again to enlarge it. "And look at her shoulders." With an index finger, Boomer traced along Sophie's neck and shoulders while Greg and I watched. "They're squared, determined, like she's getting ready to rumble."

I scrutinized the photos, my brain exploding with new insight. The kid was right. Sophie may have had a gun in her mouth, but her eyes, hard as tempered steel, were fixed on something or someone specific. And her posture was rigid, her head held high. It was anything but the stance of a depressed and despondent woman.

"If I were offing myself," Boomer continued, "I wouldn't be looking around. I'd be scared shitless, probably with my eyes shut tight. But this woman . . . she looks *pissed!*"

NINETEEN

THERE IS SOMETHING TO be said for keeping the hands busy and the mind occupied.

My ergonomically structured workspace was landscaped in an ever-changing mountain range of manila folders and brownish red expanding files. As I worked, one peak grew while another lessened. Industry had become my middle name, replacing Patience, which was running low in supply.

Since arriving at the office this morning, I had feverishly typed up my notes from the meeting with our client the day before. Then I moved on to setting up the needed files and began processing the paperwork to qualify the client's company in the four new states in which it was planning to do business. It was detail work that included research, typing, and placing a few calls. Steele had promised the client that the required forms would be ready for signing by the end of next week. I planned on getting them to the client for signature by Monday. The client would be happy.

I kept my head down and my mind focused, vowing to keep Sophie out of sight, out of mind, at least until after work.

The task at hand was simple enough, and I could do it in my sleep. There were few surprises in corporate work. I knew where the project began, and could track my progress easily. The desired end was recognizable and tidy. It was more than I could say about my other project, my after-hours undertaking.

The night before, Greg had wanted to take me to dinner. But I had declined, saying I didn't have much of an appetite. As always, he had understood. I just wanted to go home, fix something simple like soup, and privately cogitate on the missing links, the phantom people just beyond the camera range—which I did until two this morning.

Who could they have been? The only thing I was sure of was that one of the people at Sophie's that day had been a woman. Only a woman could have met Ortiz at the door and passed herself off as the lady of the house.

Greg and I had tried calling Detective Frye with our findings, but the person answering his phone at the station said that he was out until Monday. She asked what it was about, saying that someone else would be happy to help me. Instead, I told her that I'd call back after the weekend.

What we had was nothing concrete, just theories based on a dead woman's gaze just moments before her death. It would have been different if the photos had shown a shoe or a hand, or something tangible that could be linked to a living being. And I only wanted to talk to Frye. One trained professional patiently listening to my amateurish and emotional speculations was enough.

Sophie's eyes, and the anger burning in them just before she pulled the trigger, had been branded into my brain as if my noggin had been the side of a struggling calf. It had bleated in pain at the sight and felt the stinging of the hot iron long after the pictures had been shut down. I thought about it even throughout my morning walk.

Today, only Ruth had been at the starting place at six. The two of us had walked together quietly, exchanging a few pleasantries. She seemed to respect my preoccupation and even asked if I was okay. I had assured her that I was, saying that I was just concerned about something at work.

Ahhh, but here I go again, digressing into Murderland, buying an adult ticket and standing in line to ride the attractions. And I had promised myself that I wouldn't until tonight. I thought about tonight and exhaled concern. Tonight I was scheduled to have dinner with the scary Mr. Hollowell.

The new project well on its way, I turned my attention to returning a small batch of phone calls that had accumulated the day before when I was out of the office. Most were clients asking about the status of their work, or requesting some last-minute changes or guidance. Mr. Wallace had called, but I had returned that call as soon as I got in. He expressed concern that he hadn't been the one to tell me about my new assignment with Mike Steele, and, like Tina, he urged me to give it a chance.

One voice mail message had been from a woman named Marcia. She had called early this morning, just before I had arrived at the office. She left no last name and no call-back number. If it was important, she'd call again.

People strolled by my desk, chatting. Two women stopped— Joan and Kelsey. Joan was a litigation paralegal, Kelsey the librarian. They tried to coax me out to lunch, but I declined, saying I wanted to clear my desk up a bit more. I hadn't given the office manager any solid dates for taking some more time off while Mr. Wallace was gone, but I knew I needed some R&R. After giving me some gentle ribbing about being too conscientious, Joan and Kelsey left, but not before extracting a promise to go out next Friday for Kelsey's birthday.

After working a while longer, I gave in to my growling stomach and went to the lunchroom to fetch my lunch from the refrigerator. I was gone less than two minutes, returning to hear my phone ringing. Looking at the caller ID display on the phone, I saw that it was Joyce, our bubbly, red-haired receptionist. Pulling a homemade tuna sandwich from a brown paper bag, I picked up the receiver and gave her a cheerful hello.

She announced that I had a visitor . . . a Mrs. Peter Olsen.

Instantly my mind went to the unknown Marcia from the earlier message. Peter Olsen had said that his wife's name was Marcia. Marcia Olsen. That must've been who called.

My lunch sack fell to the floor with a crinkly thud.

Mrs. Peter Olsen wasn't alone. She'd brought her mother, Irene Pugh, a.k.a. Gram, along for support. After introductions, Marcia Olsen invited me to lunch, saying she had to speak with me immediately. She said it was about Sophie. My tuna on whole wheat would have to take a rain check.

The three of us were seated in a booth along a bank of windows in the restaurant, oddly a member of the same chain in which I'd lunched with Peter Olsen just four days prior.

Mrs. Pugh looked very much the same as when I'd last seen her. Pearls hugged her neck, and she was wearing a slightly different version of the demure floral print dress of before.

Marcia Olsen reminded me a lot of her husband, Peter; quiet yet strong and confident. Looking at her, the word *medium* popped into my mind. She was medium in build, not fat, not thin, with medium-brown hair worn in a medium-length blunt cut. Her brown eyes were nice, but unremarkable, and her face pleasant but not outstanding. She had a nice, appealing smile. I suspected that even her temperament didn't run either too hot or too cold.

My first impulse was to like her. After all, for whatever reasons, she had allowed Sophie to follow Robbie's development over the years.

Our lunches were served. Cobb salads for both me and Marcia, with Gram ordering a chicken club on whole wheat toast. Marcia smiled while Gram scowled. I wasn't sure Gram approved of this trip to Orange County or of me. No one seemed sure of how to start beyond ordering food.

"So tell me," I began, wanting some of the questions cluttering my brain like dirty laundry answered, "did you really send all that stuff about Robbie to Sophie over the years?"

"Yes," Marcia answered evenly, without a hint of defense in her voice.

From beside her daughter, Gram gave a mild "humph."

Marcia glanced at her mother, giving her a quick frown.

"My mother never approved of that, as you can see," she said, returning her attention to me.

I kept on eating. Marcia Olsen had come to me with a purpose. She was dying to tell me something, but in her own good time. Looking over at Gram, I wished the old woman would eat elsewhere. I eyed an empty stool at the counter and wondered if it'd be too rude to park her there, if just for the next fifteen minutes.

Instead, I asked Marcia, "Why did you? I'm sure Sophie appreciated it, but not many second wives would do such an unselfish thing."

Marcia stopped eating and looked down at her salad. When her eyes met mine a few seconds later, I could see that they were starting to pool.

"Peter said that you didn't know anything about Robbie, that Sophie never even told you about him."

"That's right. Came as a complete surprise."

"She was a devoted mother, you know."

"And you're not?" Gram quipped quietly, giving me a sample of her strong accent.

"Now, Mother, stop it," Marcia said gently to the older woman, then turned her attention back to me.

"Sophie and I both loved Robbie. It was something we had in common." She smiled wanly. "You know, at first I was very jealous of her, but then, after I got to know her, I realized that I had nothing to worry about. She had no intention of returning to reclaim Robbie or Peter. She just wanted to see her child. You understand that, don't you?"

I nodded. Yes, I did understand that. Even though I was childless myself, I could understand a mother not being able to keep away from her child. I'd be the same way in similar circumstances.

In my head, I quickly rewound my meeting with Peter Olsen and played it back. He hadn't said anything about Sophie seeing Robbie after she was declared dead. And he never mentioned the two women meeting. In fact, he had been surprised to find out that Marcia had been in contact with Sophie even by mail.

"You met Sophie?" I asked, surprised. "In person?"

Marcia nodded. "Yes, at first I noticed her hanging around the school yard when I'd pick Robbie up in the afternoon. He was little, only about seven or eight at the time. I didn't know who she was at first. She wore sunglasses and usually a hat. I thought she was just another parent waiting for her child. But I knew most of the families. The school wasn't that big. Then I began to notice that this woman had eyes only for my Robbie. It wasn't every day, but every so often, maybe once or twice a month. It made me nervous. I thought maybe she was one of those crazy women who snatched kids, so finally I confronted her. Nicely, of course."

Of course, I thought to myself and smiled. I could see this mild-mannered woman approaching the big and bold Sophie.

"You never told your husband?"

She shook her head. "I didn't want to worry him or have him think I was being paranoid."

"I think it was nervy of the woman," Gram snapped in a tight, low voice.

"Mother, be still or go sit in the car. I didn't bring you here to snipe at poor Sophie, God rest her soul."

Gram might have been sterner than her daughter, but it was easy to see that Marcia didn't allow her mother to run her. Under all that medium beat the heart of a lioness. Marcia Olsen was kind, decent, and at all times the protector of her lair. It was becoming clearer how she and Sophie had bonded.

Marcia sipped her iced tea and smiled at me.

"She was so nice, Odelia. But then you know that. We hit it off right away. You know, Robbie's a lot like his mother, but more reserved. Anyway, it broke my heart to see how being away from her son was tearing her up, so I started keeping in touch with her, sending her pictures and little keepsakes. We became quite good friends over the years. Once I even invited her to one of Robbie's Little League games. Peter was out of town. I introduced her to Robbie as an old friend."

"And Peter never knew," I asked.

"No," she replied, "but he does now. At that time, I was afraid he'd tell her to stay away. Men don't understand these things. Peter and I were never able to have our own children." She looked down at the half-eaten salad in front of her, her mouth turned down. "If it hadn't been for Sophie and what she did, her sacrifice, I would never have had a son."

I reached out and touched her hand. Her fingers slipped over mine and squeezed firmly. She looked up and our eyes met. I knew she was telling the truth. Her motives had been pure, a way of thanking Sophie for giving her a family. I found myself wishing that Marcia Olsen didn't live so far away.

"You might as well tell her the rest," Gram said in a hushed voice. She had slipped an arm around her daughter's shoulders to comfort her. My estimation of the older woman went up a few notches.

I looked at Marcia expectantly.

"Peter thought . . . by the way, he knows I'm here today. We discussed the whole matter and thought you should know the entire story. He said you're looking into the suicide. That you don't believe Sophie killed herself." She leaned toward me, her jaw set. "We don't believe it either."

Marcia dug into her purse and presented me with the baby shoes from the fancy box. They were still in the resealable bag. I took them and looked at her, thoroughly puzzled.

The waitress came and cleared our plates.

"There's something inside I think you should see," Marcia said after the waitress refilled our drinks and left.

I opened the plastic bag and removed a baby shoe. Looking inside, I found some paper and extracted it. It was an old, tightly folded clipping, actually two of them, from an Orange County newspaper. After carefully opening the yellowed paper, I scanned one article, not sure of what I was supposed to see. Then I read it again, slowly, carefully, and from the top. I did the same with the second article.

The first clipping was a story about a baby's death, dated seventeen years prior. The baby in question had been a boy with Down Syndrome. He was eleven months old when he was found dead in his crib. The live-in nanny, named Bonnie Sheffley, had been suspected of suffocating the child. All who knew the girl claimed it impossible, including the dead baby's parents, who stood emphatically by their trust in her.

There was a photo of Bonnie Sheffley above the piece. She was a comely girl, plump and rosy, with curly blond hair and an angelic smile. The article said she was just twenty years old.

The second article was a small follow-up piece to the first. It announced that the nanny had been cleared of all suspicion, with the final determination being that the baby had died from crib death.

The baby's name was Jonathan Hollowell, son of John and Clarice Hollowell of Newport Beach.

I leaned back in the booth, my eyes still focused on the newspaper held limply between my fingers.

"There's more," Marcia said. "In the other shoe."

The other shoe was still in the bag. I was almost afraid to lay a hand on it, scared of what might be lurking within the scuffed white leather. Yet I wanted to know. Like a kid told not to touch the stove, I had to reach out a hand to see for myself what hot meant.

Again, I fished out a newspaper article. This one was even older, dated twenty-two years ago. It was about an accident, a fatal hit and run. The victim had been a prominent Orange County businessman named Kenneth Woodall. Woodall had been struck and killed as he was getting into his car in front of a shop on the Pacific Coast Highway. The driver of the other car was never found, but witnesses claimed that the car had been swerving erratically just before it slammed into Woodall.

According to the short bio at the end of the piece, Kenneth Woodall owned a real estate development firm called Woodall Development Corp. He was survived by his wife and young daughter.

His wife's name was Clarice.

"Did you know about this before?"

"No," Marcia responded, her voice almost a whisper. "When Peter brought home the box you gave him, I went through it. I found those articles just as you did, inside the shoes."

Alarms were going off in my head, popping like kernels of corn in a hot, oily pan.

To an objective eye, the articles meant nothing, just tragedies occurring in the same family. But both had connections to Hollowell. Sophie had hidden them, kept them for years for a reason. Hollowell had asked if Sophie had left anything for him. Maybe he was talking about these. But he couldn't have been. Newspaper articles were public record. Anyone could look these up in the archives of the newspaper or a public library with excellent resources. Unless . . . unless Sophie had the means to bridge them into something incriminating, something more than what they appeared. I looked down at the aging paper and knew that I held in my damp hands a key to unlocking the truth about Sophie's supposed suicide. I just had to find the right door with the right lock.

"I don't know what these mean, Marcia. But I intend to find out."

"Odelia," Marcia said, looking me dead in the eye, "there's something else."

I braced myself, waiting for the next blow.

"We're afraid of John Hollowell, of what he might try."

"Ya," Gram interrupted, her voice filled with passion. "Let him try!"

"Mother, please!"

The old woman ignored her daughter's plea. Pointing a knobby index finger in my direction, her eyes burning coals behind old-fashioned glasses, she leaned forward.

"That man touch one hair on my Robert's head," Mrs. Pugh said in a low, harsh whisper, "or harm my daughter or Peter, I swear I kill him! I have shotgun. I know how to use it."

"Mother, stop it!"

So much for warm cookies and milk at grandma's house.

The old woman relaxed, leaning back in the booth. Her face was flushed and determined. Marcia looked drained, ready to sob.

What in the hell did Hollowell have to do with the Olsens?

Lunchtime is supposed to be a time of rest, a break in the activities of the day. I was exhausted from all this information and emotion, and thought about crawling under the table for a much-needed nap. Sleep seemed like the ideal escape hatch right now.

"Tell Odelia the rest," Gram urged, patting Marcia's shoulder gently.

Marcia looked at her mother, then at me, her face as pale as fresh milk. For the first time, I saw fear in her eyes—butt-naked fright. I snapped out of my fatigue and waited for what was coming, knowing it was important.

Marcia Olsen swallowed, then said, "You see, Robbie isn't Peter's. He's John Hollowell's son."

TWENTY

"I'M NOT ASKING YOUR permission, Steele, I'm telling you. Advising you. Informing you. Call it what you will."

My voice was even, my tone matter-of-fact as I stood in front of Mike Steele's modern chrome and black lacquered desk. The office was done in black, white, and silver, with a splash of primary color here and there. The whole room looked like it'd been lifted from some artsy-fartsy modern museum. Steele was sprawled lazily in his leather swivel chair, pivoting back and forth like an antsy kid waiting for recess. Every time his chair moved, it squeaked. His impudence annoyed the hell out of me, but I kept my face a blank.

"I'm taking a few days off next week, at least Monday and Tuesday," I informed him for the second time in less than two minutes. "And it's already been approved. I just wanted you to know."

"That's very inconsiderate of you, Odelia," he said in a voice dripping with reproach. "You know I need to get those qualification papers out to Hilldale. I promised them by next Friday."

He was always difficult when I wanted to take time off. It was one of the reasons I seldom did. Mike Steele and I had been working

189

together in an edgy relationship for nearly five years. During that time I had maxed out my vacation accrual because I was too intimidated and weary to fight for what was mine. And when I did, I always had Mr. Wallace there to grant me the time off in spite of Steele's objections. Soon, that buffer would be gone and I would be on my own with this jerk. I had better be ready for battle.

With ceremony, I dropped an unsealed Federal Express package on his desk. Inside were the documents he was talking about, prepared and ready for signature.

"They're going out tonight," I informed him. "Hilldale will have them Monday morning by ten thirty."

Steele stopped playing in his chair and sat up straight. He pulled the stack of documents halfway out of the envelope.

"Nice work," he said tightly, his jaw clenched.

Stuffing the papers back into the package, he shoved it across the desk in my direction. I'd taken the teeth out of his power play, a most grievous sin.

Gathering up the package of documents, I started to make my exit. With barely a glance in his direction, I said in a very professional manner, "Everything else due early next week is also completed. The other matters can wait until I return."

After sealing the overnight package and dropping it off for the five thirty pickup, I went back to my desk. I continued working, getting things organized so I wouldn't come back to a mess on Wednesday. Or maybe Thursday. I had asked Mr. Wallace for two days off, with a footnote that I might need one more. He hadn't minded. Steele was the control freak. But Steele wasn't stupid when it came to office politics. He knew better than to try to overturn an approval of vacation time given by Mr. Wallace, especially for no good reason other than spite.

After my lunch with Marcia Olsen and Granny-Get-Your-Gun, I decided to sink my teeth into Sophie's murder in a big way. I now called it murder with absolutely no looking back. There were too many arrows pointing in that direction to ignore. Still nothing concrete in the evidence department, but after seeing those photographs and reading the articles Marcia gave me, I didn't have a dog hair's doubt. Neither did I doubt that Hollowell was buried up to his neck in dung. I just couldn't prove it . . . yet.

I checked the time—5:10. In about three hours I would be sitting across from Hollowell, trying to make nice-nice while rooting around for information that could nail him or his accomplice.

I felt exhaustion wash over me once more. It had come and gone in waves all afternoon. Since lunch I had been working feverishly, getting projects for next week done and out the door in record time. Thankfully, I ran an organized desk and was able to prioritize and complete assignments easier than most. I planned on working another hour and a half, giving myself just enough time to get home, shower, and dress for dinner.

After stretching out my kinks, I filled my mug with the dregs of the day's coffee and prayed I didn't drop face-first into my entrée tonight. Here and there during the afternoon I had done some on-line research on Hollowell. Not as much as I would have liked, but time had been tight. I believe in the saying that knowledge is power, and I wanted to be as fully armed as possible before I met him again.

A few days ago, before meeting him for the first time, I ran Hollowell's name through a California public records check. I found the purchase of his home and other real estate dealings, but not much else. That was when I first learned that his wife's name was Clarice. I also did a check on his company, Hollowell-Johnson Investment

Company, under the California Secretary of State website. The corporation had been listed, along with its registered agent. It had been in existence about twenty-five years. Printing the information, I had filed it away for a rainy day. Now, with a lull in the day's activities, I pulled it out, reading it for possible clues. The Secretary of State's website listed only limited information. My experienced eyes scanned each morsel of data, looking more for what wasn't reported, than for what was.

Hmmm. What have we here? I did some quick calculations.

Sophie was forty-seven when she died. Peter Olsen had said that both he and Hollowell were just one year older. That meant that Hollowell was about twenty-three when this company was incorporated. That seemed mighty young to begin a new and thriving corporation, but it could be done.

Still, it could be a toehold.

I plugged in the web address for the research site used by most lawyers and law firms. After providing my password, I did a search under California Business and Corporation Information. Several hits popped up. I focused on the first one, only to find the same information I had discovered on the Secretary of State's site, except that this also listed John Hollowell as the president and chairman of the corporation. Not surprising, he was the big cheese of the whole shebang.

Scrolling down, I clicked another possibility, but it was just a fictitious name filing. Hollowell-Johnson Investment Company had filed the appropriate forms in Orange County to do business under HJ Financing. That had been about nine years ago. The next search result was similar, only this time the filing had been in Los Angeles County. The information for both was straightforward and unremarkable. It was the description of the next search item, the fourth finding, that caught my eye.

In the State of California, if a corporation wishes to change its name, it must file a Certificate of Amendment with the Secretary of State. According to the records I found online, Hollowell-Johnson Investment Company had once been called Woodall Development Corporation. The change had been made eighteen years ago.

Yanking my tote bag from my side desk drawer, I rummaged through it, locating the old newspaper clippings. I scanned the dates quickly.

Woodall died twenty-two years ago. Baby Hollowell died seventeen years ago. Somewhere in between, John Hollowell had married Woodall's widow, sired a son by her, and changed the name of her dead husband's company to his own name.

Nice work if you can get it.

Quickly, I input a new search command—this time for Woodall Development Corporation.

Scanning the list of short descriptions for each search result, I settled on one promising hit. It was the corporate information for Woodall Development Corporation at the time of its incorporation. I read the computer screen, then compared it with the printed page of information for Hollowell-Johnson Investment Company.

The registered agent for both Hollowell-Johnson and Woodall Development had been someone named Glenn Thomas, not unusual since it had been a simple name change. The address for service on the registered agent was an address in Santa Ana. Thomas was probably an attorney or officer of the corporation. Too bad the entire slate of officers wasn't listed on either website I was using; it would have been helpful. California requires that each corporation file a Statement of Officers with the Secretary of State's office, but a copy could take three to seven working days to obtain.

Glenn Thomas. Glenn Thomas. I'd heard that name before. But where? My memory was working hard to jog a pebble loose, but to no avail.

Checking my watch again, I noted that it was almost six. I still had some things to get done before I left for my working vacation. Reluctantly, I closed down the site, but not before printing the new information out.

Glenn Thomas. The name lingered on my tongue along with the bitter, cold coffee I was drinking. I knew it would come to me. These things always nagged me until I remembered them, usually in the shower or in the middle of the night.

"You come to the restaurant, Greg Stevens, and I will personally steal the wheels off your chair and leave you up on concrete blocks!"

Cradling the cordless phone between my left ear and my shoulder, I continued getting dressed for my dinner date with Hollowell.

"It's not safe, Odelia," Greg replied. His voice was strong and insistent. "You shouldn't go alone."

I was wearing my relationship undies—black silk bra and matching hi-cut panties—not a hole or loose elastic in sight. Looking in the full-length mirror, I suddenly wondered why. This wasn't a real date. And I certainly didn't intend for Hollowell to get this close to skin. But it felt good, and lately I hadn't had much chance to dress up. I had even shaved my legs.

I sat on the edge of the bed, phone in one hand, sheer black pantyhose in the other.

"It's a public place. What's he going to do, whack me in front of God and everyone?"

More than once during this conversation, I wished I hadn't told Greg about the two newspaper articles or the corporate stuff. Maybe it was naive on my part, but I didn't expect him to react quite so strongly.

Fortunately, I hadn't told Zee yet about the new developments. She wasn't home when I called after work, so I just left a message that I was going out to dinner. I knew she'd be as agitated as Greg if she knew about Hollowell's past.

It was a ritual, a safety device Zee and I had set up a long time ago. No matter where I went, if I was on a date with someone new, I would call and leave the information with Zee and Seth, or at least on their answering machine. If I ever ended up a missing person, it would give them some clue where to start looking. I'd done the same when I met Greg for breakfast.

I stopped dressing and tried to reason once more with Greg.

"Besides, look at Hollowell's track record. If the articles do link him to those deaths, it certainly doesn't look like he gets his own hands dirty. Seems to me he's more of a remote-control kind of killer, not a hands-on killer." There was a pause. "And he'll never loosen up with you there, admit it."

"I could just be there," he insisted, "in the background. You know, blend in."

"No."

I tried shouldering the phone while I struggled into my hose. It wasn't working.

"Greg, hang on a minute."

I put the phone down. First, I slipped one foot into the silky fabric, then the other, working the nylon up my legs, a little at a time, one side at a time. Standing, I finished pulling the tight weave up and over my generous behind, grunting along the way. God, I hate control-top pantyhose. Every time I wore them, I waited for the elastic fibers to give, exploding like thousands of wild, broken springs capable of putting an eye out.

Satisfied finally with the fit, I picked up the phone again. "Sorry, just had to pull on my hose."

"Too bad you don't have a webcam," Greg said with a wicked laugh. "I would love to see that."

"You wish, mister."

We laughed together, easing the tension.

"Seriously, Odelia, please be careful. You'll have your cell phone with you, won't you?"

"Won't fit in my evening bag." It was true. My favorite evening bag was a satin envelope not much bigger than a thank-you note. It barely held essentials such as keys, driver's license, money, linen hankie, and lipstick.

"Damn it, woman! Take a bigger bag! Better yet, call me just before you see him and leave the phone on so I can hear everything."

"Greg," I said with a sigh, "I'll be fine. I promise you I'll call as soon as I get home."

"Promise?"

"Cross my heart, bra and everything."

"One more promise, Odelia?"

"You're using up precious promises, Greg. You might want to bank a few for later."

He chuckled, then said in a serious tone, "Promise me you'll use valet parking."

"Valet parking?"

"Yes, valet parking. Promise me you won't park in some lot where he can walk you alone to your car. I need to know that you'll be standing in front of a well-lit building with other people when he says goodbye to you."

I hesitated, thinking about his request.

"Damn it!" he said, almost shouting. "I'll even pay for it."

Now I felt bad. He was genuinely concerned about me and I was yanking his chain.

"Greg," I said softly and seriously, "I promise to use valet parking. And I promise I'll call tonight. And thank you for being so sweet and caring. It's much appreciated. Really. Now I have to finish dressing. Talk to you later." I hesitated. "I *promise.*"

I hung up and slipped on my dress, thinking about Greg and wishing I was dressing to go out with him instead of Hollowell. I was wearing my favorite outfit, a black lace sleeveless sheath with a low-cut neckline. The hemline ended a couple of inches above my chubby knees. Sticking my feet into low spiked heels, I looked into the mirror, taking stock of the goods.

Reaching down the front of my dress and into one cup of my black silk bra, I hoisted a saggy breast, rearranging it so that the nipple looked upward under the smooth fabric. I did the same with the other side, then checked to see if they were even. My cleavage was definitely saying hello.

If Hollowell was into full figures, then he was into boobs, and that was one talent I had by the handful. There were questions to be planted and answers to harvest, and I wasn't coming home without some satisfaction. If I had to seduce the truth out of him, so be it. One BBW Mata Hari coming up!

Grabbing a lace shawl that matched the dress, I took one last look in the mirror. My palms were sweaty, my knees knocked.

I looked like a pot roast in mourning.

TWENTY-ONE

THE PARKING GARAGE LOOKED tempting . . . and free. It was after normal business hours so the ticket gate was up. I slowed just before making the turn into the concrete and steel structure. Straight ahead was the driveway for the restaurant's valet parking.

Contemplating, I pulled over to the curb. I hated valet parking, especially in Newport Beach. My car was a fifteen-year-old silver Toyota Camry. It was in excellent condition, but in car years, more than ready for Medicare. I had bought it new and saw no good reason to give it up now.

Valet attendants usually sniffed at me when I pulled up behind Beemers and Benzes. A forty-something fat woman driving an old four-door family sedan did not make their night. Let's face it, this city didn't earn the nickname *New Porsche Beach* because of its tolerance of frugality.

But I had promised Greg.

And he was right. I shouldn't put myself in any more potential danger than I had already. Moving ahead, I pulled into the valet area directly behind a brand-spanking-new Lexus. While I waited my turn, I stored my cell phone in my glove compartment after making sure the lock was activated. Yes, I had brought it. It still didn't fit into my black satin evening bag, but I figured I could call Greg as soon as I left for home.

After giving my keys to a young surfer dude wearing a valet's jacket, I entered the restaurant. I saw Hollowell immediately. Sitting at a table on the edge of the dining area, he looked confident, in control, and deadly. He was dressed fashionably in a dark silk suit and white shirt with a banded collar. I bet he and Mike Steele shopped some of the same places. He smiled slow and easy at me and stood up. Giving him my best coat hanger-induced smile, I headed his way, threading carefully through occupied tables. My walk was tenuous, my stomach knotted.

Silently I gave myself a quick pep talk. I sure didn't want Hollowell thinking I was the type to mumble to myself like a relative locked in an attic. Though I am. Something told me he wouldn't find it endearing, but instead a fault to be used against me as a weapon. He seemed the type.

"Well, hello, Odelia," he said, leaning forward to give me a quick peck on the cheek. I stiffened slightly at his nearness. "Don't you look scrumptious," he added, staring openly at my bulging boobies.

Scrumptious? Like a pastry waiting to be devoured? I murmured a thank you, sitting down in the chair he pulled out for me.

The dark elegance of his suit and the whiteness of his hip shirt set off his coloring splendidly, especially his thick salt and peppered hair. Looking around quickly, I took stock of the other patrons. Hollowell was easily the most handsome and successful-looking man in the room.

"Would you like a cocktail?" he asked, his fingers resting lightly on my hand. In front of him was a glass that looked barely touched. I guessed it to be Chivas, as before.

"Yes," I replied with a saccharin smile. "A champagne cocktail would be nice. Thank you."

He waved a waiter over and placed my order. It appeared at the table almost instantly. He held up his glass in a toast. In turn, I held up my flute.

"To new friends and possibilities," he said, clinking his glass against mine.

Having no intention of being his friend, I didn't second the toast, but kept smiling and sipped my drink. As for future possibilities, I only wanted to toast the possibility of finding enough information to link Hollowell to Sophie's murder. But I was at a loss for a tactful opening. It wasn't like I could just open my mouth and ask why he did it, or how. Tell me, John, just how many deaths *are* you responsible for?

Fortunately, he picked up the lag in the conversation.

"I'm afraid we can't be out too late tonight. Hope you don't mind."

Without thinking, I shot a barb his way, right off the top of my head. "What's the matter, wife have you on a curfew?" Crap! I wanted to entice him into loose conversation, not cop an attitude and give away my true feelings about his creepiness.

He laughed. "That's what I like about you, Odelia, you've got moxie. A beautiful woman high in spirit, with a sharp and intelligent tongue—can't beat 'em."

"Who, me? And here I always thought I was just a bitch."

He laughed deeply, took a gulp from his glass, and continued. "No, my wife doesn't have me on a curfew. Clarice and I have an understanding."

"An understanding," I repeated. "Usually that means the man wanders while the little woman keeps her mouth shut and spends his money like a drunken sailor on leave."

If he liked moxie, I'd give him moxie by the mouthful. He obviously liked his word duels scrappy. It made me wonder about his sexual preferences.

He gave me his signature chuckle. "Sounds like you've been married."

"Nope," I said, shaking my head. "Never. But I've been hit on by many a married man with an understanding wife."

He grinned and looked at me. This time his eyes appraised me thoughtfully, completely. I could feel him weighing my worth. I took another drink. My nerves were settling, my purpose for this charade rising to the top.

"So," I said, continuing, "why can't we be out late if it has nothing to do with Mrs. Hollowell?" Inside I was relieved. I had wondered how I was going to extricate myself from his company later in the evening.

"Because," he said, leaning in, stroking the inside of my right arm with a feathery touch, "I need to get up early and drive to San Diego in the morning. There's a golf tournament. Care to come along?"

"You mean you're going alone?"

"No, not alone. With a friend. But I can take her another time."

"A friend? I'm flattered. You'd break the heart of your mistress for little ol' me?" I took another drink and gazed at him over the top of my glass. It was behavior right out of a sleazy soap opera and I knew I would rot in hell for this absurdity alone.

"Say the word, Odelia. A suite at the best hotel, a shopping spree."

I hesitated, pretending to give it thought. "The word, John, is no. Sorry."

"I'll just have to ask better next time." He smiled. "You ready to order?" he asked me.

We made our selections and Hollowell ordered a bottle of wine to go with dinner. He would have been the perfect date if not for one teeny reason. Well, okay, many *not* so teeny reasons, beginning with the debris of suspicious deaths in his life, including his own son's.

"So, tell me," I began, getting down to business, "you and Clarice have any children?"

"Aw, now why would you want to spoil a perfectly good evening talking about my family?" He covered my hand with one of his and squeezed gently, leaving it there. To the casual observer, I'm sure we looked like a comfy couple in the glow of early courtship.

"Because I want to get to know you, John," I said with a slight purr. Yep, Odelia, you are definitely going to hell.

The waiter came over with the wine just as Hollowell was about to say something. He went through the ritual of swirling a sample in his glass, sniffing it, and giving it a taste. It was a merlot, dark as black raspberries. Satisfied, he nodded to the waiter, who then served me first.

Next came our salads. Finally, we were alone again.

"You were about to tell me something," I prodded.

"Yes, seeing that you're interested," he looked at me with slightly narrowed eyes, took a bite of salad, and chewed thoughtfully. "There's a daughter by my wife's first marriage. She's in her mid-twenties, married, and lives outside Chicago. We hardly see her anymore. Also, we had a son many years ago. He died suddenly when he was an infant—a case of crib death."

I studied his face. It told me nothing, a blank. He seemed neither sad nor lost in memory. His words were even and noncommittal, like he was simply giving directions.

"I'm very sorry, John."

"Long time ago," he said, giving me a slow grin.

I plowed on, trying more of a direct approach. "Did you always know that Sophie had a son?"

He looked at me strangely, his eyes narrowing again, and said, "Of course, didn't you?"

"No," I admitted, wide-eyed and innocent. "She kept real quiet about it. In fact, she hardly spoke about you. Why do you think she didn't talk to me, or any of our other mutual friends, about her son? I find it very disconcerting."

Hollowell ate on. In a few more bites he was done with his salad. The waiter came over and cleared his plate away.

"I'm finished, also," I said to our waiter.

The waiter was a swarthy man with gaunt cheeks, a thin black mustache, and eyes of India ink. He nodded silently and whisked my half-eaten salad away along with Hollowell's empty plate.

Hollowell took my hand again. "Honestly, Odelia, I don't know why she didn't talk about him. I didn't think it was a secret, though she never saw the boy. I can guess why she didn't tell you about me—jealousy. She was very insecure about me and other women. You do know that we'd been lovers for years?"

I nodded.

"She probably thought you'd woo me away from her." He reached up a hand and stroked my cheek softly. My first instinct was to back my face away from his touch, but I held firm. "She was probably right."

I thought about that. The Sophie I knew didn't have a jealous bone in her body. During our friendship, I'd met several of her male friends. She didn't seem insecure about that at all.

To protect them.

"I take it your relationship wasn't exclusive. In fact, I know that Sophie dated other men."

"True. In the last few years, I encouraged her to see others. I had been trying to break it off with her, but she wasn't happy about it. The relationship had run its course, but she kept calling me, inviting me over. Very sad."

. . . he sort of popped in.

Caught Sophie by surprise . . .

Made her mad . . .

He was lying. Looking me straight in the eye, holding my hand, he lied to me. And he was good at it. As smooth and as cold as vanilla ice cream, the expensive stuff. He surrendered no hint of conscience or hesitation. He could have been telling the truth. There were a lot of things about Sophie I was obviously in the dark about. But Greg had known the same Sophie I did. So had Marcia and Peter Olsen. Only Hollowell's story wasn't fitting.

Fortunately, the entrées arrived just as I was about to say too much. I concentrated on my grilled salmon and steamed asparagus, using the time to plot a new course. I decided to dig in a different direction.

"You said last time that you suggested the website to Sophie. May I ask why?"

"Money, mostly." He hesitated. "You do know that she worked for me for a long time?"

"Yes," I answered, "but I only learned that recently."

"A few years ago, we started going our separate ways, doing less business together. But after years in one company, she didn't want to start over at another. Besides, she liked it—the website. And was good at it. Have you seen the site?"

"Yes, I have." I thought about the photos posted in the Members Only section. "John, are you the man in the photos on the site? The one having sex with Sophie?"

He stopped eating and leaned back in his chair. He looked at me in silence for a bit, only opening and closing his eyelids every once in a while. The action reminded me of a lizard sitting on a rock, it having been easy to make the leap to the reptile family.

Finally, he said, "Why are you so curious about me and Sophie, Odelia?"

I shrugged. "Just nosy, I guess. I feel, now that she's gone, that I really didn't know her very well. It's hard for me to understand what drove her to suicide."

He looked at me again in silence, his face still a blank page, except for his eyes, which were busy evaluating.

"Do you have any idea what Sophie did for my company?"

"She was a computer consultant."

"Yes, initially she was a computer consultant." He gave me his sly grin. "Later, she was a consultant who used her computer."

He paused, moving closer to me before speaking.

"Her title was Acquisitions Consultant," he told me in a low voice. "But in truth she was the company whore."

. . . *Hollowell's private whore.*

I shifted uncomfortably in my chair and put down my fork. My appetite hadn't been good all evening. Now it was totally gone.

"I don't understand," I said. "You and she were together, weren't you?"

"Yes, we were. But she also worked for me." He took a bite of his salmon and chewed slowly, thoughtfully, before continuing.

"After she came down here from Santa Paula, I spruced her up, bought her clothes, and had her learn about the finer things. She was so incredibly sexy." He paused and smiled, more to himself than to me. "I'd take her to business meetings and show her off. Now don't get me wrong, she was extremely bright. She'd listen and understand everything discussed. But her real job was to close the deal."

He finished his meal and pushed his plate aside. The waiter materialized to take the plates away and to pour us some more wine. I took a big gulp.

"You know as well as I do, Odelia, that many men love the bigger beauties like Sophie and yourself." He said it with a half-grin, half-leer, his eyes grazing my chest. "So did many of my business associates, especially the foreign ones. They just adored Sophie, her looks, her brains. They lusted after her in a big way. It was her job to make sure that they had no doubts about doing business with my company. Sometimes she did the convincing during pillow talk."

"You pimped her?" I asked, trying to keep disgust out of my voice. Anger was rising inside me along with stomach acid.

He chuckled. "Not really. It was her choice. If she didn't like a man, she wouldn't sleep with him, of course. But she would still attempt to flirt and woo him into signing the deal. I paid her a monthly retainer, a handsome amount. She also got bonuses after the deals closed.

"A few of these men saw her regularly afterward. They gave her expensive gifts, jewelry, trips. They'd fly in from Brussels, London, even from the Middle East; do business with me, monkey business with her. It wasn't like she was turning tricks on a seedy sidewalk.

She kept them happy, which made me happy. Most were married, of course."

"Of course," I echoed. "And no doubt to skinny women who looked good in society photographs."

Hollowell put his hands up, palms outward. "Hey, I don't make the rules. I only play by them."

I wanted to slug his lights out and was astonished by my self-control.

According to both Peter Olsen and Greg, Sophie was so in love with Hollowell that she was addicted to him. If she could give up her son for the scumbag, she'd do just about anything to keep him.

But one big piece wasn't fitting. She had Hollowell's son. Why didn't she use him for leverage?

"Sophie was in love with you," I said, looking at him squarely. "She probably would have done anything to please you. And you took advantage of that."

He grinned and leaned back again in his chair. "Maybe at first I did, but you can't tell me that later on she didn't enjoy it."

He was obviously trying to shift the initial responsibility away from himself. It was okay to use and manipulate someone as long as they eventually got used to it and maybe even accepted it. My jaw ached from clenching my teeth to produce a fake and faint smile.

"So once she stopped working for you, she started the website?"

He smiled again, but this time is was a slick, oily smile. "More like she fell into it. You see, some of these guys enjoyed being filmed with Sophie and she accommodated them, for a price. That was her own business. Later, when computer cameras became so hot, she'd put the photos on disk. When these adult sites began getting big, I suggested that she try it." He took a long drink of wine, almost draining his glass.

"Let's face it, she wasn't getting any younger. And even though Sophie was still very beautiful, these wealthy and powerful men wanted younger women. Middle-aged they could get at home. The jump to an adult website was a natural; a new twist on an old favorite, so to speak. Many of these guys paid handsomely to be seen live on the Internet screwing her brains out. They'd pick a time, tell their friends, then broadcast the sex. From what I saw of those sessions, identities were well concealed."

I took my own big gulp of wine. "Was Sophie still on retainer to your company when she died?" I asked after I swallowed.

"No, I haven't paid her anything in over a year, maybe more." He gave his annoying chuckle. "Those photos you saw weren't me, they were of her special friends. Her paying customers." He waived the waiter over.

"Odelia, you look like you need a good, strong cup of coffee."

I nodded numbly. Hollowell told the waiter to bring two coffees and the dessert menu.

"Will you excuse me, Odelia?" he said, pushing his chair back. He left the table and headed in the direction of the men's room.

Elbows on the table, I lowered my head, resting my cheeks in the V of my open palms.

Sophie a high-priced corporate call girl. It seemed unbelievable and utterly fantastic. She was bright. She was educated. She could have gone anywhere, been anything. Why this? Was it just the money? Or was she that in love with this cold-hearted bastard?

The more my overloaded brain rummaged through what Hollowell just told me, the more I wondered what other kind of hold he could have had over Sophie. But from the newspaper articles recovered from the baby shoes, it seemed more likely that Sophie might have had something on him.

And what about Robbie? Hollowell didn't give the slightest indication that he knew that Robbie Olsen was his son. He just grazed over any mention of him. Was it possible that Sophie successfully hid Robbie's parentage from his own father?

"Talk to me, Sophie," I muttered into the air.

"You feeling okay, ma'am?" It was our waiter, hovering by my elbow.

"Yes, I am. Thank you."

I straightened up as he placed two cups on the table and poured fresh coffee into them from a silver pot. He left behind cream and sugar, also in silver containers, and two dessert menus.

I wanted to leave. It was just nine thirty, but I didn't know how much more I could stand hearing. Music drifted in from the bar area. It was a pleasant tune, a popular ballad. I could hear someone singing, telling me it was a live band. The melodious voice ran over me like warm milk. I gave into it, letting my brain relax for the moment. This detective stuff was hard work.

Hollowell returned to our table, settling himself in his chair as if nothing unusual had been said. He seemed smug. His physical beauty existed no more in my eyes. Replacing it was an ugliness no plastic surgery could cure.

When the song was over, I felt revived and recharged. I called upon my so-called moxie to keep going. Hollowell could be lying, covering for his own despicable deeds. And even if he wasn't, it didn't take away the fact that Sophie was a good-hearted woman who loved people and helped many, including yours truly. She was still my friend and she needed me.

I wasn't through with Mr. John Hollowell just yet.

"Tell me something, John," I said, leaning forward on my elbows, my hands clasped in front of me. "Why didn't you ever marry Sophie?"

For the first time, I saw Hollowell falter and thought I saw fleeting and genuine pain cross his face. Just as quickly, he collected himself.

"Like I said, Odelia, I don't make the rules, I just live by them. It's no secret that fat girls from poor country families are not exactly executive wife material."

TWENTY-TWO

BRINGING THE CELL PHONE proved to be a good decision. So was parking with the valet. I silently gave thanks for Greg's good sense.

After coffee and dessert, Hollowell and I adjourned to the bar, where we danced and sipped brandy. Well, he sipped brandy while I had a ginger ale. I wasn't used to this much drinking in one night; a before-dinner cocktail and wine during dinner had been my limit. It was also best to keep my head clear in his presence.

We danced and chatted superficially until eleven, when he said he had to head home to get ready for his trip to San Diego in the morning. He invited me to go once again, and once again I declined coyly.

Between dinner and saying goodnight, I tried my best to loosen more information from him. It was the only reason I tolerated his presence. But he had given up all he was going to for the night, and deflected my subtle and not-so-subtle queries deftly. Even letting his hands wander around my hips and butt during slow dances didn't let down his guard.

In front of the valet, I had allowed him to give me a chaste kiss. Without witnesses, I'm sure I would have been prying his mouth and hands off of me like leeches. He chuckled yet again as I climbed into my car, saying that he hoped I'd be friendlier the next time we met. It made me wonder if he was looking for another Acquisitions Consultant.

Driving away from the restaurant, I dialed Greg on my cellular. Might as well get it over with and give him some relief. I was glad I had the phone. Talking to someone I liked and cared about would cleanse me, and I needed that right now. He picked it up on the first ring. His voice was alert, sounding like he'd been sitting by the phone waiting since our last conversation.

"Hi," I said cheerfully. "Just checking in, safe and sound."

"You're not home?" he asked.

"No, and not going there. I'm heading for Sophie's. I learned a few things from Hollowell that I want to check out on her computer. Give me your password so I can access the website."

"You can do that from your own place," he said. I detected frustration in his voice.

"The site, yes, but not the hard drive," I explained. "I need to check out both."

What I planned to do was closely inspect the pictures posted in the members area again, the ones with the man or men. Then I intended to search the hard drive files for stored, captured photos of these sessions, hoping somehow to discover clues to identities.

Greg sighed. I could picture him shaking his head.

"It's late, Odelia. Why don't you wait until tomorrow. I'll meet you there and help you."

"Because I'm wide awake and curious now."

I turned the car onto the Pacific Coast Highway and headed toward Sophie's. The drive was only ten to fifteen minutes.

"Greg, did you know that Sophie was a paid escort for Hollowell's company?"

The silence on the other end of the phone wasn't lost on me.

"Greg?"

"Yes," he said in a small voice. "I knew."

I couldn't believe my ears. My question had been meant to shock him with some new and startling information. I didn't expect to be answered in the affirmative.

"You knew? Why didn't you tell me?" If we had been having this conversation in person, I would have been tempted to throw something at him.

"Because it was behind her," he said, "part of her past. She got out of it about the time she started Reality Check." He paused. "And because I didn't want your image of her tarnished any more than it already has been with the website."

I took a deep breath, then said in a very tight voice, "How dare you decide what I can and cannot handle, what I judge and not judge. I'm not a child, Greg Stevens. I don't need you to protect me from bogeymen."

Silence, then another sigh.

"I'm sorry, Odelia. You're right, you're not a child."

"And did it ever occur to you that maybe one of these men might have had something to do with her death?"

"Yes, that did occur to me, Odelia, but after thinking it over, I decided it was unlikely."

"*You* decided it was unlikely. I thought we were in this together. When do I get to mull things over and make such decisions? After all, it was my ass Hollowell was groping tonight, not yours."

"Again, you're right and I'm sorry. I truly am, Odelia."

His apology, no matter how genuine, irritated me. Wasn't it just like a man to say *I'm sorry* and think it would all magically be healed, like kissing a booboo. *Sheesh.*

Grumbling unintelligible words into the phone, I turned onto Sophie's street. Parked in front of her house was a truck with the security company's name on the side. I pulled into the driveway. There must have been a false alarm or malfunction for them to be out here at this time of night.

"Greg," I said into the phone. "A truck's parked in front of Sophie's. It's from the security company."

"That's odd. You think Iris Somers called them?"

"Don't know. There aren't any lights on in the house and everything appears quiet."

"Odelia, this doesn't feel right."

"Protecting me again, Greg?"

Quietly I got out of my car, cell phone still in my hand, and looked up and down the street. All was still. Except for a few lit windows, the houses seemed tucked in for the night.

"Everything seems normal," I whispered into the cell phone, holding it close to my mouth. "Maybe someone in this neighborhood works for the security company and brought the truck home."

I started up the walk to the front door, then heard a noise. It seemed to be coming from the side of the house, between Sophie's and the home belonging to Iris Somers. I stood still and listened, hoping it was a cat or some other small animal.

"I just heard something," I whispered again into the phone. "Hang on."

"Odelia," I heard Greg say, "please go home. I'm sorry if this sounds overprotective, but something's wrong, I can feel it."

"Shhh," I said.

I listened again and once more heard the sound. This time it sounded like a moan, a human moan. Cautiously, I walked to that side of the house, feeling my thin, spiky heels sink into the grass with each step.

The space between the two houses was narrow, only allowing for a small strip of grass. A low white fence ran down the middle, separating the properties. The hair on my arms stood like a forest as I stepped warily away from the glow of the street lights. I heard the sound again. It seemed close, maybe only a few feet away, yet I saw nothing.

I took another step and felt something under my foot. There was a soft crunch as my weight pressed down on it. Looking down, I saw something shiny. As bits and pieces of light caught the item, it shimmered. I bent down and picked it up. It was a clump of foil, more like a hat covered in crinkled aluminum.

I heard the soft moan again and moved toward it quickly. After a few steps in the near darkness, I almost tripped on a small, crumpled figure lying on Sophie's side of the fence, next to the house.

"Iris?" I asked quietly, falling to my knees next to the inert form.

The figure moaned.

I leaned closer, almost nose to nose, and saw that it was indeed Iris Somers. Her eyes were shut. I stroked her head, the gesture evoking another, deeper moan. When I withdrew my hand it was wet and sticky.

"AHHH!" I sucked in my breath along with the muted scream. The phone dropped to the ground.

Fear coursed through me, coldly flowing through my veins like an icy stream, numbing me limb by limb.

Out of the darkness, without making a sound, came a shadowy form. It hovered over me. I threw up my hands to protect myself and half-covered Iris with my body.

Something struck my head, the blow causing me to fall forward on top of Iris. Pain seared my brain, bringing tears to my eyes. Somewhere in the background, I thought I heard running, followed by the sound of an engine. I lifted up my heavy head but saw nothing. It was too late.

Moans, not much more than whimpers now, continued to come from the body under mine.

Other sounds, faint and static, were coming from somewhere else. It broke the iciness engulfing and immobilizing me. The phone—it was on the ground near me. In the darkness, I could see the digital display with its glowing, yellow-green light. I groped around in its general direction until I succeeded in picking it up.

"Odelia. Odelia, answer me!" I heard Greg yelling on the other end.

"Help," I said in a small voice, then collapsed, unable to speak further.

Time passed in waves of undulating pain. I never lost consciousness, but seemed paralyzed from the neck up. Greg's voice was no longer coming from the phone grasped in my hand. I willed myself to move, giving my body orders one muscle at a time until I managed to at least get to my knees.

Damn, my head hurt! It felt on fire on the left backside. I reached up a leaden arm and felt the aching spot. *Ouch!* But it didn't feel wet, the skin not seeming to be broken. I felt a little woozy and saw a few stars, but not a galaxy.

I turned my attention to Iris. She was still and the moans had stopped. My heart rat-a-tat-tatted like a machine gun as I placed my fingertips on her neck just behind her jaw. Never having checked a body for life before, I hoped I was doing it right. I picked up nothing, but kept softly probing the area while I used my other hand to dial for help.

Finally! There it was, a very faint, weak pulse.

"Hang in there, Iris. Help's coming."

Sirens splintered the peacefulness of the neighborhood just as I punched the phone buttons for 911.

"Thank you, dear God, thank you," I whispered into the darkness. "Come on, Iris, just a few minutes more."

I stood up and tried to make my way to the front, to flag down the authorities. It was the police, two cruisers' worth. Greg must've called them. My head felt like a granite monument.

Leaning against the side of the house, I waved to them as they pulled up to the front curb in a bouquet of flashing lights.

The security truck was gone.

The ice pack the paramedics gave me made my head hurt in a different way. The deep, tooth-cracking ache was still there, but the cold was numbing the surface pain. They told me I was lucky. Seems the blow glanced off my thick skull instead of making powerful and deadly contact. There didn't seem to be any concussion, but they advised me to go to the hospital just to be safe, especially if I experienced any nausea or dizziness.

Iris Somers wasn't so lucky. She was taken to the hospital in a coma. I was told that she had received several deep blows to the head with a heavy object.

Greg arrived about twenty or thirty minutes after the police. As soon as he saw me, he gathered me into his arms. I clung back. Now he was next to me, an arm around my shoulders, talking with

217

Detective Frye, telling him everything. Wainwright was asleep next to Greg's wheelchair, oblivious to the police milling about. I had already told my story to the police and then repeated it for Frye.

The big detective turned his attention back to me. "Tell me again, Odelia, what you saw after you found Iris."

Just as I was about to answer him, I remembered something—not something about the evening, just something out of place.

"Weren't you supposed to be on vacation or something?" I asked him.

Frye looked at me oddly, then answered. "I took some personal time, if that's what you mean."

I nodded my head slowly, very slowly. "Yes, Greg and I tried to reach you, to tell you about the photos. Why are you here if you're supposed to be off?"

Frye was sitting on a chair directly in front of me. He looked at Greg, his face volunteering no expression. Then he leaned forward, taking my free hand gently in his big paws.

"My wife is ill. She's in the hospital," he answered patiently. "My daughter is with her now." He looked again at Greg, this time communicating something just between them, maybe concern, then he focused back on me. "Take your time, Odelia. Think about what you saw after you found Iris. I want you to tell it to me again."

"I'm sorry," I told him, squinting past the throbbing in my head, "about your wife, I mean. Sorry you had to come out here tonight."

He thanked me politely, then gently urged me back on track.

I continued. "I didn't see anything, just a form. A man in black maybe."

"Think hard. Did you see his face? His shoes? What type of pants he wore?"

I dug deep into my aching head, looking for a hidden piece of memory untouched by the assailant's blow.

"His face was black," I finally said. "Not his skin, but his whole face."

"Like he was wearing something, a mask maybe? Or makeup?"

"Yes, maybe a ski mask or dark stocking, but it was totally covered. I couldn't tell any features. But I only got a slight glimpse before he hit me."

"Great, Odelia, you're doing fine."

Frye patted my hand and released it, then said, "So far, the only thing we know is missing is the computer. The monitor, printer, everything else seems untouched, just the hard drive's gone. Also, it looks like some storage disks might have been taken. Whoever did this came only for one thing and knew how to get in and out. We haven't found any fingerprints or other evidence yet. Guy knew about the security system, too. He cut out a section of the sliding glass door in the back, never touching the sensors. He also seemed to know where the motion detectors were positioned. He'd been in this house before, I guarantee it. You were very lucky, Odelia."

That word kept cropping up. I didn't feel lucky at the moment. But I knew that I could have easily been bludgeoned into a coma like Iris. I moved the ice pack over a bit to avoid freezer burn to my scalp.

"What about the security truck?" I asked.

"It was stolen, probably just before the job. The company didn't even know it was missing until we called them. The truck and its usual driver checked back into the yard around eight tonight."

An officer came into the room and leaned his head down close to Frye's. He said something, whispering the words into his ear. The two carried on a short conversation in hushed tones, then Frye looked back at me.

"The truck was just found abandoned near Crystal Cove."

"Greg," Frye said, turning to him, "you say the photos you copied from Ms. London's hard drive are at your office?"

Greg nodded. "Yes, I burned a CD and locked it in my safe, along with enlarged prints of the ones we felt were important."

"And no one knows these copies exist?"

"Only Odelia and I. Oh, and Boomer, my assistant. He's the one who actually did the enlargements."

Frye thought a moment. "You feel they're safe? At least for tonight?"

Greg grinned slightly. "Even if they're not, I can assure you that two other sets are."

Frye looked impressed. "Good, then I'd like a set of the prints tomorrow. I'll stop by your office and pick them up. How about ten o'clock?"

Greg told him fine, he'd be there.

"Also, I'd like your password to Ms. London's adult site. It's not necessary, but it'll be a whole lot easier and faster than trying to gain access using a force hacker. Unfortunately, without the hard drive we won't be able to check out other photos that might possibly be stored there. But we can at least have our lab go over the pictures of the men posted to the site."

"Sure, glad to help," Greg said.

Frye stood up, unwrapped a piece of gum and shoved it into his mouth. Then he remembered us and offered us each a piece. We declined.

"I don't want you to be alone tonight, Odelia," Frye said, chomping the gum every couple of words.

"The paramedics said I probably didn't have a concussion," I said.

"Doesn't matter. Either have Greg here stay with you, or go to another friend's, or even your family if they're around."

At the thought of going to my Dad and Gigi's, my head starting throbbing more. It was almost two in the morning, too late to call Zee and Seth. I looked at Greg's chair. I had extra space for guests, but it was upstairs.

"You're coming home with me," Greg said, almost reading my mind. "I have an extra room."

"Good," said Frye, closing the deal on my behalf. "I'd feel a lot better about that."

"So Detective," I said, reaching out and placing a hand on his jacketed forearm. "Do you believe us now?"

Frye sat back down in front of me. I put down the ice pack. This time he took both of my hands, the cold and the warm. He looked at me, then at Greg, and gave us both a small, sad smile.

"Odelia, I always did believe you. From the beginning, I thought this whole suicide thing smelled bad. But until now, we just didn't have enough possible evidence to keep pursuing it officially. Unofficially, I never put it to rest."

TWENTY-THREE

"GREG, YOU AWAKE?" I whispered, standing partially in the doorway to his bedroom.

Muted light came through a window set high over the bed. It was enough for me to make out the outline of the body in the bed located in the middle of the large room. Wainwright, curled up on a rug, gave me a few encouraging wags.

"No, Odelia, I'm not."

His voice was normal and clear, surprising me. Not a sign of sleepiness, even though it was three in the morning. He turned on the small lamp on his night stand, filling the room with a soft, non-glaring light.

"You okay?" he asked.

"Yes, just can't sleep."

"Me either."

Using his strong upper body and arms, he scooted up until he was sitting. The sheet slipped down to his waist, exposing his well-defined chest and shoulders. His torso was nicely covered with hair—not too much, just enough to make a girl sigh. He reached up and pushed his long hair back and out of his eyes. Looking at him like this, it was difficult to remember that he was paralyzed from the waist down. The only giveaway was the vacant wheelchair standing sentry next to the bed. He smiled softly at me.

"Is your head all right?" he asked. "Do you feel sick?"

"No. I'm fine." Reaching up to touch the epicenter of my headache, I felt a good-size goose egg taking shape. "I'm going to have quite a knot, though."

After Frye let us go, Greg had followed me back to my place. Quickly, I changed from my evening clothes into jeans and a short-sleeved shirt, and slid my feet into sandals. I threw some toiletries and makeup into an overnight bag, along with clean underwear and a nightshirt. The last thing I did before leaving for Greg's was to feed poor Seamus. Wainwright had waited in Greg's van.

Greg had wanted me to leave my car at home, but I insisted on taking it to his place. I didn't want him to have to drive all the way back to Newport Beach tomorrow. It wasn't all that far, about twenty miles, maybe less, but chauffeuring me around wasn't necessary. My injury would be fine. No danger lurking there, just a week or so of gradually subsiding pain and tenderness. Besides, tomorrow I had plans—plans I didn't think would meet with Greg's approval. I wanted to visit Clarice Hollowell, especially knowing that her husband would be out of town.

Greg and I stared at each other awkwardly. I was in my jammies, a knee-length oversized satin nightshirt, blushing like a school girl.

"Would it be presumptuous of me to ask if I could join you?" I asked. "I mean to talk."

Pulling open the covers on the other side of his king-size bed, he said, "You can join me to talk or sleep. Really, if you'd feel better sleeping here rather than in the other room, be my guest."

Walking around Wainwright, I went to the empty side of the bed and gingerly climbed in. It had been a long time since I'd been to a slumber party. It seemed almost as long since I'd had a bed partner, though that wasn't true. It just seemed that way.

Cautiously, I settled in and tried to arrange my doughy body in the best, most attractive position possible. It wasn't working; my bulk wasn't cooperating. I gave up and settled a pillow against the headboard and leaned back, shoulder to shoulder with Greg.

"I really am sorry, you know," he said.

"About what?" I asked, turning slightly to look at him. He was so handsome, both inside and out. Quite a switch from Hollowell.

"About not telling you about Sophie's . . . ummm . . . former occupation."

"It's okay. I know you did it because you thought it best for me. I'm just glad you were there when I really needed you to come to my rescue."

He lifted up his left arm, inviting me to snuggle close. Gladly, I took up his offer. As his arm went around my shoulders, I turned and rested my head against his chest. His other arm curled around the front of us both. I felt his lips carefully graze the top of my head near my forehead. The whole scene felt cozy and warm and natural, but most of all safe.

"Greg, something's bothering me."

He chuckled softly. "Something, as in singular? I would have thought you'd have an entire laundry list of nagging thoughts."

"Well, yes, I do," I said, laughing slightly. "But one thing in particular is gnawing at me right now." I paused before continuing. "If Robbie is Hollowell's son, don't you think Sophie would have used the kid as a pawn to keep Hollowell, at least in the early years?"

"Mmmm, maybe, but keeping Hollowell wasn't the goal. She already had him in a way. They were together over twenty years, longer than his marriage."

"Maybe Hollowell didn't know that Robbie was his. He never indicated to me that he knew."

"It's a possibility. If he knew, he might not have used her like a prostitute. After all, she was the mother of his child."

"Trust me, Greg, John Hollowell would hawk his own mother if he thought he could gain from it."

He tightened his arms, giving me a squeeze. Mmmm, he felt good.

"The Olsens are afraid of him, afraid that he'll come for Robbie now that Sophie's dead." I snuggled closer and tried to keep my mind on the topic at hand. "That seems to indicate that he knows. If that's true, why didn't he claim Robbie during all these years? Hollowell's a proud guy. The type who'd show off a smart, handsome kid like Robbie like a trophy."

"Maybe he doesn't like kids. He may have had something to do with his other son's death. You said yourself that you think he's behind both that and Woodall's death."

I thought about that, then a light went on inside my bruised head.

"Like I said, Hollowell's a proud man, not given to tea and sympathy. Jonathan Hollowell was a Downs baby, damaged and embarrassing goods to a man like Hollowell."

I shifted my body so that I was facing Greg, leaning across his strong torso, looking into his face.

"My guess is that Hollowell is in the habit of disposing of people he views as a threat to his power, even a tiny baby born with an extra chromosome. Somewhere along the line, Sophie decided to break ties with Hollowell. Perhaps she threatened to tell all if he didn't leave her alone. From what Glo Kendall said, Sophie got angry when Hollowell showed up at her door. Hardly the behavior of a woman trying to cling to a relationship."

Thanks to the pain relievers I had taken less than an hour ago, my head was beginning to feel better. My battered mind was trying to wrap around the facts and possibilities known to date and tie them together somehow. Greg let me ramble on.

"And I think you're right, Greg," I said, continuing. "I don't think the men in the photos had anything to do with Sophie's murder. Hollowell's got to be behind this."

Greg leaned forward and kissed my forehead.

"I bet," he said, his lips resting against my skin, "if we find tonight's burglar, we'll find that he's in Hollowell's back pocket. Maybe Hollowell had the computer stolen to protect his business associates."

Without thinking, I kissed Greg's chest, just below his neck. We held that position while we thought, his lips planted on my forehead, my mouth on his body. He smelled so good, so masculine.

"Or to blackmail them," I said. "But that doesn't make sense either. If he was going to blackmail these men, wouldn't you think he would have done so a long time ago? And exposing them would hurt his business more than help it. I don't think Hollowell is about money; that alone doesn't float his boat. It's power and control that gets him off, and power makes money. He needs those business contacts to further his ambitions. And he told me that Sophie was getting too old for a lot of their tastes. They wanted younger women. He's still interested in keeping these guys happy."

Greg kissed my forehead again, this time with several small pecks. "You know what that means, don't you?" he asked between smooches.

"Yes, it means that he's still in the procurement business. Just with other girls as his closers."

"Uh huh, that's my guess."

He put a hand under my chin and raised my face to his. His eyes looked into mine for just a heartbeat before he brought his mouth down onto mine for one smooth, quick kiss.

He was making it difficult for me to think.

"Sophie was trying to break away from Hollowell, that much I know for sure," Greg said, pulling me close. "Had been for a while, and I got the impression from what she told me that he was having a tough time letting her go. That would fit with what your friend Glo witnessed. Maybe he didn't care about the business end of their relationship anymore, maybe he was worried about something else, something she knew."

"Like the deaths of the baby and Woodall."

"Exactly. Maybe she was blackmailing him."

"Maybe they were blackmailing each other," I said in return. "And what about Ortiz? Who killed him, or was it really a coincidence?"

A flashback from just two days ago struck me like lightning, frying what was left of my brain. Two days felt more like two years.

"I just thought about something else Glo said, something I meant to look into and forgot. Glo told me that the drunk who killed Ortiz was someone from the company she works for, an executive, very high level."

"Do you know who she works for?"

"Let's see, I think so." I ransacked my memory. "I know this. I know, I know this," I said, squeezing my eyes tightly. "It's a state, an Indian name." *This is important, Odelia,* I told myself silently, *you've got to remember.* My eyes sprang open in triumph. "Dakota! That's it, Dakota Industries."

Greg had a computer at home. The legal research site could be accessed from anywhere with my Woobie password. I could take a look now.

"Greg, if there's a connection between Dakota Industries and Hollowell, I'll find it. Trust me."

I started to get up, but he held me close and laughed.

"I do trust you, Odelia. But can't this wait until morning? Or at least until later this morning?"

I looked at him, my face a big question mark, just as his mouth came down on mine for more than a fast peck.

Yes, I told myself, *it could wait.*

Our mouths melted together, the kiss growing in passion. Parting my lips, I welcomed his tongue like an old, familiar friend.

Reaching up an arm, I encircled his neck, drawing him closer into my hungry mouth. One of his hands explored my body, running from my waist down over a hip and thigh. Then I felt it go under my nightshirt and move upward toward my breasts, stroking my fatty flesh. I stiffened in self-consciousness and he stopped, sensing my discomfort.

"Maybe we shouldn't," he said.

"No, I want to," I told him in a whisper. "It's just been a while." I hesitated, then added, "Unless you don't want to."

He let out a soft laugh and kissed my forehead. "I've dreamed of little else since I first met you that day at the Washingtons'."

"Really?"

"Really."

I glanced at the wheelchair. "But what about . . . I mean, I've never . . ."

"Had a cripple before? Few women have, I imagine. It's different, Odelia. I won't lie to you. It takes some getting used to. But if you're willing to try, all you have to do is follow my lead and everything will be fine."

Awash in afterglow you could fry an egg on, I drove down Pacific Coast Highway. The ocean shimmered in the sun to my right. I was singing along with the radio, off-key and loud, and didn't give a rat's ass who heard me. It was mid-morning, too late for sunrise, too early for the usual beachgoer. A few mellow folks were lounging on the sand already, but they'd be gone by the time the throngs of families and teenagers descended to worship cancer-causing rays. I like the beach in the morning, finding it peaceful and fresh. Usually, it was the only time I went. Sometimes I would go in the evening to sit beside a fire ring with friends. But the midday heat and burning sun weren't kind to my fair, freckled skin, and had become a real enemy as the years went by.

A new song started and I picked it right up, even though I didn't know most of the words.

Greg had promised that the lovemaking would be fine if I allowed him to lead me through it. And it had been fine, very fine indeed.

He had been a wonderful guide and lover. Worried about hurting him with my weight, at first I had been reluctant to get on top, as he instructed. But my growing lust for him overrode my hesitations and, in the end, after a roaring climax, I had rolled off of him reborn. In truth, it was the best sex I had ever had.

We had fallen asleep in each other's arms around four and woke up together just before eight. After an encore performance, we reluctantly got up. Greg had to meet Frye and I wanted to make contact with Clarice. After showers and a quick breakfast, we went our separate ways, but not before promising to meet back at his house tonight around six. I couldn't wait.

It was during breakfast that I broke down and told him of my plan to visit Hollowell's wife. He wasn't pleased; no big surprise there. But he was smart enough to know that he couldn't talk me out of it. I also made him promise not to tell Frye. But, as with my trip to Santa Paula, he made me agree to call him at a certain time and check in. If I missed the call, I knew he'd be on Frye like butter on popcorn.

Humph. A girl gets a little bump on the head and everyone panics.

Cautiously, I touched the place where the assailant had left his calling card. The bump was raw and painful. Washing and drying my hair this morning had been tricky. In my purse was a bottle of pain relievers that Greg had let me pinch from his medicine cabinet. My injury reminded me to stop in at Hoag Hospital and check on Iris.

Poor Iris. In the end the beams did get her, just not in the way she expected. Seeing the security company truck parked in front of Sophie's, Iris must have hurried over to relate her woes, surprising the bogus technician. That was Frye's theory, and it sounded on target to me.

Right after breakfast, while Greg showered, I fired up his computer and checked out Dakota Industries. Its registered agent wasn't Glenn Thomas, as I had expected, but a man named Lowell Jensen. But under Dakota Industries, Glenn Thomas was listed as president and chief financial officer.

Excited with possibilities, I switched to the Orange County Register's site and found their archives. I typed in Glenn Thomas. Up popped a story about the Ortiz accident. That's where I'd heard Thomas's name; he was the drunk who'd killed Danny Ortiz.

With several clicks of the computer mouse, I searched for the website for Hollowell-Johnson Investment Company. I should have tried this route before, but it hadn't occurred to me. Not all companies have websites, but most did. Hollowell was a happening kind of guy. I would have been surprised to find his company behind the times.

In no time I was scanning the Hollowell-Johnson home page. It was a snazzy yet conservative site, giving visitors the idea that the company was both modern and trustworthy. I wasn't interested in its services but in the subsidiaries, the other companies it owned and operated. I found a link entitled The HJ Investments Family. Clicking on it gave me a nicely presented list of businesses under the Hollowell-Johnson umbrella. Sure enough, Dakota Industries was one of them.

I printed out hard copies of the research and tucked them into my tote.

Switching gears, I had quickly searched Sophie's website using the password Greg supplied. As I suspected, upon closer review of the photos, I could see that there wasn't one man as I had first thought, but a few different ones, each with his face concealed. From the dates imprinted at the bottom of these photos, I could also tell that they were old pictures, all taken more than a year ago, which supported what Greg had told me about Sophie getting out of the closing business.

I still didn't think any of these men had anything to do with Sophie's death. I could be wrong, but for now I was willing to go in another direction. Besides, the police were going to investigate this possibility. I wanted to trample my own ground.

TWENTY-FOUR

STILL SINGING MY HEART out, I stopped at my place for a quick change of clothes. Then I hit the road for Corona del Mar.

I parked at the curb directly in front of Hollowell's home and got out. The house looked quiet. The walkway leading from the street up a small rise to the front door was bisected by a river of circular driveway, like a moat. I crossed it, stepped up to the door, and rang the bell.

I wasn't sure what I was going to say to Clarice Hollowell. Nothing particularly clever came to mind, so I thought I'd start by asking a few questions and see where it got me. That is, if she was home. And if she would deign to speak with me.

The front door had a stained glass window set into the middle and a large picture window on the wall to its left. I tried peeking into both. Getting no answer, I rang the bell again. Still nothing.

To the right of the home, a straight stretch of driveway veered off from the circular drive. I followed it past a large, open metal gate. The driveway ended at an unattached garage large enough for three cars. It sat behind the house, off to the right. The area directly behind the house was comprised mostly of a huge redwood deck surrounded by a waist-high open fence with steps leading down into a garden. The area held an assortment of tables with umbrellas, chairs, and lounges. Both the deck and garden were abundant with flowers, shrubs, and exotic greenery. In one corner of the deck was a man-made river rock waterfall cascading into a spa. The whole area looked like a slice of paradise.

The back looked as deserted as the house. I was about to turn away when I realized that something was out of place. I stood still and waited, my nose tilted up.

A lifetime nonsmoker can pick up a whiff of cigarette smoke from a hundred yards away, much like a shark smelling a drop of blood in the ocean. And there was no doubt about it, I smelled smoke.

Venturing past the driveway boundary and into the back, I tip-toed closer to the deck. It was only a few steps up from the ground. Surveying the tables, I finally found the burning butt. It was sitting in an ashtray at the table nearest me, a table so close to the fence I'd almost missed it. Light gray wisps spiraled up into the still air.

"Either go away or say something."

The voice startled me. Placing a hand over my heart, I felt it thumping from the jolt. I stepped closer to the sound and discovered a body sprawled in a lounge chair next to the table supporting the cigarette. The figure was dressed in white gauzy material and wore a straw hat pulled down low on her face.

"So, which is it to be?" the voice demanded.

"Mrs. Hollowell?" I asked, stepping up the stairs to stand on the deck itself.

"If you're selling something, go away and save us both some time." The voice was cultured, the tone superior.

"Mrs. Hollowell, I need to speak with you."

A bony hand with French manicured nails and a diamond the size of a bonbon reached out for the cigarette and drew it close under the hat. I was near enough to hear a deep inhale, then an exhale, followed by smoke signals puffing out from under the brim. While I waited to be granted an audience, I took note of a serving tray on the table. On the tray were a pitcher and a glass. It was an empty martini glass with two green olives stranded at the bottom. The pitcher was about a quarter full.

The hand not holding the cigarette pushed the hat back from the woman's face. She looked me over from head to toe and back to the top without a word, then took another deep drag of smoke.

After exhaling, she asked, "You one of my husband's fat sluts?"

I could see that this was going to be a fun ride, right up there with getting smacked on the head with an heavy object.

"Guilty to the fat part, not guilty to being a slut, your husband's or anyone else's."

A very small smile crept across her face. "Good answer."

She sat up straighter in the lounge chair and swept her free hand toward an empty seat next to the table. I accepted the gesture and sat down.

"Would you like a drink?" She stubbed out her cigarette and picked up the tall glass pitcher, twirling its glass stirring rod gently. "I make a mean martini."

"No, thank you, Mrs. Hollowell."

Greg and I had made pancakes and sausage for breakfast. I had a hard time imagining gin mixing well with maple syrup.

She shrugged and poured herself a fresh glass. "As they say, more for me."

She sipped the drink as if in prayer, making me wonder how often she visited the altar.

"So, now, just who are you?" she asked.

"My name is Odelia Grey."

Holding her glass with both hands, she sipped again, then screwed up her face a bit. The straw hat sat back on her head enough for me to see her entire face. At first glance, I put her around my age. But a closer look made me increase my estimate. Her facial skin was pulled tight, her features pointed with a hint of being stretched. Chemically enhanced black hair framed her narrow face in a feathery, short cut that looked fresh. Her makeup was flawless. The whole look said spoiled, idle, and rich . . . very rich.

"Odelia," she said, repeating my first name. "Unusual name, isn't it?"

"I was named after a great aunt I never met," I told her.

"Odelia." She rolled it around in her mouth like one of her martini olives. "I think I like it."

"Glad to hear it," I mumbled, thinking to myself that she was half drunk and might be useless to me.

"But I must not know you," she said, looking at me over her drink. "I think I would have remembered your name."

"No, Mrs. Hollowell, you don't know me. But I need to ask you some questions. It's important to me."

"And how is it important to me?"

I hesitated, then jumped in with both feet. "It's important because it involves your present husband, your dead husband, and your son, Jonathan."

Well, that did it. Cocktail banter was over. She put down her glass so sharply, I was surprised the slender stem didn't snap. Her eyes narrowed and she leaned forward.

"Who the hell are you?" she asked in a slow, stern voice.

"I'm a friend of Sophie London's," I replied.

"So, you're not a fat slut," she said, giving a wicked laugh. "Just the fat friend of a fat slut. Same thing."

With John Hollowell, you had to dance around the questions you wanted to ask, keeping time with his personal sheet music, the whole activity frustrating, yet civil. Questioning Clarice Hollowell would be different, more like professional wrestling with headlocks and body slams. More to my personal liking, if I didn't knock her block off first.

"Did your husband kill Sophie, Mrs. Hollowell?"

"You don't mince words, Odelia. I like that." She picked up her drink and settled back in the chaise. "I heard that she was dead, of course. It was on the news. Also heard it was suicide."

"I don't believe it," I said with conviction. "And I think John Hollowell had something to do with it."

"You're a smart woman to connect the two, Odelia. But you really should lose some weight. Fat makes people look dumb, don't you know that? Or is that your cover?"

I was sitting across from a woman so thin she could have been taken for a concentration camp inmate. In addition, she smoked like a chimney and swilled martinis by the pitcher. It took a lot for me not to point out her flaws in return. But I kept silent, reining in my indignation. Clarice Hollowell was pushing buttons, looking for the one that would set me off. I wasn't about to give her the satisfaction.

"So John did have something to do with it," I said, keeping my mind on the real business at hand.

"John? My, my, so you do know my husband?" She looked me over again. "Yes, he would like you. You're attractive, well dressed, sharp, and seemingly educated. You close any deals for him yet?"

I smoothed my pink silk summer dress down over my legs, glad I had dashed home to change. I had thought it best not to face a possible society vulture dressed in jeans and a camp shirt, and had made the right decision.

"I have met your husband, yes; but there's no relationship."

She looked at my hands and arms, and so did I, wondering what she was searching for.

"You're probably telling the truth," she said, "you're not wearing the bracelet."

"The bracelet?"

"Yes, John gives all his fat sluts distinctive bracelets with a single round charm. Like a brand, but much nicer, don't you think? Usually the bracelets are in silver, but the really top-notch whores get them in gold." She laughed. "I know Sophie had a gold one." Clarice looked at me, studying me closely. "He asked you, though," she said with a leer, "didn't he? And I bet he offered you gold."

"Yes, Mrs. Hollowell, he did. But I'm not interested. My only concern is finding out what happened to Sophie."

"I love it!" She threw her head back and laughed. It was a throaty laugh that sounded too deep for her small body. "He's trying to get into your drawers and you're trying to nail his ass for murder. It'd serve him right if you succeeded."

"Did he murder Sophie?"

She shook her head. "We hosted a big brunch that day for the executives of John's company and their wives. He was here all morning and afternoon, I'm sorry to say."

"Was Glenn Thomas at the brunch?"

The mention of that name brought her up short. She hesitated before speaking. "Yes, of course. He runs one of the subsidiaries."

"Did you know that Mr. Thomas is an alcoholic?"

"Everyone knows that. So sad about that boy he killed, though."
Her voice was lowered, tinged with true sadness, as she spoke.

"He also worked for your first husband, for Kenneth Woodall,
didn't he?"

"Mmmm, you're not the police, and you don't look like a private
investigator." The sadness was gone; she was back in character. "Yet
you've done some good, solid homework. Just what *do* you do,
Odelia? You an attorney?"

"Paralegal. Corporate paralegal, actually," I told her.

"Oh, didn't go the whole way? Couldn't make the grade of law
school, huh?"

"No, Mrs. Hollowell, I *chose* to be a paralegal. Less bullshit."

I kept my eyes focused on hers. For a brief moment our wills
locked, then she looked away.

"Did Glenn Thomas kill Kenneth Woodall?" I asked. "Was he the
hit and run driver?"

"Yes," she admitted, "but if asked by anyone else, I'll deny it."

"That was your husband, Mrs. Hollowell. Why would you protect Glenn Thomas?"

"Because I hated Kenneth Woodall." Her words cut the still air
like razors. "He was a big time bastard, to both me and our daughter. Miserly and abusive. When John—"

She stopped, shocked that she'd said so much. She was giving up
a whole lot more information than I had expected, but I wasn't
complaining. I chalked it up to the booze.

"John?" I thought a moment about her slip. "That's right. You
married John Hollowell within a year of Woodall's death. So maybe
you and John Hollowell got Glenn Thomas to kill him, make it
seem like an accident."

She stared at me, her dark eyes flinty, the skin around them taut, like it would snap.

"Why should I tell you anything?" she asked.

I took a deep breath and held it. Upon blowing it out, I lit into her, hardly stopping for air.

"Because besides Sophie, a young man—an *innocent* young man—was killed. And last night Sophie's neighbor was almost bludgeoned to death. She's in a coma as we speak. And even I was attacked, almost knocked unconscious by the same assailant. Somehow these recent events are tied to those past deaths. And I'm going to find out how. Believe me, I won't rest until I do. So you can talk to me now or you can talk to me through bars, because there is no statute of limitations on murder," I said, pointing a finger at her, "and you, lady, are an accessory to at least one."

She looked at me without expression. I looked back in the same manner, hoping she wouldn't laugh at my attempt to intimidate. Truthfully, I wanted to tuck my tail between my legs and run; to change my name and move to another state so that the Hollowells and their associates could never find me.

"Why would Glenn Thomas help you and John get rid of Kenneth Woodall?" I asked, plowing on, willing my butt to stay put.

An expression scurried across her face, letting me know that she had made a decision. I waited to see which way she would go.

"Because Glenn is my brother," she said slowly, "and he hated Kenneth Woodall as much as I did."

She drained her glass and returned it to the table, then lit up another cigarette. I waited. After a long inhale and deep exhale, she continued.

"Kenneth worked for my father. He was a nobody from nowhere, but he worked hard and helped my father and brother build the company. We thought of him as family. Everyone was thrilled when I married him." She took another long drag. "About the time Jackie—that's my daughter—was born, my father died. Within months, Kenneth had taken control of the company. Turned out he'd been planning it for years, just waiting for the right time to make his move. He had set up his own company and eventually absorbed everything my father had built into it. My brother was left with nothing but a title, no real authority. I think Kenneth kept him around just to trot him out to the old customers, show them that the Thomas family still had an active part in the business."

She paused to take a puff before continuing. "Glenn's a very shy, quiet man. He never married; was given to drinking. I think he stuck it out just to keep an eye on me."

"So who thought up the plan?" I asked. "My guess is John Hollowell."

She nodded. "John was working at Woodall Development. We met at a company function. Old story, really. He was handsome and charming. I was lonely and neglected, not to mention outraged. We started an affair. Before I knew it, we had planned Kenneth's death and carried it out."

She poured herself another drink. "Sure you don't want one?" I shook my head.

"Funny," she continued. "That old saying . . . what goes around, comes around . . . it's true. Kenneth married me to gain control of my father's company. John killed him and married me to gain Kenneth's company." She gave a short laugh. "Guess that doesn't say much about my taste in men, does it?"

"And what do you think is going to come back around to bite you on your butt, Mrs. Hollowell?"

She let out an insane-sounding hoot. "Oh, it already has bitten me, Odelia. I got my comeuppance almost eighteen years ago and have been living in hell since."

"Your son?"

She turned her head out toward the lush garden beyond the deck. Her look was vacant, lost in another time.

"Jonathan was such a sweet baby," she said to no one in particular. "A good baby."

"Who killed your baby, Mrs. Hollowell? Was it the nanny, Bonnie Sheffley?"

She sighed. "Yes, she did the actual killing. I saw her. I was supposed to be out shopping, but came home early. I walked into the nursery and saw her with the pillow over his head. I screamed at her, tried to stop her, but I couldn't."

"He was already dead?"

"No, not yet. But John came in and grabbed me, held me until it was over. We watched that fat slut kill our baby."

Fat slut. The picture of Bonnie in the newspaper had shown a plump young girl.

"Bonnie and John were having an affair then?" I asked gently. It was a guess, but a safe one considering Hollowell's penchant for using overweight girls.

"Yes, right in front of me. Didn't even care if I knew." Clarice Hollowell turned to look at me. "John was embarrassed by Jonathan because he was different."

"Because he was a Downs baby?"

"Yes. He didn't even want any more children. He had his son. Didn't care a whit about my daughter."

"His son? You mean Robbie Olsen?"

"Yes, he kept telling me that one day he was going to get the boy away from Sophie and her hick husband and raise him properly. I thought that if we had our own child, he'd forget about her and their bastard. And he might have if Jonathan hadn't been born the way he was."

Clarice seemed to shrink as she told her sad story. Already thin, now she looked like a corpse draped in mummy wrappings. She seemed to be relieved by the confession, her voice more sad, less tart and aggressive.

"Did John blackmail you into keeping quiet about the baby? Did he use your involvement in Woodall's death to buy silence?"

"Very astute, Odelia. That's John's way, blackmail. Seems it's what makes the world go 'round."

"What happened to Bonnie?" I asked the question, knowing in my gut the answer would not be a pleasant one.

"Another case of what goes around, comes around," she said, smiling faintly. "Apparently, John had promised that he'd marry her when it was all over. But of course, he never intended to. He'd never divorce me. I was his ticket into Orange County society. Even most of his international contacts came from my attachments. I was his trophy wife and I knew too much. Our marriage had evolved into a rather sordid blackmail standoff."

She polished off her drink and headed for another. I stopped her.

"Maybe you should slow down, Mrs. Hollowell."

She hesitated, then put the pitcher down. "You're probably right, Odelia. I've been hitting it pretty hard lately. And no one likes an aging lush."

"Bonnie, is she still around?"

"Heavens, no! John eventually talked her into being one of his consultants, like Sophie. But she wasn't as bright as your friend. She kept nagging John about marrying her. Stupid bitch even threatened to go to the police if he didn't. Then one day, I heard that she'd packed up and moved overseas, supposedly to marry one of John's associates." Again, the asylum laugh. "When I asked John about it, he told me he'd gotten a good price for her. That's exactly what he said, got a good price for her. He told me Bonnie was somewhere in the Middle East being passed around like a party favor."

Even though it was almost eighty degrees, I shivered. It was just as I thought. Hollowell was capable of anything.

Clarice got up and stretched her frail frame. I could see now that she was wearing a white, nearly transparent, caftan. She was taller than I expected, with an attractive, almost pretty face. But her looks were going and attempts to cling to them were becoming obvious. I found myself wondering how many surgeries her face had endured to date.

She walked to the wooden railing and leaned against it, looking out over the garden. I got up and joined her. The air was redolent with a heady natural perfume.

"What do you know about Sophie's death, Mrs. Hollowell?" I asked. "It really is important."

She didn't move. I grabbed her shoulder and spun her around to face me. She looked drained.

"How many more people have to die?" I asked her firmly. "Do you really think you can keep covering up this way?"

She pulled away and started for the house. "Come this way," she said, indicating for me to follow.

We entered the house through a small service porch. From there we stepped into a grand kitchen, bedecked with professional appliances and lots of stainless steel shined to a blinding luster. In one corner, over a table and chairs, was a narrow ornamental railing close to the ceiling that held decorative utensils and vintage canisters. Clarice pulled up a step stool and started to climb, but she was unsteady.

"What do you need, Mrs. Hollowell?" I asked. "I'll get it for you."

She pointed to an old-fashioned metal canister nestled attractively between an antique beater and vintage sifter. I retrieved it and handed it to her. As I climbed back down, she popped open the top and pulled out a cassette tape.

She handed it to me, saying, "This is what kept John from trying to take Robbie away from Sophie. This is what kept her alive until now."

I held the black, unlabeled tape in my hand, turning it around. I looked at her blankly.

"It's a tape of John talking," she explained, "bragging really, about how easy it was to get away with murder. I taped it one night shortly after Jonathan was killed. John was downing drinks and babbling about how stupid my brother and I were. He threatened me on the tape that if I told anyone, Glenn and I would be convicted, but not him. He was too smart, he said. He had friends who'd protect him. It's also on the tape that he intended to get possession of his son or kill Sophie trying."

I swallowed hard.

Clarice continued. "Right after Bonnie was exonerated from charges of killing Jonathan, John became cocky. I started running a tape every night he was home, but he was very cautious. This night I got lucky. I made a copy and gave it to Sophie."

"You met her then?"

"Yes, I went to her home, the home my husband bought for her, by the way. I played the tape and gave her the copy, telling her to use it as insurance. I didn't care what happened to her fat ass, nor did I care about Kenneth's death. But one baby was dead and I wasn't about to let another child die without doing something."

"Does John know about this tape?" I asked, trying to figure how this had played out between Sophie and Hollowell.

She plucked the tape out of my hands. "Sorry, but it's my insurance policy, too. You'll just have to use that smart head of yours to find Sophie's copy."

She stuck it in a pocket of her caftan. "I honestly don't know if John knows about this tape or the copy. I certainly never told him and if Sophie did, she never told me. Every now and then we'd make contact and compare notes, more like watching each other's back. Nothing buddy-buddy, I can assure you. What I do know is that she and John arrived at an understanding. She told him that she had proof of his involvement in the murders and would keep it her secret if he gave up all interest in the boy and no harm came to either of them."

"But why kill her now, after all these years?"

"Who said he did?" Clarice looked at me, one eyebrow cocked. "John knew that if something happened to Sophie, this information might surface. It wasn't in his best interest to kill her. In order for him to kill her and get away with it, he'd have to make damn well sure of what she had on him and where the evidence was. And he'd have to make sure he retrieved it all first."

I thought about that and about how Hollowell had drilled me about something Sophie might have left for him.

"But why didn't she just take off and disappear? Or turn him in?"

It still didn't fit. Plus, I had assumed that Bonnie Sheffley might have been the woman Ortiz had seen, but now I was back in the dark about that, too. My head was starting to ache again.

Clarice looked at me a moment. "Odelia, have you ever been in love? I mean desperately in love?"

I thought about it. I had been in love, but not to the point of committing murder or harboring a criminal.

She didn't wait for my answer.

"Sophie London was hopelessly in love with John. She wasn't about to turn in the father of her child, but neither was she going to let a murderer have access to him. As for John," she said, smiling sadly, "if he were capable of loving anyone in this world, it probably would have been Sophie. He made it clear when we married that she was not going away. And I was so in love with him that I was stupid enough to think that I could change that. But his ambition and ruthlessness wouldn't let him trust or care about anyone.

"To protect her son, Sophie cut him off from both natural parents. By staying close to John, she could keep tabs on him and be a constant reminder that he needed to behave. She hadn't worked for John in quite a while, that I know. And I don't think that they had been lovers for a long time either. I do believe that both of those were her decisions, not his."

My mind was taking notes fast and furious. It made sense, yet it didn't. But if John Hollowell didn't kill Sophie, who did? And another thing was nagging at me . . . Clarice Hollowell herself. She didn't seem the chatty type, especially with a stranger. And she certainly had motive enough to kill. Maybe all those years of pent-up anger and pain had finally blown the lid off of her society restraint.

"What about you?" I asked Clarice. "Why are you still here? And why are telling me all this?"

"But I'm not here," she replied flippantly. "I'm a ghost. You're talking to a ghost, Odelia." She smiled tightly. "Why I'm telling you, I have no idea. Someone needs to know about this, so why not you? Maybe fate brought you to my patio . . . especially today." She laughed and I got the feeling the joke was private.

She picked up an unopened pack of cigarettes that was sitting on the kitchen counter and unwound the cellophane. Then she stopped and put the pack back down. Her mood changed back to serious.

"Until now, I stayed because if I left, John would have found me and harmed both me and my daughter. Unfortunately, I don't have that threat on tape. After several years of worrying and keeping Jackie almost tied to me, I finally sent her off to boarding school, only allowing her home for short breaks. She doesn't know why, but has always assumed that I preferred her stepfather over her. Someday I hope to make her understand. But it actually hasn't been that bad. John and I go our separate ways most of the time. There haven't been any more incidents since Jonathan. But with Sophie's death, I knew that things would heat up again. Then this thing with Glenn."

Another thought occurred to me. It was a long shot, but why not?

"Mrs. Hollowell, did you by any chance call Robbie Olsen recently?"

She gave me a half smile. "Boy, you don't miss a trick."

The doorbell rang. Clarice looked at her watch.

"That'll be the limo," she told me.

She strode through the house with me on her heels. The society maven had returned in full force. Just as she started up the curved, polished stairway, she stopped and glanced back.

"Yes, I called Robbie. I wanted to make sure he was okay. After Sophie died, I became afraid for him." She smiled sadly. "After all, Odelia, I am a mother."

The doorbell rang again.

"Be a dear and tell the chauffeur to wait. I'll be right down. I just have to change my clothes."

I looked up at her, rooted to my place by confusion.

"Don't just stand there, Odelia, let him in. He can at least start loading the luggage."

Huh?

I walked to the front door and noticed for the first time a pile of expensive matched luggage stacked neatly in the entry hall opposite the stairway. On the hall table was a designer handbag. Resting on top of the handbag were airline tickets and a passport.

Opening the front door, I came face to face with a tall young man in a chauffeur's uniform. He looked Latino and held himself professionally.

"You arranged for a limousine, ma'am?"

"No, not me. Mrs. Hollowell will be right down." I looked up the stairs and then at the luggage.

"Shall I take these to the car?" he offered.

"Yes, she'd like that."

While the driver loaded enough luggage to keep a family of four clothed for a month, I stood by like a reluctant lady-in-waiting. I noticed photos on the wall in the hallway, pictures hung in well-planned groupings. But some photos were missing, taken from the wall recently from the look of it. I studied those still in place. Some showed Hollowell with various people, even a few celebrities. Others were family shots of John and Clarice with a sullen little girl. Some, taken more recently, showed the Hollowells in golf attire at charity tournaments or dressed to kill at formal functions. In the photos, Clarice had auburn hair worn in a pageboy that hung just below her chin. Today her hair was short and black.

But I'm not here. I'm a ghost.

Clarice Hollowell was skipping town.

I was about to snoop at her tickets and passport when I heard her coming down the stairs. She was dressed in a navy blue pantsuit that I suspected was Chanel. Large sunglasses shielded her eyes. She appeared to be in total control, about to take a leisure cruise rather than fleeing a crime.

"But what about your brother, Mrs. Hollowell?" I asked as she stood in front of me. "He needs you."

"He's already gone, dear," she said, giving me her signature tight smile. "Jumped bail this morning while we were talking."

She picked up her purse, tickets, and passport.

"Are you married, Odelia?" she asked cheerfully.

I shook my head.

"A little advice, then; if you ever marry, don't be a fool and mingle everything. Keep something aside just for you and keep it a secret. A girl's got to have her own money, because money can buy a lot of things, dear. Ciao!"

Before I could say more, she scampered down the walk and climbed into the waiting limousine, leaving me to lock up.

TWENTY-FIVE

IN SPITE OF EFFORTS to give it a homey feel, the hospital cafeteria still clung to that certain cold ambiance that only institutions could muster. I sat across from Detective Frye, sipping a Diet Coke and munching on an egg salad sandwich. He was going over his notes, questioning me from time to time for clarification. My nerves were strung so tight, I would have given anything for a bacon double cheeseburger to calm them down.

Even before the limo carrying Clarice Hollowell had left the driveway, I was dialing Greg's office number, hoping to catch Frye. But I had missed him. I quickly gave Greg a rundown. He said he'd get in touch with Frye and have him call my cell phone. In the meantime, he ordered, get the hell out of there.

He didn't have to tell me twice. Even though I really did want to poke around, I didn't want any chance of running into John Hollowell. People have a way of coming home early when you least expect it. Case in point: Clarice witnessing her baby's murder.

Frye called me as I was driving to Hoag Hospital on my way to see Iris. They probably wouldn't let me see her, but I still wanted to stop by. Frye said he was already at the hospital and that he'd meet me in the cafeteria.

On the phone I told him about Clarice Hollowell and her brother taking flight. Frye was particularly concerned about Glenn Thomas.

"Odelia," Frye said, after taking a big gulp of coffee from the cup in front of him, "can you describe Clarice Hollowell again for me? We've units at or heading to all the airports now, but I'd like a better, more concise description." He had just polished off a ham and cheese sandwich in record time.

"I can do better than that." I opened my tote and pulled out a framed picture of John and Clarice Hollowell. I had lifted it from the wall of portraits before leaving, thinking it might help. "This looks exactly like her, except for the hair. It's now very short and black, and I don't think she was wearing a wig."

Frye looked at the photo and chuckled softly. "You've got a good head on you for this type of thing, Odelia. Both you and Greg. Probably from watching too many cop shows."

I grinned my thanks. "I wish I had the tape to give you. I should've just knocked her down and grabbed it from her. She looked like she hadn't had a good meal in months. I know I could have taken her."

"No, you did fine." He took another drink and looked at me. The only expression on his face was exhaustion with a capital E, but I could've sworn his eyes were twinkling just the same. "She told you she gave one just like it to Sophie?"

"Yes, but we didn't find anything like that when we were packing her things. She probably hid it just like she did the newspaper clippings."

"Could it be in that box you gave the Olsens?"

"That contained mostly photos and records, flat paper stuff, except for the booties. But I'll call and ask them to look through it again."

"Good. We'll need to go through all her things. I'll get a warrant for that. Stuff still at the house in boxes?"

I nodded. "You need a warrant even if I give you permission?"

"Yes. It's probably not necessary, but it keeps things on the up and up."

"Something's bothering me, Detective." I started to tell him my concerns when I looked up to see Ruth Wise entering the cafeteria. She strolled in, scanning the place. When she spotted us, she brightened, then looked concerned. I waved her over.

"Ruth," I said, "how nice to see you. What are you doing here?"

She was dressed in a khaki skirt and plaid blouse. Her hair was down, parted on the side, and worn soft around her face. It was the first time I'd seen her out of her exercise clothing, and she looked even taller. She approached us slowly.

"I . . . um . . . came to see a friend. She just had a baby, or is about to have a baby. I came in here for some coffee," she explained, looking shyly at Frye. "I'm sorry I disturbed you."

"Not at all, Ruth," I said, smiling. I made the introductions and the two shook hands. Ruth seemed a bit flustered around the detective.

"Well, I should leave you two to your business," Ruth said. "Will I see you on Monday, Odelia?"

"Maybe. I have the day off. Might just sleep in, though I really should walk."

"Walking will do you good, Odelia," Frye said. "As long as you don't overdo it with that bump on your head. It'll get your mind off things, rejuvenate your spirit. Isn't that right, Ruth?"

Ruth looked at him, offering a shy smile. "Yes, that's right. It's good for lots of things."

"Okay, then, I'll do my best to make it."

I watched Ruth walk away and head for the cafeteria line.

"She's such a nice young woman," I told Frye. "Only been coming to our walks a short while. I'm sorry she's seeing Reality Check in such turmoil."

He smiled slightly. "So what else is on your mind, Odelia?"

"Oh, that. It's about Clarice." I took a sip of soda. "If I was sneaking out of the country, I wouldn't be packed like I was going on safari. I'd take one carry-on and wouldn't use a limo with a full liveried driver."

He gave it some thought before answering. "I doubt that when Mrs. Hollowell made the arrangements, she thought she'd run into someone just before leaving. She probably has a fake ID and passport and was just planning to blend in with the other international first-class passengers."

"You think you'll nab her before she gets on the plane?"

"Might. Thanks to you, we got the word out quickly to look for someone with that description. We're checking out the limousine companies as well. Once we find the right one, we'll know exactly where they dropped her off."

"She didn't think her husband killed Sophie or had her killed. If not him, then who was there that day?"

"That's the big question, Odelia. There are several possibilities. Might have been one of her website playmates. Could still be the Olsens. We do know that one was a woman. One thing is for sure, they've covered their tracks well."

I shoved aside the remnants of my lunch. "The only connection we have to Hollowell at this point is Glenn Thomas. He killed the only witness."

"Correct. That's why it's important to find him." Frye polished off his coffee. "I have to get going, but I want you to do something for me."

"Sure," I said, eager to assist in the case.

"I want you to go back to Greg's and stay there. At least through tomorrow. Leave the rest to us, please."

"But I can help."

"You've already done quite a bit. But I want you someplace safe. I've already spoken to Greg about it."

I felt my feathers ruffling. "What about me, don't I get a say?"

"This time, no." Again I saw a slight dance in his blue eyes. He consulted his watch. "Greg will meet you at your place in about twenty or thirty minutes. Throw some things together, then go with him. If anything comes up, I'll call you there or on your cell phone."

Surrender wasn't something I swallowed easily. It was in the same category as okra. But I could see I was outgunned, so I chose to behave civilly instead of childishly.

"Is your wife still here, Detective?" I asked. "Or are you here to check on Iris?"

"Both, actually." He hesitated, sighing deeply. "My wife has been sick for years. She has ovarian cancer."

My heart thumped in icy fear at the dreaded words. Against my will, tears started to form. "I'm so very sorry."

His lips made an effort to give me a tired smile. "Thank you."

"What about Iris? They won't tell me much."

"It's not good, Odelia," he said, shaking his head slowly. "She's had surgery to relieve some of the pressure on her brain, but she's still in a coma. We finally managed to locate her family. They're flying in late tonight from Baltimore."

I lowered my head in sorrow. Iris Somers was an annoying kook, but she certainly didn't deserve this. Neither did Mrs. Frye.

I had indeed been lucky.

TWENTY-SIX

A SOUND WOKE ME. It was a dull thud, something heavy hitting wood. In my sleep-laden haze I thought it was my bladder knocking audibly, asking for attention. I started to stir.

"That's only Wainwright," Greg assured me. His eyes were closed, an arm curled around me. "It's his doggie door."

I couldn't put off peeing any longer. Slowly I lifted back the covers and started to ease out of bed, looking for something nearby to throw on me.

"What's the matter?" he asked.

"My nightshirt, where is it?"

"Around here somewhere." He shifted away from me and adjusted himself in the bed so that he was slightly sitting up. That accomplished, he ran his fingers through his long, thick hair. "You don't need it. It's just us."

I snorted softly to myself. Just us was enough. I looked around for a substitute. In the movies women always hopped out of bed and threw on something of their lover's. No matter how rumpled, they always managed to look sexy in oversized shirts with rolled-up sleeves.

Greg had no shirts hanging about and even if he did, I doubted if they would fit. So much for movie glamor. I started to pull at the sheet I clutched to my body.

"Odelia, I mean it," he told me, playing tug of war with the sheet. "You don't need to cover yourself. In fact, I don't want you to. I want to see that luscious body."

I gave him a look of skepticism.

It was silly, really. It wasn't our first time together, but our second, yet this morning seemed different. We had an established sexual relationship now and I didn't want to blow it by having the reality of my size thrown in his face. I would have been less self-conscious if it had been just a one time, heat of the moment fling, but I knew after last night that this had potential. That changed everything.

"Okay," he decided with determination, "we'll check out each other."

With a single toss of the covers, Greg gave me a full visual of his lifeless legs. It was a view that until now I had avoided. The limbs, thin and much paler than the rest of him, seemed not to belong to his strong and buffed upper body. He scooted himself to the edge of the bed and grabbed the nearby wheelchair to pull it close. Making sure the wheels were locked, he hoisted himself up on his muscular arms and swung his butt into the chair. The move was quick and efficient. I had seen him do it before, but this morning even that was different. The uselessness of his legs was a glaring fact; something that couldn't be ignored.

"There," he said, once he was settled in. "Here I am, skinny legs and all."

His charm and cockiness made me laugh, and his courage made me brave. With my own toss of the covers, I uncovered myself and hopped out of bed completely, standing in all my lumpy glory before him. I nervously watched as he checked me out from top to bottom. Then he tossed me a lecherous wink. I could feel an involuntary blush begin to creep upward from my toes to my scalp.

"Now walk toward the door, baby," he said. "Let me see you strut your stuff."

"You're joking?"

He shook his head. I rolled my eyes and very self-consciously walked to the door and back again.

"Nah, you can do better than that. Straighten those shoulders and lift those boobies," he coached. "Let's see some pride in that swagger!"

He was making me laugh, and laughing made my need to urinate more pressing. With one last effort, I squared my shoulders, tucked in my gut as best I could, and lifted my chest and chin. I concentrated on walking slowly and gracefully to the door, much to his delight and cat calls. Once there, I turned around and gave him a vampish glance over my shoulder.

"Gotta pee, big boy, see ya in a few."

When I returned, he was gone. Locating my errant nightshirt, I slipped into it. I wasn't quite ready to strut my stuff throughout the house. I found Greg in the kitchen, feeding an eager Wainwright.

"Scrambled eggs sound good to you?" he asked.

"Sure. In fact, I'll even whip up my famous messy eggs."

"Don't tell me, you cook them in the pan, shells and all," he said with a grin.

"Close," I answered, pulling eggs and other ingredients from the refrigerator. His fridge was well stocked with fresh items, making me feel guilty about my own nutritional disaster at home. "Scrambled eggs with chopped veggies and cheese. Like an omelet, only not neatly filled and folded. Think of a nicely made bed versus a rumpled one."

He laughed. "You're on."

"You always in such a good mood in the morning?" I asked as I began chopping zucchini, along with green and red peppers.

"Only when I wake up with a beautiful woman at my side."

"Hmmm." I could feel myself blushing yet again. "Be careful, Greg, I could get used to this."

"That's my plan."

Greg's sink, cabinets, and appliances were built lower than the norm, which was fine by me since I'm short. I moved around the custom kitchen comfortably, feeling quite at home.

"Greg, what happened to you?" I asked as I grated Swiss cheese into a bowl. "What happened to your legs?"

Greg rolled over to the coffee maker and poured us both a cup. He set mine on the counter and took his to the table.

"You don't have to talk about it if you don't want to."

"No, Odelia, it's okay. You should know, and I don't mind talking about it. At least not after all these years."

He poured milk into his coffee and offered me some. I shook my head.

"When I was almost fourteen," he began, "I was horsing around with some cousins who lived up north. I was visiting them for the summer. We were coming home from fishing and goofing off along the way. You know, skipping rocks, bugging each other. Being normal adolescent wise-guys.

"There was an old, short, wooden bridge along the way, built high above a small river. Joey, who was fourteen already, dared me and Slick—that's my cousin Seymour, who was twelve at the time—

to cross the bridge tightrope style. You know, walk along the top of the railing."

"God, I can see this coming already," I groaned.

"We'd done it before, many times in fact. But that morning, it had rained and the railing was slippery. It was also old and wiggly. Joey, being the one who made the dare, went first, followed by his brother. I was last. They both made it across, although Slick had a few tense moments. I wasn't so lucky."

"You fell, of course," I said, scooping the chopped vegetables into the hot frying pan and tossing them with a bit of butter and salt and pepper.

"Of course. The railing jiggled from side to side and the wetness just helped it along. But I didn't just fall into the river. I was almost across when it happened, so when I started to fall, I was partially over the embankment. On the way down, I hit some rocks jutting out and kind of ricocheted into the river. Joey said I looked like a pinball going down, bouncing from the rocks to the ground and then into the water."

"I'm so sorry, Greg."

"It was just a foolish accident. Stuff like that happens."

We were both quiet for a moment. The sound of sizzling filled the room. I started scrambling the eggs in a bowl, getting ready to add them to the pan.

"You seem so okay about all this, Greg. So accepting. Didn't you ever get angry about what happened?"

He started setting the table. "Of course I did. Still do. But I work through that anger every day, taking it just one day at a time. Anger won't bring back my legs. It'll just mess up my life."

My forced retirement from investigative work at least gave me time to spend with Greg. Saturday night he took me to dinner and a movie. It was a good old-fashioned date, complete with flowers. After, we made love. Today we planned on simply relaxing and hanging out together.

I stole looks at Greg as I popped some bread into the toaster and mixed the cheese into the cooking egg mixture. He was placing jam and butter on the table, looking very domestic and very yummy at the same time. I wondered if I could ever totally accept his handicap, the age difference, and my own body. But then, maybe that was *my* disability; an invisible, crippling insecurity I would have to work on day by day to overcome.

I served up the eggs and toast. Greg poured the orange juice. Wainwright settled under the table. All that was missing was one cantankerous green cat.

The rest of the day was near to perfect. I called Zee to let her know where I was and what was happening. After I calmed her down and assured her that I was safe and that the bump on my head was just a bump, Greg, Wainwright, and I adjourned to the beach.

I still couldn't get a handle on who the people were at Sophie's the morning she killed herself. It plagued me even though I promised Greg to let it be. I ran all the possibilities over and over inside my head like a broken record, making myself nuts.

Greg knew I was stewing about it. I could tell by the looks of disapproval he shot my way when I was overly quiet. But like meat and vegetables simmering in a broth, facts and theories bubbled away in my heated brain. Finally, I couldn't help myself.

"Greg, do you think that maybe the woman Ortiz saw that morning was one of Hollowell's bimbos?"

He let out an exaggerated groan. "You're not going to let this go, are you?"

"Not until I have some answers."

"You're going to drive yourself insane, Odelia."

"Well, at least give me a road map so I can get there faster."

"Okay, okay," he said, laughing. We were seated, looking out at the ocean, he in his chair, me on a concrete bench. He pulled me close and kissed me. "You're like a dog with a bone. Might as well let you chew on it until you're done."

I smiled and kissed him back. "Thanks. It'll be easier on you in the end, trust me."

"I can see that," he said. "So what's the question again?"

"Clarice Hollowell said something about her husband giving all his women, his 'fat sluts' actually, the same bracelet. Sophie had one just like she described. I returned it to Hollowell the first night we met, and he tried to give it to me."

"Really?" Greg's interest in the subject was really aroused now. "Did he offer you a job, too?"

"No, but he asked me to go to San Diego with him. But you know, now that I look back, he did ask if I wanted to go on cam. Maybe he was looking for Sophie's replacement."

"You go on cam, fine with me," Greg told me. "But only for my personal enjoyment, you hear?"

"But you didn't mind Sophie being on camera."

"No, but I wasn't involved with Sophie. At least not like we are. Had she and I become lovers, I probably wouldn't have been able to handle it. I'm not *that* open-minded."

His reply made me happy.

"So did you take the bracelet?"

"No, of course not. But what if some of the other girls he uses in his business are also on adult websites? We'd be able to tell who they are by the bracelets."

"But only if they're wearing them."

"Are there that many BBW webcam sites on the Internet?"

"You're asking me?" he asked innocently. I gave him my "get real" look and he caved with a sheepish grin.

"Not really. At least there aren't that many listed on the webcamera index sites." He looked at me, his head tilted to the side. "You want to go back and check it out right now, don't you?"

I gave him my best begging look.

TWENTY-SEVEN

AT FIRST HAPPY TO see me, Seamus was ready to move out and return to the coyotes when he realized that I had returned home Sunday night with Greg and Wainwright in tow. He would just have to get used to it, I told him, cradling his big sassy body in my arms, or start spending more time alone.

His hisses were interspersed with kitty growls, and his tail flicked like a snake as he watched Wainwright enter his turf and settle comfortably in a corner of the living room. The dog, oblivious to the evil eye being cast on him by the cat, looked at Seamus and wagged his tail.

"We won't stay long," Greg told me. "You look tired."

I was tired, but most of all frustrated. Our research into the world of Big Beautiful Women websites had yielded zilch. It had seemed like a plausible theory to me, the idea of looking for distinctive bracelets with a single charm. It hadn't taken long. There weren't that many adult webcam sites featuring large women, and none of them wore the telltale bracelet, or much else.

"Are you sure," he asked for the umpteenth time, "that you don't want to stay with me again? You can bring Seamus. We'll give him the entire guest room to roam."

"Thanks, Greg, but I'd rather sleep here tonight," I said. "Not that I don't want to sleep with you, just that I feel I need some time to myself. It's been a crazy few days."

Few days, my foot. Since Sophie died, my life had been nonstop lunacy. She had been gone only two weeks to date, and I felt like I'd been trapped in a carnival fun house for years. I was no longer young and dynamic, and I was feeling the news in spades. Come to think of it, I don't think I was ever young and dynamic. If so, I'd remember. But, of course, the mind is the first thing to go. That and the ass, followed closely by the boobs.

"What are you going to do tomorrow?" he asked.

I shrugged. "Get some rest. Maybe talk Zee into going with me to get a massage and a facial. You know, girl stuff. Might see a movie. We'll see. I also have a lot of paperwork from the attorney to go over about Sophie's estate. Maybe I'll look at that, too."

Sophie's place itself was off-limits. The police were still sifting through everything, looking for the tape.

Frye had called earlier to touch base, reporting two things. One, that they hadn't found the tape or anything else that might incriminate Hollowell yet. And two, that they had apprehended Glenn Thomas at John Wayne Airport in Orange County, but not his sister. Seems Clarice Hollowell had the limo driver drop her off at LAX, but disappeared before getting on the plane. Airline personnel recalled seeing her at both first-class check-in and in the VIP lounge, but no one remembered her after that. Her bags had flown from Los Angeles to Chicago, but she never got on the plane.

She had either been abducted or was one smart cookie. After spending over an hour with the woman, I voted for the latter.

"Whatever you do," Greg said, looking a bit dejected, "have fun and be safe."

I smiled and walked over to him, Seamus still in my arms. He rubbed the cat's scruff and scratched him behind his ears. Seamus, being easy like his mother, started purring. I bent down and gave Greg a kiss goodbye. That kiss turned into another, this time deeper and longer. Then another. We were so engrossed in our long goodbye, neither noticed Wainwright creeping up to get a whiff of Seamus.

Suddenly, the cat in my arms became a tangle of claws, teeth, and bloodcurdling howls. The animal broke free of my grasp, but not before inflicting scratches on my arms and one small one on Greg's chin. Once free, Seamus made a dash for a high place. The highest ledge in the room belonged to the top shelf of my wall unit. On the shelf was one of my most expensive nativity pieces. I held my breath as the cat landed next to the porcelain image and tiptoed around it. Then he crossed to the next shelf, putting distance between the dog and himself. He finally settled on the last top shelf. Resting on that, waiting to be properly hung on the wall, was the needlework sampler Sophie had left me. I blew out trapped air, knowing my valuables were safe and sound.

Peace restored, Greg and I said goodbye again; this time, a quick kiss sufficed. I held out my hand to Wainwright. As polite as ever, he sat down and offered me a paw. We shook. Then, like father like son, the animal lunged his large head forward to give me a kiss. I felt his big tongue lap my chin. At the same time, I caught a glimpse of Seamus flying over my shoulder, heading for the dog. Pandemonium reigned as a startled Wainwright fled the outraged cat. Greg, helpless to give chase, barked orders at Wainwright. The poor dog, cornered and trying to avoid the claws coming at him, snarled at Seamus and showed his teeth. Thinking twice about attacking, my green cat turned yellow and scampered up the wall unit again. This time he wasn't so dainty. Down came the sampler, smashing its glass front.

The room became eerily still.

Sharply, Greg ordered his dog to him. This time Wainwright obeyed, his tail hanging sheepishly low. Scolding the golden retriever, Greg directed him over to the door and told him to stay. The animal lowered himself down onto the carpet by the front door and looked at us with eyes full of remorse. Seamus, on the other hand, sat on the top shelf of the wall unit looking smug and innocent. *Yeah, right,* I thought, watching him coolly lick his paw and comb his whiskers. *Figures I'd live with the evil child.*

"I'm sorry, Odelia," Greg said, wheeling closer to where I knelt retrieving pieces of glass from the carpet.

I picked up the broken sampler and handed it to Greg. Only the glass seemed shattered, the frame was intact, the stitching unharmed.

"That's okay," I told him. "I should've known better. Seamus is very jealous and possessive of me. He probably thought Wainwright was going to bite me, not lick me."

With the largest pieces of glass in my hand, I went into the kitchen to dump them and bring back the hand vacuum. I wanted to get all the glass now before I forgot and missed some of it.

While in the kitchen I heard Greg call to me. "Odelia, come here quick."

I dashed into the living room to find him fondling the front of the sampler. There was a slight bulge in the middle. Outlining it with his fingers, we could both see it was a semi-flat rectangle.

My heart was in my throat, my fingers crossed.

Greg turned the frame over. It was thick, like a shallow shadow box frame. He started pulling off the cardboard backing. Sure enough, underneath was a cassette tape surrounded by padding.

The phone rang, bad timing unless it was Frye. I looked at the caller ID readout and noted it was a blocked call. Damn. I danced around indecision. It just might be Frye calling. I grabbed the phone.

"Hello," I answered.

"Odelia, it's me, Glo," the caller said in a Southern twang. "I heard you got clunked on the head. You okay?"

"Yes, I'm fine, Glo. Sore, but fine." Grabbing my tote, I dug around in it until I found Frye's card. On it he had written his private cell phone number. "But I can't talk now," I said excitedly. "You know, I never thought Sophie committed suicide; neither did Zee. Now I think I finally have enough evidence to prove it, and maybe even who's behind it. I have to call the police."

"But she shot herself," Glo said. "People saw her."

"I know, but I think someone made her do it. Possibly John Hollowell. I'll talk to you later, maybe tomorrow morning."

"Okay." She hesitated, then added, "And, Odelia, if it's true, I hope you put him away to rot forever."

I smiled into the receiver. "Thanks for calling, Glo, it was very sweet of you."

After hanging up, I dialed Frye. Within minutes, he returned the call. He was at the hospital, less than three miles away. Soon the three of us were seated in my living room, listening to Hollowell's recorded bragging and threats. I had insisted on hearing the tape before turning it over to the police.

My body shook as I listened. Greg noticed and reached over to clutch my trembling hand.

I knew Hollowell was dangerous, but the sound of his voice so coldly boasting about his past deeds and future plans made me dizzy with a combination of fear and anger. It was inconceivable to me how anyone could use and discard human beings in this manner, reducing them to the status of single-use paper goods. I knew, of course, that people did it all the time. I wasn't naive. The cold, hard facts exploded in our faces almost daily from the news. But those things happened to the proverbial other people, not to my friends and certainly not to me.

In my dogged search for the truth, I had uncovered the underbelly of Sophie's life. And in turn, it had exposed me to the shadowy side of the street on which I lived, worked, and played every day in blissful ignorance and contented boredom.

My life would never be the same. In the split second it had taken for that bullet to travel from the gun's chamber into Sophie London's mouth, penetrating her brain, I had been unwittingly altered forever. It was still to be determined if it was for the betterment of my future existence.

TWENTY-EIGHT

WALKING WAS DEFINITELY NOT on my list of favorite things to do on a day off. As I parked my car and forced myself to get out and look for the others, chocolate glazed donuts danced a can-can in my head. The lure of sweet pastry, devoured along with hot, steaming coffee, tempted me to forget the whole thing and leave.

Decisions. Decisions.

For the time being, good sense won out. I locked the car and wandered over to the starting point. It was about fifteen minutes to six by my car clock. I was early, but thought I could use the extra few minutes to enjoy the morning and reflect on recent past events. I was surprised to see Glo there already, stretching and waiting. When she saw me, she waved cheerfully.

This was good. Just what I needed. Donuts never looked happy when you approached and were physically incapable of waving. Exercise with good friends never left you feeling guilty either.

I smiled at her. "Good morning, Glo."

"Mornin'," she said back. "You ready to get that blood movin'?"

"The spirit's willing but the body's reluctant."

"I know what you mean." She stretched a bit more. Today over her usual shorts and T-shirt, Glo was wearing a light windbreaker against the morning dampness.

Overhead, birds soared. The air was filled with nature's music. The day was fresh and clean, like yesterday never happened. There was a new beginning every twenty-four hours, like a cosmic do-over.

There were very few people exercising this morning, just a couple of diehards jogging devotedly. I took a deep breath, filling my lungs to capacity, then exhaling to depletion. Then I inhaled again. A sense of peace washed over me. I really was glad to be here.

"Wonder if many are coming this morning," I said, doing a bit of stretching of my own as I spoke. "I ran into Ruth on Saturday and she said she'd be here."

Glo looked at her watch and shrugged. "It's already six. Maybe we should start."

"Really? I thought it was still a bit early, at least according to my dashboard clock."

"You know how undependable those things are." She gave a little laugh. "Mine's never worked, except for the day I bought the car. Besides, they can catch up—it's not like we're speed demons."

"So true."

We started down the trail, shoulder to shoulder.

"So, what's happenin' with this murder thing?" Glo asked. "Do you really think Sophie didn't commit suicide?"

"Yes, I do, though I'm not sure yet who exactly was there when it happened. I just know that Hollowell had something to do with it—and that executive from your office, Glenn Thomas."

"Mr. Thomas! You're kiddin'?"

271

"No, I'm not. He's John Hollowell's brother-in-law and has possibly killed for him before." I looked at Glo. "Did Sophie help you get that job at Dakota?"

She thought about it. "No. Come to think of it, when she found out I'd gotten the job, she didn't want me to take it. I don't remember her givin' me a reason though. Anyway, I didn't listen 'cause I needed the work."

"She was probably trying to protect you."

"From what?"

"John Hollowell, most likely."

I glanced back while I walked, but there was still no sign of Ruth. Maybe she changed her mind or succumbed to the evil donut spirit in my place. I turned my attention back to Glo.

"Seems Hollowell has a thing for big women," I told her. "He likes to woo them and use them. It's probably why none of us knew about him. Sophie was most likely trying to keep us out of his clutches. And after meeting him, I can see why."

Glo was quiet for several steps. "Well, thankfully, the job's turned out okay. Even with this thing about Mr. Thomas, the place is still runnin' smooth."

"He tried to leave the country this weekend," I told her. "But the police caught him."

"No kiddin'?" she asked again.

"No kidding. The young man he killed was the only person who could identify who was at Sophie's the day she died."

Now it was Glo's turn to swivel and look behind us.

"Guess we're the only ones who made it today," I said to her.

"Sure looks that way."

We continued walking until we passed a bend in the path. Thick growth and shrubbery at the curve blocked the view behind us. If the others were back there, they wouldn't be able to see us until they reached this point themselves.

Suddenly, Glo stumbled. I reached out to help her.

"Don't worry, Odelia. I just tripped over my own laces."

She crouched down on the pavement next to the dirt horse trail to tie the laces on her sneakers. Just as she did, I noticed something shiny on her wrist . . . something familiar. It was the exact same bracelet Sophie had, but in silver.

I dropped to my knees and seized Glo's wrist.

"Where in the hell did you get this?" I demanded, holding onto her tightly.

"I . . . uh . . . Blaine gave it to me . . . this weekend," she said in a halting voice. "It's our anniversary."

This weekend, my XXL ass. I had seen it before on Glo's wrist, but now the distinctive style meant something to me. With a wrench of her arm, I turned her wrist over to get a good look at the charm.

"Owww, Odelia, you're hurtin' me."

I ignored her and read the disk. It was engraved with two sets of initials, just as Sophie's had been, but this charm had *JH* on one side, *BS* on the other. Hollowell was recycling bracelets again. Only this time, he didn't even bother changing the charm.

"You're one of Hollowell's fat sluts," I said, using Clarice's term. My voice was low, filled with disbelief.

Glo said nothing, but looked at me in the most peculiar way. Gone was the self-effacing naiveté, gone was the panic; in its place was hatred as concrete and solid as a freeway overpass. The face was the same, but the person I was looking at was not the same Gloria Kendall I knew. Momentary fear pulsed through me like an electrical current.

This new Glo quickly looked around, searching up and down the path.

I shook off my initial surprise and fright. "What do you know about Sophie's murder?" I asked in a tone so harsh I surprised myself.

She remained silent as she brought her eyes in contact with my own. Again, I felt fear try to take hold. Instead of giving into it, I gave Glo's wrist another hard twist. She squealed in pain and reached over with her other hand to try and pry my iron grip from her wrist.

"Tell me," I demanded, "or I swear I'll beat it out of you." I raised a hand to strike her. "Tell me!"

Another transformation took place in Glo Kendall. As I twisted her arm, she started to sob. It came out in little mewing whimpers, growing in volume, and her face returned to the softness I was used to seeing.

"Tell me," I demanded as I slapped her face hard, my stomach buckling as my flesh struck another's in anger for the first time in my life.

"It was an accident," she said, choking on her tears. "We didn't mean for her to pull the trigger. Honest. We were just tryin' to scare her."

"Who's we? You and Hollowell?"

She shook her head. Her crying grew louder. "No, me and Blaine. It was his idea. He wanted Sophie's customers."

"You're screwing guys for Hollowell?"

She dropped her head low. "John Hollowell got me my job at Dakota. In return, I did him every now and then." She was sniveling, not looking at me. "Then John told me I could make some real money entertaining his customers. We really needed the cash, so I said yes. Blaine knew about it. We did okay, helped pay the bills, but nothin' great. John said that Sophie had all the really rich customers. When he told us how much money she made, Blaine got kinda crazy."

Drunk with outrage, I raised my hand again. After a split second of hesitation, I lowered it slowly. It just wasn't in me to batter anyone into submission. With my free hand, I grabbed the front of her windbreaker and shook her hard.

"Sophie helped you, you little ingrate. She befriended you, cleaned you up, gave you hope." Tears flowed down my cheeks in half anger, half heartbreak. "We all trusted you, Glo."

"I know. I'm so sorry." She let out a wail and covered her face with her other hand, the one I wasn't holding in a death grip. "I swear, we didn't know she'd do it. Blaine thought we should threaten her son, you know, just to scare her."

"You threatened her son?" I asked, my mouth hanging open in surprise. "You didn't even know she had a son until I told you the other day while walking."

Glo swallowed hard. "I lied. I knew she had a son. John Hollowell told me once. So Blaine told her that if she didn't get out of the business and turn her customers over to me, he'd kill her son."

She looked at me for the first time since I'd pounced on her. Her face was swollen and splotchy, but something was still amiss. Somehow, I couldn't see Hollowell talking to Glo Kendall about Robbie, not even if he didn't tell her the boy was his. But Hollowell had bragged and been caught on tape, so maybe he would talk to a mistress after a few drinks.

"What did Blaine say to her?" I asked, still full of rage. "Tell me exactly, then remember it, because you're going to repeat it to the police word for word."

"What's going on here?" asked a voice from several feet away.

I looked up. It was a jogger, running in place.

"Nothing," I snapped at a guy wearing red running shorts and a black tank top. "Just found out my friend here's been screwing my husband."

He shook his head in disgust and went on his way.

Glo swallowed. Her nose was runny with slimy mucous. I gave her another hard shake to get her started again.

She let out another wail and reluctantly continued. "Blaine said he'd tell her son she was a whore, then he'd kill him. But no matter what Blaine said, Sophie refused to cooperate. Just kept sayin' over and over that she didn't know what we were talkin' about, that she had no son and no customers."

"You've been had, Glo," I said with bitter sarcasm, "and in more ways than one. Sophie hadn't worked for Hollowell in a long time. He told you that crap to hook you in to his disgusting world. What else did Blaine say to her? What happened to make Sophie pull the trigger?"

Glo stared at me and said nothing. I gave her wrist another turn, this time cranking the whole arm behind her back. She screamed.

"Tell me the truth, Glo."

"It was all her fault!" she yelled. "She's the one who pulled a gun on Blaine and pissed him off. She shouldn't have done that. She pulled a gun out of a drawer, but Blaine saw her do it and pulled his out first."

The words spilled out of her like vomit.

"Blaine went nuts thinkin' she was tryin' to kill him. He's got a crazy temper. He almost shot Sophie right there and then. Instead, he told her the deal had changed. Now she'd have to die. Her life for the boy's. When she didn't back down, he made up all sorts of gory details about how he was gonna kill the boy." She started sobbing loudly again. "He didn't mean it. He was just tryin' to *scare* her!"

"Yeah, sure." I let her go, throwing her down onto the dirt trail. "So the kid from the security company saw you that morning?"

She rubbed her wrist and nodded. Moving toward me slowly, Glo held a hand out in supplication.

"Please, Odelia, help me. I didn't mean to hurt Sophie. I loved her."

"You sang 'The Lord's Prayer' at her service, Glo," I said in a small voice lost in tears. "You sang, knowing that you'd killed her." I felt drained, old, and broken. "How could you?"

Wearily, I started to get up. It was time to drag her sorry ass back up the trail to my car. Frye could take it from there.

"You gotta believe me, Odelia," Glo begged.

Unable to stand the sight of her, I turned and walked a few paces away from where she huddled on the ground.

"It was an accident," she whined. "We would never harm Jonathan."

We both must have realized her slip at the same time because just as my eyebrows shot up and I spun around, something whizzed by, nicking my shoulder. I looked to the side to see torn fabric, then I felt a sharp sting turning to pain. I clutched my shoulder and blood appeared, staining my heavy T-shirt.

Frozen by shock, I looked at Glo. She had gotten to her knees and was facing me. Her right hand was in the pocket of her windbreaker and the pocket had a big hole in it. I stood still, numbed by disbelief, as she rose to her feet. Slowly, she pulled her hand and the gun out of her pocket. She waved it in the direction of a stand of trees and high shrubbery.

"Start walking, Odelia, slowly, in that direction," she commanded—without a Southern accent.

I put my hands up and started moving in the direction she'd indicated.

"Oh, for God's sake, Odelia, put your hands down." Glo laughed slightly. "I'm not robbing you, we're just going to have a little talk."

"Talk?" I asked. "Talk about what? How you and Blaine killed Sophie?"

"That's old news, Odelia. And for the record, Sophie died because she was stupid."

We reached the edge of the trees and she directed me into the grove a few feet. Once we were out of view of the trail, she told me to stop.

"Now," she said, standing a few feet away with the gun aimed at my ample gut, "let's see if you're smarter and more cooperative than Sophie."

"I don't understand, Glo," I said truthfully, my eyes glued to the barrel of the gun.

It was the first time I had ever seen a gun up close and personal. Needless to say, it was making me nervous. Perspiration broke out on my forehead and upper lip. It trickled down the side of my face like hot fudge over a scoop of ice cream. I wanted to wipe it away with my sleeve, but didn't dare.

"I don't know anything about Sophie's business with Hollowell. I found out about it after she died," I said, trying to keep panic out of my voice.

Glo laughed. "I believe you, Odelia. But it's not the sex business I'm talking about. That was just to throw you off to buy me time when you surprised me this morning. What I really want is information about her son."

"Her son?" I asked in disbelief.

"Yes, her son. More importantly, I want to know about John Hollowell's son."

"I still don't understand."

Glo rolled her eyes in disgust. "Blaine should've clubbed you harder Friday night. Just like one of them fat baby seals everyone gets worked up over."

She took two steps closer and raised the gun so it was aimed at my chest. Forget the sweating; now I had to pee.

"Don't play dumb, Odelia," Glo said to me. She twitched her up-turned nose. "Tell me where I can find Hollowell's son and I'll let you go."

I didn't believe that for a minute. "What does her son have to do with anything?" I asked.

"I just want to know how to reach him, that's all." She purred the words sweetly, almost slipping into her phony Southern accent in an attempt to sway me. For a moment, I got a glimpse of the Glo Kendall we all knew.

"If Sophie wouldn't tell you, why should I?" My voice was getting thick. I cleared my throat. "That's what happened, isn't it? Sophie wouldn't tell you anything about her son. She knew you were going to hurt him, maybe even kill him. But why?"

"We asked her nicely, Odelia, we really did," she explained, ignoring my question. "But she wouldn't talk." Evil Glo smirked. "She even tried to deny that she had a son. Finally, we just had to threaten her. When she pulled her gun on us, we had to let her know we meant business. Blaine didn't just tell her what we were going to do to the boy, he told her what we were going to do to her to make her talk. That's when the stupid bitch shot herself."

So, I thought to myself, for the second and final time, Sophie killed herself to protect Robbie. I felt tears sting my eyes and clutched my searing shoulder, but it wasn't my physical pain that was making me cry.

"So, Odelia, tell me about John and Sophie's son and I'll let you go," Glo said, sweet as pie. "Otherwise, you'll just have to join Sophie. The two of you can shop the big mall in the sky together." She laughed.

"This time, Glo, everyone will know it's murder," I said, trying to keep my voice steady. "There'll be no doubt."

She adjusted her grip on the gun and took aim.

"But why, Glo?" I asked in earnest. "Sophie only wanted to help you." Soon it wouldn't matter why, but I needed to buy some time.

"An eye for an eye, Odelia. It's as simple as that."

"Revenge?" I moved my foot slightly, shifting my weight from one leg to another. My shoulder still hurt but I was beginning to get used to it. "This is about revenge? What did Sophie ever do to you except help you?"

"Sophie never did anything to me. She was just plain stupid—a casualty of war, you might say."

"Like the security guy?"

She shrugged. "Hey, Glenn Thomas had already killed for John Hollowell, so why not for someone else?"

I looked at her incredulously. "You made Glenn Thomas kill Danny Ortiz? But how?"

Bad Glo grinned. "It was easier than you think. You see, I know all about John Hollowell's evil deeds, even those from twenty years ago. I know who, what, when, and where; everything but where his son is."

My brain shushed the pain in my arm so it could think. Suddenly, a piece of the puzzle, the piece lost on the floor under the table, was found. The bracelet . . . a silver bracelet with the initials *BS* . . . could mean Bonnie Sheffley. They sure didn't stand for Gloria Kendall and I quickly ruled out *bull shit*. But Glo couldn't be Bonnie, she wasn't old enough.

"How do you know Bonnie Sheffley, Glo?" I asked, forgetting the gun and looking straight into her eyes.

She looked straight back, her eyes as hollow and cold as the end of the gun pointing at me.

"Bonnie Sheffley was my mother."

TWENTY-NINE

ALTHOUGH I HALF EXPECTED her to say that, the shock of actually hearing it nearly knocked me off my feet. I staggered back a few steps.

"Careful, Odelia," Glo said, realigning her aim. "You wouldn't want me to think you're trying something."

"But I thought Bonnie was . . . I mean, she's been gone a long time."

"You mean, you thought she was sold into white slavery by John Hollowell, and she was. My mother had me when she was in high school. I don't know who my father is. She stashed me with her grandmother in Hemet when she went to work for the Hollowells as a live-in nanny. One day she came to visit me and gave me this." Glo indicated the bracelet. "She said she was going away to marry a very rich man and soon she'd send for me. She was so excited. She actually believed that scumbag Hollowell had arranged a marriage for her with a wealthy older man overseas. We never heard from my mother again. Grammy tried calling the Hollowells to see if they knew where she was, but got nowhere."

Her voice started to crack. She sniffed, cleared her throat, and continued.

"About three years ago, my mother showed up in Hemet out of the blue. Her grandmother was dead and I was living in her trailer with Blaine. My mother was half crazy and a diseased drug addict when she finally came home. A year later she died."

"If you want revenge, why not kill Hollowell? Why his son?" I asked as I cautiously shifted my weight again. My lower back was starting to hurt more than my shoulder from standing still so long.

"I told you, Odelia, an eye for an eye. That's why." She wiped her face with her free hand. "I want that bastard to suffer. Killing him outright is too good for him."

I couldn't argue with that.

"Before she died, my mother told me everything. She told me how Hollowell got his company, how he was blackmailing his wife and her brother, and about Sophie and Hollowell's bastard son. She learned a lot living in that house, listening to the fights that went on constantly. She even told me about Jonathan and her role in his death, and how Hollowell had promised to marry her as soon as he divorced his wife, then changed his mind and found her a rich husband instead. There was no rich husband, of course, just a pimp a hundred times worse than Hollowell." Glo coughed her smoker's cough.

"The last year of her life my mother spent in confession, with me as her confessor. When she died, I decided whatever it took, I would get back at Hollowell for what he did to my mother." Her voice faltered, but Glo cleared her throat and continued. "My mother told me all about Sophie London, so I checked her out and found out about Reality Check. I took on Blaine's accent and made up a story about moving here from Tennessee. I figured it was just a matter of time before I found out about her son, but as the months dragged on, I got antsy to get it over with, so Blaine and I decided to force her to talk."

Glo paused, then took a step forward. "Now, Odelia, where can I find Hollowell's son?"

I took a step back, then another. Twigs cracked under my feet and low shrubs brushed my legs. I shook my head slowly.

"Come on, Odelia," Glo said, again wiping her face. "Tell me and then you can go home and get ready for work. It's that easy."

Without a word, I slowly backed up through the scrub another few steps. Glo moved forward, matching my pace. A small animal scurried over her trespassing feet, spooking her. She gave a short, low squeal.

As soon as I saw her falter, I moved as fast as my fat, middle-aged body could go straight at her . . . and tackled her as if a Super-bowl ring was at stake.

Upon impact, the gun flew from her hand and we tumbled into the dense growth. Her arms and legs wrapped around me like a python. I struggled to free myself, but it was difficult. With every move I was dragging her two-hundred-pound bulk around like dead weight.

I fought like a madwoman. My heart was pounding, my breath coming in short gulps. I thrashed around in her arms until I managed to turn over, taking her with me. We rolled over and over, through the prickly brush, coming to a halt under a low-hanging tree with me on top, our faces inches from each other. Glo looked frightened, understanding that she'd lost control. In the rolling her legs had come free. My weight was pinning her down. Still, she had a tight grip on me.

Freeing an arm, I grabbed her hair and started pounding her head against the hard earth. This was life and death. Suddenly, I wasn't squeamish about smacking her around. I keep raising her head and slamming it against the ground until she let go of me.

Just as I disentangled myself and got off of her, Glo tripped me. She scrambled to her feet and leveled a hard kick to my ribs as I was trying to find my own footing. I went sprawling back into the dirt and almost passed out from the pain.

Shaking my head to clear it, I saw Glo scurrying through the brush on her hands and knees. Even in hazy pain, it only took me a second to realize she was looking for the gun.

Taking off through the maze of low branches and thick brush, I ran wildly. My legs were being torn by sharp undergrowth. My chest heaved. Even with the regular walking, I wasn't in very good shape. I was exhausted, my side felt shattered, and my head hurt where I'd been hit just a few days before. I made a dive into a thicket of dense growth, hoping for cover to give me time to rest.

I head footsteps coming closer and willed my breathing to slow down, to be quiet. Soon the steps retreated and headed in another direction. With as much stealth as I could manage, I started crawling deeper into the bushes on my stomach, mud smearing my clothes and body. Small critters scattered. Slowly, I got up onto my feet but kept crouched close to the ground. I could hardly make a dash for my life on my belly, and I'd be damned if I'd die in the slime, inching along like a snail.

Die! I might die. My body began shaking. I commanded it to stop and surprisingly it did. I had to keep alert.

Gently pulling apart some branches, I peeked out to see Glo methodically walking through the bushes. Here and there she kicked aside undergrowth. The gun was held ready in her hand. She was dirty from our earlier tumble. Her face, tracked with tears mingled with dirt, reminded me of a stone gargoyle.

"Come out, come out, wherever you are," she taunted as she walked. Frustrated, she moved away from my hiding place and headed in the opposite direction, searching new patches of dense shrubbery.

It was now or never.

Just up ahead I could see the trail again. It wasn't far, maybe a few yards. It was also in the open, where I had a better chance of people seeing me and helping. Where I was now, I could be killed and my body hidden for days. To my right, the overgrowth ended and an embankment, naked and raw with erosion, plunged downward.

I looked again. The trail was above me, close but up a slight incline, which would slow my getaway.

A shot was fired. It hit the dirt a few yards from my feet. I ran like hell for the trail, screaming the whole way to draw attention.

Just as I reached the hard, packed dirt of the horse trail, there was another shot. I pitched forward, then wobbled backward and staggered down the incline. A few missteps later and I was headed down the embankment. Scorching pain radiated down my left leg, and I knew I'd been hit.

On my back in scrub still damp with morning dew, I did a quick check. Nothing vital had been hit, but my left side from my hip down was screaming violation and every move was torture. Rolling over onto my stomach, I scrunched as close to the ground as I could, flattening myself against the side of the slope. Slowly, I started moving sideways and down, trying to get away from the trail above. I couldn't see anyone, but she was up there. I could hear her heavy smoker's cough brought on by the exertion.

Pain or no pain, I made my way down the steep embankment like an upside-down crab. With each movement of my left side, I bit my lip. Below me were marshy shallows and another trail, a small dirt nature trail. *Not much farther, Odelia, you can do it,* I told myself. My chest ached, my breathing was shallow. *Faster, girl, faster.* Then I looked up and turned to stone.

Standing above me was Glo Kendall. A sick grin stretched grotesquely across her filthy face. One hand clutched a gun, and that gun was pointed down the embankment directly at my head.

I closed my eyes tight and thought of my father.

"Police," someone nearby shouted. It was a woman's voice.

My eyes popped open at the sound, and I looked back up the slope. Glo Kendall still held her gun, but it was no longer pointed at the top of my head. Now she had it aimed at someone on the trail, someone out of my line of vision.

Again, someone yelled "police," this time followed by other words I couldn't make out.

The shot from Glo's gun rang loud and angry, defiling the clean morning air. Then I heard a blast from another direction. I watched as Glo teetered at the edge of the trail above, the gun still in her hand. Then she lifted her arm and re-aimed down the trail. I heard a shot, answered instantaneously by another. Glo turned and staggered, then dropped down the slope, plunging toward me. I tried to move out of the way, but my injury prevented it. Her body struck mine and together we tumbled down, coming to rest on level ground near the marsh.

Her weight was resting on my left side. The pain was so intense I thought I would die from it. I tried to move her off me, fearing she would come to and decide to finish me off with her bare hands. Finally,

I managed to roll her over. I gasped. Blood covered her windbreaker in the middle of her chest. Her eyes were open, her mouth slack.

Everything was spinning, drowning me in dizziness. The pain didn't matter anymore.

THIRTY

THE FLOWERS FILLED THE sterile hospital room with springtime and my friends filled it with love. If my ass didn't hurt so much, I'd actually enjoy my situation.

Since I was positioned on my side, both Greg and Zee crowded on the same side of my bed. Each looked appropriately worried, yet relieved. They'd both been here the day before when I'd had surgery to remove the bullet from my left buttock. So had my father. Even Mike Steele showed up with a huge bouquet and asked when I'd be back at work.

I must have passed out yesterday. The last thing I remember was being sprawled at the bottom of the slope with Glo Kendall's dead body. When I came to, Ruth Wise was kneeling over me, checking me for injuries. So much of Glo's blood was on me, it had taken her a while to realize that most of it wasn't mine.

I'd been shot in the bottom, the bullet lodging in my blubbery behind, but thankfully not penetrating deep enough to hit any bones and cause serious damage. I'd also been grazed on the right shoulder.

Once again, call me lucky. But I was more than lucky, I was blessed.

"The doctor said you might be able to leave the hospital tomorrow," Zee said. "If not then, the day after." She got up and nervously fussed with my covers. My experience had dropped her into a mode of frenzied care-giving.

"Yes," I said, giving her half a smile. I was still on painkillers and enjoying it as much as possible.

A knock came at my door. "Hello?" someone called in. It was the Olsens, Peter and Marcia. Surprised, I waved them in.

"When we heard, we just had to come," Marcia said, her smile barely masking her worry.

Greg wheeled out of the way. The Olsens stepped forward. Marcia leaned over and kissed my cheek. Peter patted my hand. Zee and Greg introduced themselves. Marcia was holding a large tin, which she placed on the nightstand.

"My mother sent these for you," Marcia told me. "They're cookies, all her best recipes."

News had traveled fast. I was shot yesterday and already today I'd had lots of visitors, most bearing gifts. And it was only the middle of the afternoon. I was truly touched.

"Please tell Mrs. Pugh thank you for me," I told Marcia. "I'm sorry I didn't get to tell her myself."

"She and Robbie are minding the store," Peter said.

The room went quiet.

"Does Robbie know?" I asked quietly, as if the boy might be in the next room.

Marcia and Peter tossed each other looks. Hers was pleading, his tight and firm.

"Not yet," Marcia said. "But we're discussing it. After all, he's not a child, and John Hollowell may still stir up trouble."

"No need for him to ever know," Peter added in a low tone. "We can just send him away to finish school. Somewhere out of Hollowell's reach."

"How are you going to explain the money from Sophie's estate?" I asked. "It's about a million dollars."

Both Olsens looked at me with surprise. Peter Olsen's mouth hung open. Then, like a trap, he shut it.

"It's a difficult call, I know, and not mine to make," I said honestly. "But I do have one request."

Marcia squeezed my hand. "Anything, dear."

"I have Sophie's ashes. I'd like you to bury them at her grave in Santa Paula. No funeral or anything. I just want her to go home and be with her family, where she belongs."

Again, all was still, then Peter said, "We can do that." His eyes were sad and damp. "Least we can do, considering she died twice to save Robbie."

The rest of the visit was pleasant and gave me a chance to study the Olsens. They seemed a happy couple and well suited to each other. Sophie may have been Peter's passion, but Marcia was his mate, both in soul and heart. It was easy to see it in the way he looked at her and held her hand. On their way out, they almost bumped into Detective Frye. He stopped them and directed them back into the room.

"I have some news," he announced. "And it's something you folks will want to know, too."

All eyes expectantly turned to him.

A nurse came in just as he started to speak. It was someone I hadn't seen before. "There are entirely too many people in this room," she said with authority.

Frye flashed his badge. "Just a few minutes, please. Then we'll thin out the crowd."

The nurse eyed the badge, then me, with more than a fair amount of curiosity. With a disapproving look, she left.

"John Hollowell is dead," Frye announced bluntly after the nurse departed.

Peter Olsen put an arm around his wife. Zee gasped. Greg caught my eye. He looked surprised but not heartbroken. I felt the same.

Frye continued. "His car was found abandoned near Camp Pendleton. He was in the trunk, trussed, and shot in the head execution style. Looks like a professional hit."

Peter was the first to speak. "Can't say that I'm sorry, Detective."

Frye nodded somberly, but said nothing.

Hollowell was dead. Did I feel sorry about it? To be truthful, no. But I felt I should be. Just over two weeks ago I might have been. Three weeks ago, I would have mourned the loss of any life, even that of a killer's, thinking of it as a waste of a precious gift. Today, I only had sympathy for his victims. I had changed a lot in a short time.

After more goodbyes, the Olsens left to drive back to Santa Paula.

"We found Blaine Kendall," Frye said after the Olsens left. "Apparently, he and his wife had a major argument yesterday morning before she hooked up with you. She shot him and left him for dead. Fortunately for him, we got to their place right after Glo Kendall was killed."

Frye paused and took out a pack of gum. He offered it around. Zee took a stick but was too nervous to unwrap it. It slipped from her fingers onto the bed. I picked it up and removed the foil for her. When I held it out to her, she collapsed into a nearby chair in tears. Greg rolled over and put his arms around her. She cried into his shoulder.

"His story matches what she told you, Odelia," Frye said, continuing. "And it was Blaine Kendall who stole Ms. London's hard drive and assaulted you and Iris Somers. When they read that she had shot herself over the Internet, they worried that they had been caught on camera, too. Blaine Kendall has a criminal record back in Tennessee, mostly assault and burglary. It's a long one, starting when he was a kid, but nothing hardcore. Glo Kendall's record was clean, except for some minor things when she was a teenager. They hooked up a few years ago when Blaine moved to California."

"You think they killed Hollowell?" Greg asked.

Frye shook his head. "Doubt it. Bullet didn't match Kendall's gun. And, like I said, the hit was professional, very sophisticated and well planned. Not at all the work of a small-time criminal."

Another mystery, I thought, but this one I didn't care about.

"What about Iris?" I asked. "Any improvement?"

"She's stabilized," Frye told us with another slow shake of his head. "But still in a coma. May be for a long time. Her family is going to fly her back to Maryland and get care for her there."

"Every time I think that the same thing could've happened to you . . . ," Zee started to say, trailing her words off. Greg gave her a comforting squeeze.

"But it didn't, Zee," I said, trying to comfort her myself. "It didn't and I'm going to be fine. Better than ever."

She smiled at me. Zee Washington has a beautiful smile, large and glorious, and today it did more for me than the painkillers.

"Takes more than a bullet in my ass to get me down," I assured her. "Although I am concerned about the surgery. Will one side of my butt be shaped differently now? You know, flatter? Bad enough I have a huge behind without it being lopsided."

Everyone laughed.

Zee wiped her eyes and nose with a nearby tissue. "You'll just have to get liposuction to even it out."

Laughing, Greg left Zee and wheeled closer to me. "I have to go back to work, sweetheart. I'll see you later tonight." We both leaned over, meeting halfway for a nice, sweet kiss.

"I'll go with you, Greg," Zee told him. "I need to get home before the kids start rolling in." She gave me a quick kiss on my forehead, promising to come back later with Seth and the kids.

After they left, Frye milled about.

"Alone at last," I joked.

He smiled wearily as he pulled up a chair next to my bed and sat down. He stuck another piece of gum in his mouth. I could tell he was only half with me.

"Your wife still here?" I asked in a gentle voice, my joking gone.

"Yes, but they're releasing her in a few hours."

"That's wonderful."

"For now," he said, his voice distant. "At least until the next time. My daughter's coming by to help take her home."

I shifted in the bed, my good side getting tired of supporting my weight. I had two options . . . my side or my stomach. But it was difficult to visit with people floundering on my tummy like a beached whale.

"She's going to die soon," Frye said sadly but frankly, "in a year or two the doctors say, maybe less. Hard to say with these things. I just hope it's sooner than later. She's been in a lot of pain for a long time."

"I'm sorry, Detective. Kind of puts my butt wound in its proper perspective."

"That wasn't my purpose in telling you that, Odelia," he said, running his hands over his tired face. "And I shouldn't be unloading on you like this." He looked at me and gave me a small, tired smile. "And please call me Dev."

"No problem, Dev," I said, smiling back. "And thank you. You've been there for me these last few weeks. Smart of you to plant that policewoman in our group. Ruth was literally a lifesaver."

Frye leaned forward, resting his elbows on his knees, hands clasped in front of him. I could smell the spearmint from his gum.

"I have a confession, Odelia."

I waited, wondering what was left to tumble my world. Was the big and burly Frye really the emaciated Clarice Hollowell in disguise? At this point, nothing would surprise me.

"Ruth wasn't on assignment," he said. "She's with the Tustin PD. She was there as a personal favor to me, keeping tabs on you and the group on her own time. I had a hunch either that something might turn up within Reality Check or that the killer might be targeting the group."

"That's some favor."

"Well, Ruth owes me," he said, winking. "She's my daughter."

THIRTY-ONE

DOROTHY IN *THE WIZARD of OZ* was right, there's no place like home. Didn't matter how humble, or where, or even if it was a farm in the middle of twister country, home was home . . . period. There's also nothing like the sandpaper tongue of your very own avocado green cat licking your chin at five in the morning either.

After being discharged from the hospital, I went to stay at Casa de Washington for a few days. It was nice, though Zee killed me with excessive care, the kids drove me around the bend with questions, and Seth did me in with lectures and warnings.

It's so nice to be loved.

Jacob was tasked with riding his bike over to my place every day to feed and play with poor Seamus. He wanted to bring him home but his dad, allergic to cats, nixed the idea. Greg had offered to take him while I convalesced, but I didn't think that was a good option either. I planned on getting Seamus and Wainwright together again, but only when I was there to referee. Greg is more than capable of taking care of himself and running a successful business, but a wheelchair is no match for a headstrong feline in a catch-me-if-you-can mood.

Per doctor's orders, I could return back to work two weeks after the shooting. That time would be up in four days, and I was looking forward to returning to the grind. Being away from work gave me too much time to think about everything that had happened. Mostly, I thought about Sophie.

Sophie London, my friend, was in the sex business. That was a fact. Zee and I discussed this, as did Greg and I. I understood how she got into the lifestyle, just not why she stayed so long. It could have been for a multitude of reasons, but we'll never really know. Greg had said that Sophie got an emotional lift from the website. The members, as well as the others who paid her and showered her with gifts, had accepted and adored her just as she was. To them she wasn't fat, stupid, lazy, or slovenly—all the attributes usually assigned to the overweight. In their eyes, she was womanly perfection.

Honestly, that would be enough to tempt me.

Reality Check would go on, with me at the helm. We had a meeting last night at Zee's. It was the first one since Sophie's death. Almost all of our regular supporters were there. They had come out in droves to voice their support of the group, its work, and me. It had been an emotional and overwhelming evening.

It was agreed that I should pick up and carry on the work begun by Sophie. I consented, but not because of any sense of obligation to Sophie's memory. Reality Check was capable of creating change—woman by woman, life by life. It was a chain reaction with an exciting future.

In the end, I did it for me.

After parking my car under one of the few shade trees in the parking lot of Fashion Island, I walked into the open-air mall. My wounded haunch was still stiff and sore, but it felt good to move and exercise it.

Hannah Washington's eighteenth birthday was Sunday. Seth and Zee were having a birthday brunch for the family and close friends. While recovering at their house, Hannah had dropped numerous hints about an outfit she wanted. Unfortunately, it was at the dreadful store where I'd last been humiliated. Zee told me to get her something else, but I said no. What are aunties for? Especially honorary aunties who'd just had a near-death experience.

I walked into the uptight establishment, telling myself to just buy the item and leave. Making my way to the young women's department, I spotted the skirt and matching top almost immediately and easily found the color and size Zee had given me. So far, so good.

The cash register island was just a few steps away. Manning it was the same girl who had sneered at me the last time, the charming Jody. Sheesh, what were the odds?

She was standing with another clerk who wore so much dark eye makeup she looked like she'd just been released from the clutches of the underworld. The two were chattering away. I placed the garments on the counter and waited to be helped. Both salesclerks glanced my way, then turned their backs to me, continuing their conversation.

Another customer walked up. From her skin, I guessed her to be close to my age, but she was dressed like a teenager in an immodestly short skirt and a tight top showing off unnaturally perky breasts. Around her neck hung pounds of gold. Her hair was dyed blond and worn very long, down past her shoulders. Immediately, the two clerks stopped talking. The one with the heavy eye goop left, while my favorite clerk turned to help the aging Barbie doll.

Impatiently, I shifted my weight to my good side and waited. Snide comments were waiting in line inside my mouth, eager to be released. *Be nice,* I told myself. *Don't agitate yourself for no good reason.*

The customer and Jody were knee deep into a conversation about which designer was still in and which was—God forbid— passé. I looked around for the other clerk, but she'd disappeared. Probably attending a séance on her break. I scanned the place for another nearby cash register, but noticed none. Guess the stuff was free.

Finally, Jody rang up the woman's purchases. I scooted Hannah's birthday present across the glass counter in her direction. She looked at the garments, then proceeded to help two bubbly young women who had just walked up. Jody greeted them like old friends. I stopped her.

Ignore me once, shame on you. Ignore me twice, look out.

"Excuse me, but I was next," I told her pleasantly, with a smile even.

Jody rolled her eyes at me. "You'll just have to wait your turn." She turned back to the young women, whispering something. They all giggled.

"I don't think so," I said, pushing the garments closer to her. "I've been standing here all along and you know it. I was even here before that last customer."

She cast a sneer my way. "So what, Orca. Shop somewhere else if you don't like it." They all giggled.

I gave the two young customers a look that made them back up, telling Jody they'd see her later. As they retreated, I eased my bulk over, positioning it to the side of the cashier area, right next to Jody. My butt hurt like hell, making me dangerously close to insane.

"I'm shopping here and I'm shopping now," I said in an even tone, locking eyes with the insolent brat. "So why don't you just call your supervisor over and we'll get this problem squared away."

She picked up the garments and started sorting through them, looking for the tags, almost tearing the fabric in the process. I placed my hand on top of the clothing, stopping her.

"Get your supervisor," I told her again. "Now."

"She's not here."

"Then get her manager."

"He's not here either."

"So," I said, starting to enjoy the little game in spite of my physical discomfort, "you're telling me that you're the top dog in this large and noted establishment at this very moment?"

She looked at me with pure hatred, then I saw her glance in the direction of a professional and stylish-looking woman across the way in the next department. Something told me this was the elusive supervisor. And something about the way Jody looked at her told me that Jody feared her and possibly unemployment.

"That's your supervisor, isn't it?" I asked, indicating the woman and stepping even closer to Jody.

When Jody didn't say anything, I gently put my foot over the toes of one of her high-heeled clad feet and applied a teeny-weeny bit of pressure.

"Ow," she said and tried to pull her foot out from under mine, but I held it by applying more weight.

The woman across the way noticed us and took a few steps in our direction. She was dressed in an expensive and classy suit. She smiled at me, then looked at Jody. There was a slightly weary look in her glance at the clerk.

"Finding everything you need?" she asked me.

"Yes, thank you," I replied sweetly. "Jody here is showing me the care tags on this garment." My foot pressed down a little more and I felt the girl's body tense. "They put them in the oddest places these days, don't they?"

The woman gave me a gracious smile, then tossed a worried glance at Jody.

"I'm glad Jody is being so helpful," she said pointedly before wandering off.

"Jody," I said, once her supervisor was out of earshot, "the next time I come in here, I'm going to make sure I come to your register."

The girl looked at me with undisguised fright, the cockiness gone.

"No matter what I buy," I continued, "in fact, even if I'm just window shopping, every time I come into this store I'm going to seek you out to help me."

I gave her toes one last squish and released them. She let out the breath she was holding and hopped lightly on one foot.

"Remember, Jody, you are now my favorite clerk and I am now your worst nightmare . . . a customer who is too big to mess with."

THE END

"With a legendary curse, a possibly murderous little person, ruthless heirs, charismatic thugs and quick-change sex . . . a lively caper that will keep you guessing right till the end."

—Kris Neri, award-winning author
of the Tracy Eaton mysteries

"Even better than her first . . . a major hoot! Odelia is indeed a piece of work . . . lovably feisty, a lady with attitude, her own unique, entertaining take on the world, and a heart as big as her hips . . ."

—Thomas B. Sawyer, best-selling author
of *The Sixteenth Man*, former head writer/
producer of *Murder, She Wrote*

"You will laugh, you will cry, you will bite your nails."

—Sue Hartigan, *All About Murder Reviews*

The following excerpt is from the forthcoming Odelia Grey mystery *The Curse of the Holy Pail*, coming in February 2007.

BY THE AGE OF forty-seven, I had technically broken nine of the Ten Commandments. Although I'm still a bit fuzzy about the whole graven image thing. For example, when I was eleven, on a dare, I stole several candy bars from a drugstore. And in high school, telling the fifth-period gym class that Sally Kipman was a lesbian would definitely be categorized as bearing false witness. But in my defense, it was only after she told everyone I was fat because I was pregnant.

Still, I always thought that I would make it to heaven with the Sixth Commandment intact; that going through life without killing another human being would be a piece of cake.

But I was wrong. And now here I am . . . ten for ten.

And it all started with my birthday.

I was born to be middle-aged. It fits me like comfy flannel pajamas that are worn and washed until they are faded and thin; clothing with no eager need to prove anything or be something else . . . it just is.

Today is my birthday. As of two-seventeen this afternoon, I, Odelia Patience Grey, wandered into my forty-seventh year as absent-mindedly as someone who arrives at the supermarket only to realize that they really intended to go to the dry cleaners. I am comfortable with being forty-seven years of age and embrace it with enthusiasm.

I never felt young, not even when I was. When I was sixteen, my family claimed that I behaved more like a thirty-two-year-old. But it's easy to act older in a family suffering from arrested development. Given the choice, I would not go back and relive my life for anything. My time is now and, from the looks of it, getting better with each passing year, every marching month.

The evening news drifted in from the television in the bedroom. I listened as I pulled, stretched, and smoothed my round face into alternative looks. A female newscaster was giving a follow-up report on the shootings three days prior at a community center. Five people had been injured, including three children. Two later died. The shooter shot himself at the end, just before the police captured him. It had been a crime fueled by racial hate.

I stopped fussing with my face and looked into my eyes as they stared back from the mirror. The green was dulled with sadness. I could never understand how some people could treat life so cavalierly. Did they think that once the trigger was pulled, they could yell "cut" and their targets would magically resurrect like TV actors between scenes?

A deep sigh crossed my lips . . . a barely audible prayer for the victims and their families.

The news program was turned off. A moment later I felt a strong hand caress my fat behind through my slinky nightgown. As I leaned back into the warm palm, the hand stopped to cup the fullness, giving my bottom a familiar squeeze. I closed my eyes and smiled. This was love, and love always conquered hate.

"In some cultures," I said with sass, still not turning around, "you'd be forced to marry me after that."

"I think that's a sentence I could live with," my groper answered.

The fingers of his hand did a tickling tap dance on my left buttock and one finger lovingly found the slight indentation left by a bullet last year . . . a bullet fired by a killer hell bent on making me her next victim. Then the fingers went back to a loving caress. Since the shooting, Greg favored that side of my bottom. The hand on my butt moved up to encircle my thick waist and pull me close. Only then did I turn to look at him as he sat in his wheelchair next to where I stood.

I bent down and kissed him lightly on the lips, tasting something unusual but identifiable. "I can still taste the cigar you smoked tonight," I said, crinkling my nose. "No doubt you got it from Seth Washington."

Greg reached up his other hand and placed it on my other hip, turning me so that I fully faced him. "Don't blame Seth," he said, giving me his best puppy dog eyes, "I brought the cigars."

I bent down and kissed him again, this time a little longer and deeper, letting him know that I didn't really mind the cigar taste.

Greg had thrown me a birthday party tonight at one of our favorite Italian restaurants. Most of our friends had been there, including my closest friend Zenobia Washington, better known as Zee, and her husband Seth. Now it was just the two of us bedding down for the night at Greg's place . . . the best part of the day.

"Thank you for the party, Greg. It was wonderful."

"You're welcome, sweetheart," he said, taking one of my hands and kissing the palm. Holding it tightly, he turned the wheelchair and headed out the bathroom door, tugging me along. "Come to bed, Odelia, I have a big surprise for you."

I laughed. "I just bet you do."

If I had known that forty-seven was going to be this much fun, I would have done it years ago.

It is not against the law to be a nincompoop. If so, I would have a rap sheet as long as my arm.

Fortunately for me, no one was witnessing my most recent slide into childish stupidity and self-pity. I was wallowing alone like a pig in a mud puddle, or, in this case, in a tub of chocolate pudding the size of a child's small sand pail.

Now, there are comfort foods, and then there are comfort foods. This particular item was my supreme tranquilizing grub. I had other favorites, but they were mere bandages eaten to soothe minor emotional aches and pains. But this, the one I fondly call bucket-o-puddin', was akin to full-strength prescription-only drugs when it came to emotional eating.

When I was a little girl, my mother often made chocolate pudding. In those days, it came in a box and we cooked it on the stove. It began as a brown sugary powder that was mixed with whole milk and then stirred constantly over low heat. That was my job, the stirring. With a wooden spoon I would gently stir and stir and stir, making sure that the precious brown mud did not stick to the bottom of the pan and scorch.

The pudding brand was My-T-Fine. I understand it's still made today, but I haven't seen it in years. My-T-Fine chocolate fudge pudding is one of those happy childhood memories that have disappeared from my life without explanation, just as my mother did when I was about sixteen.

Normally, I'm not that fond of pre-made puddings, but not long ago I stumbled across a new brand in the supermarket and decided to give it a whirl. It tastes almost, but not quite, like my beloved My-T-Fine.

I was sitting on my sofa, knee deep into the bucket-o-puddin', watching the movie *Robin Hood, Prince of Thieves*. It's one of my all-time favorites. Not because it starred Kevin Costner, but because it boasted the British actor Alan Rickman cast as the Sheriff of Nottingham. I have a thing for Rickman. In my eyes, he is right up there with My-T-Fine chocolate pudding.

Sitting patiently on the floor to my left was Wainwright, Greg's golden retriever. Greg was out of town and I was doggie sitting. To my right, ensconced regally on the sofa beside me, was my big, sassy cat Seamus. About a year and a half ago, his fur was tinted green after being terrorized by some local preteen hooligans wielding food coloring. It's now back to its original champagne color, but I swear that every now and then I still see a hint of emerald in the sunlight. As I looked at my cat, he turned to look back with frank royal arrogance, leaving no doubt in my mind that cats have never forgotten they were once looked upon as gods.

After taking a big bite of pudding, I put a small glob on the spoon and fed it to Seamus. He licked it eagerly, almost as obsessed as his human mother. Knowing that chocolate was bad for dogs, I tossed Wainwright a Snausages treat from the bag resting on my lap. The animals seemed happy to join me in my comfort food binge.

The reason for this slide into chocolate sedation was the little black velvet box sitting on the coffee table in front of me. It was closed tight. Inside was a breathtaking diamond engagement ring.

Before leaving to attend a convention in Phoenix, Greg had asked me to marry him. He had popped the question in bed the night of my birthday, and was surprised and hurt when an eager reply did not gush forth immediately. We had talked about it into the wee hours of the morning, but I was still no closer to a decision. However, he had made it quite clear that he expected an answer when he got back Thursday, just four days from now. Truth is, I just wasn't sure. I mean, I love Greg and our relationship is wonderful, both physically and emotionally. But do we belong together for the long haul? That's the million-dollar question. As compatible as we are, I'm not sure that we want and need the same things to be happy over the next twenty or so years.

I put the dilemma and the pudding on hold long enough to shout at the TV. "Go ahead, Alan, cut out his heart with a spoon!"

"Hello," I barked into the phone.

"I would have thought your disposition would be at least a little better at home," the person on the other end commented.

Damn, it was Mike Steele, one of the attorneys from the office. Correction, the attorney I hated from the office. Michael R. Steele, Esquire, was the poster boy for arrogance.

Michael Steele is the firm's problem child, a real pain in the ass to everyone, overly demanding and rude. His redemption is his brilliance in the field of law. In that he is top notch. And while he does not like me any more than I like him, he, in turn, respects my knowledge and experience.

And here he was, calling me at home on a Sunday afternoon. Now I was really annoyed. This was beyond pudding therapy.

"What do you want, Steele?" I asked without ceremony.

He got to his purpose quickly. "I need you to stop in on Sterling Price tomorrow before coming to work. Take your notary stuff. He has some documents he wants notarized, in addition to giving you something to bring back to me. I told him you'd be happy to do it. Sounds like some simple acknowledgments."

"Gee, thanks, Steele, for asking me first," I said sarcastically.

Actually, I didn't mind, though I was not about to say that to Steele. I like Sterling Price. He is one of my favorite clients and his office is not too far out of my way. I just wanted to give Steele some grief for not checking with me first.

"He's expecting you at eight sharp," Steele said curtly, then hung up.

The corporate offices of Sterling Homes are located in Newport Beach just off of Von Karman. Unlike most buildings that house multi-million dollar businesses, it's a two-story sprawling structure with redwood trim and a peaked roof. Set back from the busy street and surrounded by park-like grounds that included lots of trees and picnic tables, it has an attractive yet artificially rustic appearance. The company had spent a great deal of money going for the mountain retreat theme, which I found to be both refreshing and disturbing plunked down in the middle of the sterile architecture of Orange County. I pulled into the entrance and followed the driveway as it wound around behind the building to a large parking lot. It was just a few minutes to eight and the parking lot was mostly empty.

Once through the main entrance, I approached the receptionist. After asking my name and checking her appointment book, she informed me with a smile that Mr. Price's office was upstairs and all the way down the hall to the left. He was expecting me, she said pleasantly, and, after having me sign in on a guest register, directed me to an area just past her desk where I had the choice of taking an elevator or stairs to the next floor. My body begged for the elevator, but since I had missed my usual morning walk, my conscience opted for the stairs.

Walking down the upstairs hall, I encountered no other employees. From a distance came the lonely sound of a single computer keyboard being put to use. It sounded like it was coming from the opposite direction. I found Price's office exactly where the receptionist had said it would be. The door was open. I poked my head in and saw Sterling Price busy at a small kitchenette that had been discretely hidden behind folding doors. I knocked gently on the doorjamb.

Price looked up and smiled. "Come on in, Odelia." He gestured toward a small conference table to the right side of the office. "Please have a seat. I won't be but a minute."

After placing my briefcase on the table, I unpacked my notary supplies and sat down to enjoy the view from the large picture windows that lined one wall. Price's office took up the whole end section of the second floor that looked out over the prettiest part of the grounds. From his office viewpoint, there was no sighting or even suggestion of the office buildings and traffic that hovered so close. Somehow I was sure that was not an accident.

I had never been here before. I had met Sterling Price many times, but usually in our office and once, recently, at Mr. Wallace's retirement party. He and my former boss were very old friends, having grown up together in Orange County when it was nothing more than miles and miles of orange groves. Like Mr. Wallace, Price was in his seventies. He was on the short side, a bit pudgy and slightly balding. He was also outgoing and charming. His brown eyes twinkled when he spoke and his laugh and good humor came easily. But his easygoing nature aside, the man had built an empire in the construction and sale of upscale housing developments, garnering critics and even enemies along the way, most notably among those concerned with the disappearance of Orange County's natural wildlife and vegetation.

The other walls of his office were lined with attractive bookcases, many with glass doors. Here and there, a painting or a grouping of framed photographs interrupted the shelving. I scanned the shelves from where I sat and then did a double take of the glassed-in units.

"Would you like some coffee, Odelia? I just made a fresh pot, a special blend I make myself every morning . . . a combination of French Roast and Sumatra."

"No, thank you, Mr. Price."

"You don't know what you're missing," he said teasingly as he waved the pot at me. It was less than half full.

With one deep sniff of the rich aroma, I caved. "Sure, if you have enough. Black, please."

He gave me a not-to-worry gesture and poured some for me. "This was the end of a bag," he said, "but I'm sure there's more stashed away. Carmen never leaves me coffee impaired." We both laughed.

He carried two navy blue mugs emblazoned with the Sterling logo in bold silver to the conference table and settled into a chair to my right. The coffee smelled wonderful and tasted even better. A big improvement over what awaited me at my office.

"And please, Odelia, call me Sterling. Goodness, we've known each other many years now," he said smiling. He lifted his mug up and took a big whiff of the rich steam before continuing. "My staff usually comes in around nine o'clock. I wanted to get this taken care of before I got buried in my daily routine," he explained between sips of coffee. "Thank you so much for coming here before going to your own office."

"It was no trouble at all . . . uhhhh . . . Sterling," I said, trying on his first name like a pair of narrow shoes. He smiled again. "Happy to do it for you. I'm just surprised that your assistant isn't a notary with you being in real estate development."

"Carmen is a notary, but she's taking a few vacation days off this week. Actually, we have a couple of notaries on our staff but these papers are personal." He looked at me directly. "I'm sure you understand."

And I did. There was nothing like tidbits of the boss' personal life to fuel lunchroom gossip. It was the same in law firms.

My attention kept going back to the items behind the glass doors. "Um, are those lunchboxes?" I asked, pointing in a very unladylike way to the items on the shelves across the room.

Price looked over to where I indicated and gave a hearty laugh. "Yes, as a matter of fact they are. I collect them. Have for years." I must have had a puzzled look on my face because he laughed again. "When we're done here, I'll give you a tour of my collection."

"If you have time," I said politely. "I don't want to take up too much of your morning."

"Nonsense." He gave me one of his twinkling looks. "Besides, I never miss a chance to show them off, especially the jewel of my collection."

We finalized the papers quickly. The notarizations were simple acknowledgments just as Mike Steele had said they would be. Then Price indicated a couple of good sized stacks of expanding folders.

"I need Mike to go through these documents. No rush. But I'll have them sent over later. They're too much for you to carry."

I nodded my appreciation of his courtesy. Mike Steele, on the other hand, would have just loaded me up like a pack mule in a mining camp.

"I'm glad you're still working with Mike, Odelia," he said as I packed up my briefcase.

Well, that makes one of us, I thought.

"I'm sure he's no picnic to work under," Price added, much to my surprise.

Suddenly, I wondered if I had slipped and verbalized my comment, but I was pretty sure I had not.

"But he's a brilliant attorney and needs someone like you to keep him organized and in line."

"I do my best," I told him honestly, trying to keep sarcasm out of my tone.

"God knows you did wonders with Dell," he said, chuckling, referring to Wendell Wallace. "Now come along and let me show you one of the world's best lunchbox collections. Just leave your things there."

Following his instructions, I left my stuff on the conference table and followed him over to the glass cases where there were, indeed, lunchboxes—dozens of them. The shelves were filled with colorful metal boxes, most of which were adorned with pictures of cartoon characters, comic book heroes and TV legends. They brought back memories, and I recognized many of the boxes childhood friends had carried to school every day.

"I didn't realize people collected old lunchboxes," I said in amazement.

"My dear, where have you been?" he teased. "It's a very popular hobby, especially among men. And it can be increasingly expensive as the years go by and these boxes become even rarer."

"Which one was your first?"

He smiled broadly and opened up a glass door to remove one particular lunchbox. It looked well used, with small dents and scratches. Adorning the front, back and sides were scenes from the TV show *Gunsmoke*. On the box's front was Marshall Matt Dillon, jaw set and gun drawn. Price held the box lovingly, almost cradling it.

"This was my son Eldon's lunchbox when he was a boy," he explained. "He loved anything with a cowboy theme, particularly this TV show."

Something struck me as off. I racked my brain but could not remember a son named Eldon. In fact, I could have sworn Sterling Price's son was named Kyle. I had just seen the name Kyle Price on some of the documents I notarized. A son named Kyle and a daughter named Karla—twins; that's what my middle-aged memory bank was dredging up.

"I didn't realize you had another son."

Price looked at the lunchbox as he spoke, his voice in a monotone. "Yes, I had a son named Eldon. Unfortunately, he had an accident. Fell from a tree when he was eleven and broke his neck."

"I'm terribly sorry."

He nodded acknowledgment of my condolences and continued. "Years later, I was reading an article about the hobby of collecting lunchboxes and remembered that we had kept this stored away. That was the beginning. I have more than a hundred now, most of which I purchased after my wife's death about eight years ago. She thought it silly, but always kept her eyes open for them like a good sport." He extended an arm toward the boxes lined up before us. "These are among my favorites in the collection."

"And this Gunsmoke one is your prize box?"

"Only for sentimental reasons, dear lady. Value wise, it's only worth about one hundred fifty to two hundred dollars. It would be worth more if it were in better condition."

I swallowed hard. Two hundred dollars for a kid's beat-up lunchbox that still reeked of sour milk seasoned with rust. Sheesh.

He put the lunchbox back in its place and picked up the one displayed next to it. "This . . . this is my crown jewel; the ultimate lunchbox; every collector's dream acquisition."

Price held the box out for my inspection, holding it gingerly by the top and bottom as if it were made of glass. It did not look like much to me, but then what do I know? I tote my lunch in paper sacks and old Blockbuster Video bags.

Except for a dent on one of its corners, this particular lunchbox did not have the bumps and bruises of the one before it, but neither was it festooned with colorful pictures. It was rather plain, the metal painted a dark blue. On one side it sported a primitive watercolor of a cowboy riding a horse and twirling his lasso over his head. Around the horse's hooves were some quickly drawn grass tufts and in the background a few cactus plants. The picture was not even painted on the box but stuck on. The TV cowboy depicted in the drawing was unknown to me.

Okay, what was I missing here? I kept looking at the box hoping a clue to its desirability would pop out of it like a genie from a magic lamp. My eyes traveled up to meet Price's smiling face, quite sure that I looked as dense as I felt.

"Is it safe to assume that this lunchbox is worth more than the *Gunsmoke* one?"

He gave a mischievous laugh, almost a childish giggle. It was plain to see that Price delighted in showing off this particular treasure.

"Would you believe, Odelia, at least a hundred times more?"

In my mind, I quickly threw a couple of zeros after the two hundred dollar figure. "Holy shit!" I gasped, then immediately slapped my hand over my mouth. *Holy shit,* I thought in horror, *did I really just say holy shit to a client, and an important one at that?*

Price let loose with a real guffaw.

Ashamed of my unprofessional behavior, I apologized. "Mr. Price, I am so sorry. That was very inappropriate of me."

He laughed, reached a hand up, and patted me warmly on my right shoulder. "Sterling, dear, remember? And actually, Odelia, that was very close to my exact words when I first learned of its value." He leaned toward me. I could smell the coffee on his breath. "I paid twenty-seven thousand eight hundred dollars for this trinket," he confessed with a sly whisper. "Just over a year ago." He nudged me good-naturedly. "Go ahead, say it. Say what you really want to say."

"Holy shit," I said, this time with reverence and without apology.

Price laughed heartily. "You're probably too young to know this, but have you ever heard of the cowboy star Chappy Wheeler?" I shook my head. "His real name was Charles Borden and he was from Newark, New Jersey. In the 1940's, he found his way to Hollywood and eventually landed a TV series, appropriately called *Chappy Wheeler*. It was the first show of its kind, the forerunner of the classic cowboy genre shows like *Hopalong Cassidy, Roy Rogers* and even *Gunsmoke*.

"This lunch pail," he explained, holding the box up for my inspection, "was the prototype for the first known children's lunchboxes depicting TV stars. See the artist's signature at the bottom of the picture?"

I looked closer and saw what looked like a tiny Art Bender scrawled near a bit of prairie grass.

"This is an original drawing. This box, Odelia, started it all. Years ago, it was nicknamed the Holy Pail. Cute, eh?"

I was puzzled. I watched a lot of TV as a kid, but could not remember a Chappy Wheeler, not even in reruns.

Price put the box back behind the protective glass and shut the door gently. "Wheeler was murdered in 1949," he explained as if reading my confusion. "Found dead in his bungalow on the studio lot. His killer was never found. The *Chappy Wheeler* show was cancelled and the lunchbox never manufactured. This box is all that remains of that promotional dream. Supposedly, it's cursed." He laughed softly.

I found the story fascinating, though hardly worth nearly thirty thousand dollars. "So which did become the first children's lunchbox?" I asked.

"This one," he said, pointing to a box behind another glass door. On it was a character I knew well—Hopalong Cassidy. "This box debuted in 1950."

I strolled along the shelves looking at the different boxes. Except for a few that appeared to be in pristine condition, most showed signs of minor wear and tear. Many, I was sure, had a history of being proudly carried to and from school in the saner more innocent times of the 50's and 60's.

I stopped short in front of one of the cases and stared at a lunchbox. It was black. On the front was Zorro, my favorite childhood TV character. What can I say, Zorro and the Sheriff of Nottingham . . . I had a thing for men in knee-high riding boots even then.

I sensed Price coming up behind me. "Was that your lunchbox, Odelia?" he asked. "We're always drawn to our own."

I shook my head, more to clear my mind of memories. "No, it wasn't. But I wanted this one as a kid." I turned and looked at Price. "My mother said it was a boy's lunchbox. She made me carry a pink one with flowers and ribbons on it." I made a face. "Ugh."

He chuckled. "Junior Miss."

"Excuse me?"

"Junior Miss. That's the name of the lunchbox you probably carried to school."

"Hmmm. All I know is that it wasn't very cool."

Price laughed again. "You had good taste, Odelia. Too bad your mother didn't listen. Today the Zorro box is much more valuable than the Junior Miss."

Somehow, I knew that without being told.

"A lunchbox worth thirty thousand dollars! Are you kidding me?"

I shook my head and finished chewing the food in my mouth before speaking. "Nope, telling you the truth."

The question had come from Joan Nunez, a litigation paralegal in our firm. She and Kelsey Cavendish, the firm's librarian and research guru, were treating me to a birthday lunch at Jerry's Famous Deli. In between taking bites from a mammoth Rueben sandwich and slurps of iced tea, I filled them in on my morning introduction to lunchbox memorabilia.

"Amazing," Joan said slowly as she played with her fries, dragging one through a puddle of ketchup. She was around forty, small boned, with dark features and expressive eyes, and very proper in her demeanor.

Kelsey plucked at the sleeve of my blouse. "Pssst, hey, look over there," she whispered.

Joan and I moved our eyes in the direction Kelsey indicated with jerks of her chin. It took me a while, but finally my gaze focused on what Kelsey wanted us to see. Mike Steele . . . and he was not alone. He sat in a booth on the other side of the restaurant with Trudie Monroe, his latest in a long line of assistants. Trudie had only been working at Woobie for about three weeks. She was a sweet woman about thirty years of age with a pixie face, long coppery hair and a cute figure . . . and knockers, big knockers. In addition to Steele, Trudie was assigned to Jolene McHugh, a junior associate at the firm. She also did work for me on occasion, though generally I found it faster and easier to do my own secretarial work.

"You think they got nekkid yet?" Kelsey asked, imitating her husband's Texas twang. Kelsey was a plain, tall, and angular woman in her mid-thirties with a firecracker wit. She had married Beau Cavendish four years earlier after a whirlwind online courtship. He was a teacher in Houston at the time and relocated to southern California just before they married. Like Kelsey, he was delightfully funny and his accent added to his folksy charm.

"You mean naked," Joan corrected her.

"Naw, girl. I mean nekkid." Kelsey looked at both of us in mock disgust before explaining. "Naked is when you don't have any clothes on. Nekkid is when you don't have any clothes on and you're up to no good."

Joan looked over at the couple and frowned. "I'm sure Trudie told me during her first week at Woobie that she was married."

I took a big draw of iced tea from my straw and pondered the budding relationship of Steele and his new secretary.

"Hard to say if they've been nekkid yet," I said, "but I bet he's working on it."

Kelsey and I giggled. Joan's frown deepened.

Later that afternoon at the office, two boxes were delivered to me from Sterling Homes. One was quite large and addressed to Mike Steele; the other, a small one, was addressed to me personally. I opened the smaller box. Inside was a lunchbox, the very same Zorro box I had seen earlier in Price's office, along with a handwritten note.

Odelia, every child should carry the lunchbox of her dreams. —*Warmest regards, Sterling*

I could not believe it. I picked my way through my Rolodex until I found the number for Sterling Homes. I was so excited and overwhelmed my fingers had trouble punching the numbers. The value of the lunchbox was anyone's guess. It was enough that this generous man had given it to me. I also had doubts about whether or not I should accept it. The call went through, but the receptionist informed me that Mr. Price was not answering. I thought about asking for his assistant, then remembered that she was off for a few days. At my request, I was put through to his voice mail, where I left a stumbling and gushing thanks for the box. I also made a mental reminder to write a proper thank-you note later tonight.

"Cool lunchbox!"

I looked up at the enthusiastic comment and my eyes fell upon Joe Bays, the firm's mail clerk and jack-of-all-trades. Being rather roly-poly, Joe filled every inch of the doorway as he stood staring at the Zorro lunchbox on the edge of my desk. I detected a hungry look in his eye.

"You know about lunchboxes, Joe?" I motioned for him to come in and sit in the small chair across from my desk.

"A bit," he said, still eyeing the Zorro box. He reached for it, hesitating slightly. "May I?"

"Sure. I just got it today. It was a gift."

He sat down and picked it up. Turning it gently in his stubby fingers, he rotated it to see all of the pictures on the front, back and four sides of the box. He opened it and I heard the still familiar click of the metal latch and the squeaking of hinges. Inside was a matching thermos that I had already discovered. Joe put the box down, twisted the plastic top off the thermos and then followed suit with the stopper. He inspected both then peered inside the glass bottle as if looking through a telescope.

"This is in fine condition," Joe pronounced when he was through. "Just a few dings here and there from use. Where'd you get it again?"

"It was a gift," I answered, "from Sterling Price. You know, our client, Sterling Homes."

"Wow, nice gift. Might be worth a couple hundred bucks."

I almost swooned. Now I knew I had to give it back. It was too expensive a gift to accept from someone I hardly knew. Since Joe obviously knew something about lunchboxes, I gave him a rundown of my trip to Sterling Homes that morning. When I mentioned the Holy Pail, his eyes widened and his mouth hung open, creating a fleshy tunnel in the middle of his boyish face.

"The Holy Pail," he said slowly, quietly, almost with reverence, more to himself than to me. He slumped back in his chair in disbelief. "Wow. You really saw it?"

I nodded. Obviously, Joe was not someone who needed an explanation about the Chappy Wheeler lunchbox. Joe had a quiet way about him. He was very shy and introverted, especially around the women in the office. He always seemed comfortable with me though, and I assumed it was because I was old enough to be his mother.

"I saw it with my own eyes," I assured him.

He looked at me eagerly, like a puppy hoping for a treat. "You know, they say it's cursed. Bad luck for its owner."

Of their own accord, my eyes rolled in amused disbelief.

Mike Steele entered my office and picked up the lunchbox Joe had replaced on my desk.

"Things so tough at home, Grey, you can only afford a used lunchbox?"

"It was a gift, Steele, from Sterling Price."

He raised one trimmed eyebrow and looked me over. "Really? I thought the old boy was engaged." He snickered. "His fiancée might not like this, not to mention your own squeeze."

I chose to not dignify his comment with a comeback. Instead, I indicated the larger box that sat on the floor and said, "He also sent this box over with it. Documents for you to review, I believe."

"Wrong, Grey, documents for *you* to review. We're looking for anything that might help us break Sterling's contract with Howser Development should the need arise. Look for suspicious chinks in their paperwork." He caught me checking out the size of the box. "Don't worry, Grey, we don't need them right away. There's a dispute brewing between the two companies that may or may not turn into something. We just want to be prepared in the event it does turn ugly." He put the lunchbox down and turned to leave. "Just complete the review within the next two weeks. I wouldn't want it to interfere with your love life."

Grrrrrrrr.

Once at home, I turned on the TV, stroked the cat, and promised the dog a walk after dinner. A short trip to the kitchen and I was back with a handful of Fig Newtons as a before-dinner appetizer.

To my surprise, the evening news was reporting on an event in Newport Beach. Usually, nothing very exciting happens in Orange County, except maybe exceptionally high surf or government corruption. I paid closer attention to the TV and saw a photograph of a familiar face plastered in the upper right-hand corner of the screen. At the bottom of the screen were the words *Breaking News*. A reporter, young, handsome, and mahogany colored, was onscreen reporting live from the scene. In the background was the corporate headquarters of Sterling Homes.

I fumbled with the clicker and aimed it at the TV to turn up the volume.

"It has been confirmed," the reporter said with deliberation into the microphone held tightly in his hand, "that Sterling Price, CEO and founder of Sterling Homes, the prestigious real estate development company headquartered in Newport Beach, was found dead this afternoon in his private office."

Wainwright never let the falling cookies hit the floor.

WWW.MIDNIGHTINKBOOKS.COM

From the gritty streets of New York City to sacred tombs in the Middle East, it's always midnight somewhere. Join us online at any hour for fresh new voices in mystery fiction, book club questions, author information, mystery resources, and more.

Midnight Ink promises a wild ride filled with cunning villains, conflicted heroes, hilarious hazards, mind-bending puzzles, and enough twists and turns to keep readers on the edge of their seats.

MIDNIGHT INK

MIDNIGHT INK ORDERING INFORMATION

Order by Phone
- Call toll free within the U.S. and Canada at 1-888-NITEINK (1-888-648-3465)
- We accept VISA, MasterCard, and American Express

Order by Mail
Send the full price of your order (MN residents add 6.5% sales tax) in U.S. funds, plus postage & handling, to:

> Midnight Ink
> 2143 Wooddale Drive, Dept. 978-0-7387-0863-8
> Woodbury, MN 55125-2989

Postage & Handling
Standard (U.S., Mexico, & Canada). If your order is:
> $24.99 and under, add $3.00
> $25.00 and over, FREE STANDARD SHIPPING

AK, HI, PR: $15.00 for one book plus $1.00 for each additional book.

> International Orders (airmail only):
> $16.00 for one book plus $3.00 for each additional book

Orders are processed within two business days. Please allow for normal shipping time.
Postage and handling rates subject to change.

Photo by Ivo Lopez

ABOUT THE AUTHOR

Like the character Odelia Grey, Sue Ann Jaffarian is a middle-aged, plus-size paralegal. She lives in Los Angeles with her two cats, B and Raffi, neither of which are green. She writes mysteries and general fiction, as well as short stories and occasional poetry.

Sue Ann is the current president of the Los Angeles chapter of Sisters In Crime, an international nonprofit organization dedicated to the mystery genre.

In addition to writing, Sue Ann is sought after as a motivational and humorous speaker, and she is the founder of Fat Chance Promotions, which provides marketing and promotional workshops and coaching for writers of all genres.

Visit Sue Ann on the Internet at either of the following addresses:
www.sueannjaffarian.com or
www.fatchancepromotions.com.

CPSIA information can be obtained at www.ICGtesting.com
Printed in the USA
LVOW05s2201301014

411364LV00014B/278/P

9 780738 708638